W9-CEL-869

continued . . .

Praise for the novels of
Susan Johnson

HOT LEGS

SUSAN JOHNSON

BERKLEY SENSATION, NEW YORK

THE BERKLEY PUBLISHING GROUP
Published by the Penguin Group
Penguin Group (USA) Inc.
375 Hudson Street, New York, New York 10014, USA
Penguin Group (Canada), 10 Alcorn Avenue, Toronto, Ontario M4V 3B2, Canada
(a division of Pearson Penguin Canada Inc.)
Penguin Books Ltd., 80 Strand, London WC2R 0RL, England
Penguin Group Ireland, 25 St. Stephen's Green, Dublin 2, Ireland (a division of Penguin Books Ltd.)
Penguin Group (Australia), 250 Camberwell Road, Camberwell, Victoria 3124, Australia
(a division of Pearson Australia Group Pty. Ltd.)
Penguin Books India Pvt. Ltd., 11 Community Centre, Panchsheel Park, New Delhi—110 017, India
Penguin Group (NZ), Cnr. Airborne and Rosedale Roads, Albany, Auckland 1310, New Zealand
(a division of Pearson New Zealand Ltd.)
Penguin Books (South Africa) (Pty.) Ltd., 24 Sturdee Avenue, Rosebank, Johannesburg 2196,
South Africa

Penguin Books Ltd., Registered Offices: 80 Strand, London WC2R 0RL, England

This is a work of fiction. Names, characters, places, and incidents either are the product of the author's imagination or are used fictitiously, and any resemblance to actual persons, living or dead, business establishments, events, or locales is entirely coincidental.

HOT LEGS

A Berkley Sensation Book / published by arrangement with the author

PRINTING HISTORY
Berkley trade paperback edition / June 2004
Berkley Sensation edition / May 2005

Copyright © 2004 by Susan Johnson.
Cover art by Jan Cobb.
Cover design by George Long.
Interior text design by Kristin del Rosario.

ISBN: 0-425-20355-7

BERKLEY® SENSATION
Berkley Sensation Books are published by The Berkley Publishing Group,
a division of Penguin Group (USA) Inc.,
375 Hudson Street, New York, New York 10014.
BERKLEY SENSATION and the "B" design are trademarks belonging to Penguin Group (USA) Inc.

PRINTED IN THE UNITED STATES OF AMERICA

10 9 8 7 6 5 4 3 2 1

ONE

DAMMIT, I COULD KILL THE SOB, CASSIE THOUGHT, scowling at the pile of bills on the card table. Not really, of course, but wishful thinking about payback for her lying, cheating ex-husband was front and center in her brain.

She was sitting on a card table chair in her very nice, very large, very *empty* kitchen because Jay had taken everything when he left. Okay, okay, the division of property had been agreed on months ago after much haggling, but that didn't mean she couldn't still be pissed in the echo chamber of her more or less stripped interior, trying to deal with the bills before her. Nor was she likely to mellow out until Jay and his irritating divorce lawyer stopped trying to fuck her over *even now* on every teeny, tiny detail of the settlement. He had nearly everything he wanted already. She wasn't about to give him the painting she'd bought on their honeymoon, despite an apparent misunderstanding about the phrase "painting of the North Shore" in the settlement agreement. She'd given him the smaller landscape of Grand Marais, so

screw him. Like he'd screwed anything that moved during
much of their marriage, as she'd discovered much too late
for a supposedly intelligent, twenty-first-century female.

And after apparently playing the field like a bachelor during their five-year marriage, he'd left her for the requisite
bimbo—young, blonde, and richer than she could ever hope
to be. Maybe if Tami Duvall could carry on a conversation
without mentioning cute clothes and like the sweetest color
of nail polish or the problem with keeping the white leather
upholstery in her convertible, you know, really, really white,
Jay would have less time on his hands to badger *her*. Cassie
had enough problems trying to figure out how to make the
house payment without any added pressure from Jay Sibley
III, which should have been a warning flag when she first
met him. What family from Biwabik, Minnesota, would
name their son "the third," for God's sake? The main street
in Biwabik was only four blocks long, after all.

Jay's new girlfriend cum fiancée had a family estate on
Lake Minnetonka—tennis courts, a putting green, a covered
pool for the Minnesota winters or for those days when the lake
was too choppy for morning laps—along with a couple extra
"cottages" that alone had rated a spread in *Architectural Digest*.
So Jay hadn't wanted the house, understandably. He and Tami
had decided on Swan Cottage, he'd said with a smug smile
during the preliminary divorce discussions. And because he
was leaving Cassie the house, he'd magnanimously settled for
its contents to furnish the partially finished cabin up north he
wanted—along with his car, motorcycle, four-wheeler, boat,
and every other man toy they owned.

Theoretically, the division of property was fair enough.
Cassie had the house she loved—a real plus. Unfortunately,
it was essentially unfurnished and much too expensive to
maintain—definitely a minus. Along with the additional
negative of having been left after five years of marriage for a

woman she found so unbelievably shallow she felt as though she was in the center of a clichéd drama titled *Every Aging Frat Boy's Fantasy.*

As a favor to her, maybe the high-performance fuel injection in Jay's new red Porsche would fail as he crossed some railroad tracks as it did in cartoons. Nobody ever actually got hurt in cartoons—even if they fell off a cliff—so she could daydream without freaking out. Let's face it though, he was more likely to live a totally perfect life with darling Tami behind the security gates of the Duvall estate.

On the plus side, her voice of reason reminded her, the divorce was final and she was no longer *obliged* to deal with Jay or his annoying lawyer.

There. Consolation.

Sort of.

Because she was still facing a pile of bills unlikely to be paid with the meager balance in her bank account, and no matter how she scratched out or rearranged the numbers in the two columns on the legal pad, the sizeable deficit in her budget remained. Damn. Where was a magic voodoo chicken when you needed one? Or that pot of gold at the end of the rainbow she'd actually believed in as a child? Even her lottery tickets were useless; she didn't have one number that matched, despite the fact that she'd splurged and spent twenty bucks this week. How abjectly unlucky was that?

Her homicidal impulses rejected as impractical, not to mention illegal, and her financial straits acute enough to require a large bottle of Prozac, Cassie turned to the only consistent, tried-and-true, handy-dandy lifeline of consolation in her world gone mad.

Pushing herself up from the card table that served as desk, kitchen table, and makeshift computer stand, she slid across her beautiful inlaid maple floor in her Tasmanian Devil slippers, reached for the freezer door handle of her

Sub-Zero refrigerator, and fervently hoped she still had enough double fudge, extra nutty, Rocky Road ice cream to see her through her really devastating crisis of faith.

There it was like a secular Lady of Fatima—perhaps even a slight glow emanated from the frost-covered container—the cylindrical equivalent of perfect love, eternal friendship, and God's goodwill.

One last pint of Edna Mae's handmade ice cream stared back at her.

Perhaps there were silver linings after all.

TWO

WHEN THE PHONE RANG SEVERAL MINUTES later, Cassie hesitated, torn between the last glob of chocolate-covered almonds buried in gooey marshmallow at the bottom of the container and the call. She scanned the caller ID. There were people who would lose in a contest with chocolate-covered almonds.

But not Liv! Cassie lunged for the phone. "Where have you been?" she shrieked. "I've been trying to call you all night! You didn't leave a message on your machine! I've been going nuts! I just finished a pint of Rocky Road ice cream because of you!"

"I'm in Memphis, waiting for a connecting flight home. I had to fly to Atlanta this morning to cover my boss's meeting when he called in sick. And don't blame me for your ice-cream consumption when you know damn well it's Jay's fault."

"You must be psychic."

"I don't have to be. I've been listening to your marriage woes for months—and you eat ice cream every time anything goes wrong. I strongly suggest you buy stock in Edna Mae's."

"Don't bring up money. I'm bummed. I need a shoulder to cry on."

"Cry away. And tell me what Jay did now."

"He didn't leave me enough money, that's what he did."

"He didn't leave you *any* money. You were too nice. Didn't I tell you going for the jugular is normal in divorces?" Liv specialized in labor law, but she'd gone through a divorce the past year so she understood of what she spoke.

"I know, I know. Can I help it if I wanted to be fair?"

Liv snorted. "With Jay? Hello. He wouldn't recognize the word if it hit him over the head with his favorite nine iron."

Cassie sighed. "I really didn't want to be beholden to him, either."

"As if he'd notice."

"Well, his teenybopper fiancée might, and I don't feel like looking like a shrew to a millionaire's daughter. Call me crazy or insecure—okay, *insecure* is the right word—but it's the pits to be left for a younger woman. It makes me feel old when I'm not."

"Damn right you're not. If you were, I'd be, and thirty-two's *not* old."

"I know. But little Tami Duvall is *twenty*-two. Christ, she was twenty-one when Jay met her."

"And he was thirty-eight. Idiot."

"As if you or I are going to change the centuries-old tradition of men marrying women young enough to be their daughters. And I'm not trying to. Each to their own, blah, blah, blah."

"You still should have made him pay more than you did."

"In hindsight, you're right. But it's too late, so just tell me everything's going to be all right. Tell me the sun will rise tomorrow on a brand-new shiny day and my money troubles will be over."

"You're screwed, sweetie, but it's *not* too late. Let me sic Jack Donnelly on Jay, and your troubles really *will* be over. How does the phrase 'IRS audit' sound to you?"

"Jeez, Liv, I couldn't be so brutal and sleep at night."

"Suit yourself. Believe me, you'd never make it in the dog-eat-dog world of adjudication. Look, if it'll help," Liv added, "I can lend you some money to tide you over."

"Thanks, but I've been thinking I probably should jack up my courage and ask Arthur for a raise."

"Something you should have done a long time ago," Liv observed in her smooth-as-silk client tone.

"Easy for you to say. You only have to deal with lawyers who think the sun rises and sets on them. Arthur holds the strong belief that he *is* the sun—which makes him blithely unaware that he's actually a monumental ass."

"You still have to deal with him, sweetie, if you want a raise. On the other hand, he's only a man," Liv added with the sardonic edge she used—postdivorce—when referring to the opposite gender.

"Unfortunately, he's a man who doesn't understand there are people in the world without trust funds. I've been avoiding his lecture on frugality and thrift that he trots out every time one of the museum staff asks for more money. This from a director who spends more on travel each year than some third-world nations. Asshole prick."

"Atta girl . . . *now* you have the right attitude."

"If he'd curtail even a fraction of his international meetings and museum tours"—Cassie's voice took on a rising heat—"every curator could have a lavish raise and perhaps aspire to a modicum of his Sun King lifestyle."

"You go, girl."

"Everyone knows his quote unquote research trips to Istanbul last year had nothing to do with research unless a Topkapi intern who was young enough to be his daughter counts."

"Whoa—perfect . . . casually mention that. I doubt his newest wife will appreciate a rival so soon after their marriage."

"Get real, Liv. I can't bring that up. I want a raise. I don't want to get sacked for libel."

"You could say you were doing him a favor—you know . . . making him aware of the gossip. Tell him you don't believe the sordid rumor, but you thought he'd like to know what was being brooded about."

"Would that be like—I don't know—say . . . blackmail?"

"Such an unsavory word; I like to think of it as negotiating."

Cassie slid down on her spine and stared at the leering Tasmanian devils on her slipper toes. "Which is why they pay you the big bucks," she said with a sigh, knowing she could never be so brash, "and I'm eking out a living."

"Doing what you like—don't forget that, Curator of the Year."

"That was two years ago, and you like what you do, too, for a lot more money."

"Believe me, I have my days when I wonder if the word *ethics* has disappeared from the language. But then I remind myself that I wasn't the one to coin the phrase 'life isn't perfect.' So buck up, kid, there's no reason Arthur can't pay you more. Be a grown-up, and go ask him."

"I guess I have to, don't I," Cassie muttered. Liv was an in-your-face kind of woman, while Cassie only aspired to that degree of testosterone. "Okay. I'll do it. First thing tomorrow."

"If you need some money to get you through in the meantime, just ask."

"I might. But I'd prefer getting it from Arthur's tightwad grasp."

"I wasn't as nice as you in my divorce, sweetie. I've enough to lend you whatever you need in case things don't work out—hey—they're calling my flight. I'll talk to you tomorrow."

And the phone went dead like it often did with Liv.

She could have been a man with her style of good-bye.

THREE

WHEN NEWS OF THE MISSING RUBENS WAS released to the press, Bobby Serre was already on the first leg of his flight from Budapest to Minneapolis. With Bobby's reputation as the best bounty hunter in the rarefied world of mega-priced art, Arthur Northrup had tracked him down within hours of discovering the theft. Nominal friends like so many in the incestuous world of art, Arthur had been able to coax Bobby from his vacation villa overlooking the Danube with the practical assessment that solving an art theft in Minneapolis shouldn't be too time-consuming.

"Nothing ever happens in this provincial city. You should be in and out of here within the week."

Bobby had grumbled because he'd only just settled in, but he agreed in the end because Arthur's assessment was probably right. In his experience, outside the major metropolitan areas of the world where professionals operated, thievery in the hinterlands wasn't rocket science. This was probably a quick cut-and-snatch done by some wacko who didn't have a clue how to fence the canvas once he had it.

Bobby had already alerted all his contacts in the art under-world to be on the lookout for an oddball trying to market the Medici panel. But he still had to go and have a look for himself. Fortunately, amateurs always left a trail a yard wide.

Shifting his frame in the first-class seat, Bobby tried to find a comfortable position for sleep, but no matter how he turned, something was in the way. The design matrix for commercial aircraft didn't take into account his size, the width of his shoulders, or the length of his legs. After the fifth "Sorry" to the passengers in front of and beside him, he gave up any further thought of rest, flicked on his reading light, took out Arthur's e-mail, and reexamined the three-page, single-spaced summary of the robbery. He'd talked to Arthur briefly before boarding, and after a more thorough reading of Arthur's report, the heist was beginning to feel more like an inside job. Maybe. He was getting a gut feeling—not that his gut was always right, but it was often enough to put him on the scent. He began jotting notes in the margins—observations, questions, what-ifs, maybes.

As a matter of routine, he'd already asked for a list of mu-seum employees, complete down to the temps and docents. Once in Minneapolis, he'd take a look at the crime scene and then begin the tedious task of checking out each em-ployee—including Arthur's newest lady love.

Even in the midst of his crisis call, Arthur had mentioned the new, fabulous Jessica. *Some things never change,* Bobby thought. Arthur could always be counted on for his predatory instincts and short attention span. Hopefully, this one would last longer than wives number one and two, who had barely redecorated the house before finding their husband in bed with their successor. What Bobby could never figure out was why Arthur married them. One marriage had been more than enough for his own misery threshold. Staying single was sav-ing him a helluva lot on decorating costs *and* aggravation.

FOUR

EARLY THE NEXT MORNING, AFTER A BREAK-
fast of wheat toast and milk austere enough for a Trap-
pist monk, Cassie sat before a one-of-a-kind Boulle
desk, waiting for Arthur to finish his phone call. She was seriously going to have to remember to go to the grocery store
tonight, she decided, the taste of dry, unbuttered toast still
a bad memory. If she hadn't had to arrive at work so perversely early, she could have stopped at Wendy's and ordered
those little frosted rolls that were one of her favorite ways to
greet the day on those mornings when she could ignore her
nutritional conscience.

But she'd had to be at the museum at what was, for her,
the crack of dawn in hopes of speaking with Arthur alone.

The museum director prided himself on being in before
anyone else. Go figure what turned someone on. She glanced
at the clock. Seven-thirty. Definitely a record for her, besting
her previous record of eight-thirty the time she had to meet
the president of Sweden when he was donating two paintings
from the Thorvald Museum before flying out of town at ten.

Trying to appear poised and professional despite the ungodly hour, she straightened her skirt over her knees and suddenly noticed a glaring stain. *Damn, that's what comes of dressing while I'm still asleep.* Quickly covering the blotch with her hand, she leaned forward slightly in what she hoped was a casual pose.

A poised woman would ignore such minor issues, she reminded herself. One's inner spirit is more important than superficialities of dress.

Unfortunately, Arthur was a neat freak, and she was still not as fully assured as she would have been had she read more than the first chapter of *A Woman's Journey to Her Soul* (perhaps Sarah Bainbridge dealt with her current situation in later chapters). She adjusted the position of her hand to better conceal the sizeable spot. Arthur took pleasure in pointing out what he perceived as deficiencies in his staff's appearance, the result, no doubt, of his obsession with custom suits, starched shirts, perfectly knotted ties, and spit-shined shoes.

But despite Arthur's unmanly focus on sartorial splendor, he was far from the museum director stereotype. Tall, lean, and muscled (compliments of a personal trainer), his attractiveness further enhanced by the cachet of a private fortune, he was the antithesis of the effete, vaguely androgynous, professorial style of man so often found at the helm of museums. It helped, of course, that his grandfather had endowed the museum with its original seed money and that the Northrup family continued its charitable largesse. Both had been instrumental in Arthur's appointment as director at the almost unheard-of age of thirty. So when Arthur referred to the Minneapolis Museum of Art as *his* museum—a frequent, odious tendency—he actually meant it.

God, he was annoying, as was his soi-disant field of expertise. Byzantine architectural decorative design—come *on.* How esoteric could one be? Or dull and derivative? Take your pick.

Cassie fidgeted as Arthur droned on. Had she not been reduced to a state of abject poverty, she'd not have waited like a lowly petitioner while he discussed the theft of the Rubens with one of his acquaintances, Chip by name. Nor would she have approached him at such an unfortuitous time.

The robbery had been front-page news that morning, and for a brief moment, she wondered how much the Rubens would realize in the illicit art underworld. The brokering fee alone would pay off her house, not to mention allow her a life of luxurious comfort.

"I can spare you five minutes, Cassandra," Arthur briskly said, suddenly putting down the receiver, his voice breaking into her reverie centered around a sunny villa on the Mediterranean, a full staff of servants, and the scent of bougainvillea. "What do you want?"

Your fortune instead of my bills. "I apologize for the timing." *Be courteous and polite,* she reminded herself, returning his uncivil scowl with a smile. "You must be besieged, and if I didn't need a raise in order to save my house, I wouldn't bother you."

"Didn't you get a settlement?" His voice was sharp with impatience.

"I have the house."

"Why not sell it?"

"I'm not looking for advice, Arthur." She spoke with restraint, but her temper was rising. She knew the extent of his personal fortune as well as his venal self-interest and total lack of empathy for anyone he didn't consider a potential donor—namely her. But she refused to wimp out. "I really need a raise," she said, holding her temper in check.

"This isn't a good time, Cassandra. The museum's just lost the Rubens. Couldn't you wait until the dust settles?"

"If I had your trust fund I could." So much for politesse.

"Perhaps a financial planner could help you."

His implied criticism overlooked the fact that one needed money with which to plan. "Thank you for the suggestion, but I'm in danger of losing my house, Arthur. I need money now, not in five years."

Arthur tapped his manicured fingers on his desktop, his irritation clear. "I can't put through an increase now even if I wanted to with everything in turmoil." He grimaced slightly so his perfect white teeth gleamed for a second before he exhaled in frustration. "If you don't mind working with Bobby Serre while he's here, I *could* siphon some consultant fees your way—I suppose," he begrudgingly added.

"Until I get my raise?"

"Being pushy detracts from your femininity, Cassandra."

"You can be sued for comments like that, Arthur. I don't have to look pretty to get a raise."

His sudden smile oozed charm. "You *do* look damned good even with that bad haircut."

"I'm recording this conversation for my lawyer, Arthur. Save your charm for what's-her-name—Sarah's successor."

"Jessica."

She repressed the impulse to say, *How long will she last?* considering it bad form after he'd promised her what were generally lucrative consultant fees. "When will Serre be here?" *Stay focused. Think of the added money and not Arthur's reptilian gaze.*

"Bobby likes redheads."

"What a coincidence. So do I." She made a mental note to carry mace for Arthur's hotshot bounty hunter. Everyone knew Bobby Serre, the art world's most celebrated cowboy who always got his man. Renowned for his low-key approach, equally notorious for the beautiful women in his life, he'd been better known for his prowess on the football field before he wowed them at the University of Michigan with his eye for art forgeries. The University Gallery had lost half their collection as a result of his expertise, while the Detroit Museum had had to downgrade a dozen of their masterpieces to "school of" status. Graduate school at Harvard had only added to the luster of his reputation, and once free of the ivy tower, he'd gone on to a globe-trotting life highly reminiscent of a James Bond movie.

Arthur tipped his head and winked. "How fortunate. You have the same taste. Bobby should be here by evening. I'd suggest a haircut before tomorrow morning. Be in my office at eight."

Like hell she'd get a haircut. "I'll be here," she said. "And thank you," she forced herself to add, although it took every ounce of courtesy she possessed after that remark about a haircut. She wasn't auditioning for Bobby Serre's bed, thank you very much. If rumor were true, he had all the women he could handle anyway.

And after Jay's recent betrayal, the male gender as a whole was on her shit list.

FIVE

AFTER THE THEFT HAD BEEN ANALYZED AT length, Arthur smiled at Bobby over drinks late that evening and lifted his glass in salute. "I'm supplying you with a hot little bedmate while you're in town. One of my curators. Lush green eyes; great tits; a tall, pre-Raphaelite-style redhead with the best legs I've ever seen. A touch prickly at times, but they're always more interesting in bed, aren't they?"

Bobby's brows rose fractionally. "I don't want a bedmate."

"Suit yourself. She's your assistant then—to fetch and carry."

"I don't need an assistant, either."

"Do me a favor."

"I am doing you a favor. I'm cutting my vacation short and finding your Rubens for you."

"Look, she needs the money. Her husband walked out on her, she's left with a house she can't afford, and I'm helping her out."

Bobby's gaze narrowed. "Why?"

Arthur shrugged. "I don't know. Maybe it's her big boobs and great legs. Maybe she pleaded her case well . . ."

"Maybe you're hoping to lay her yourself."

Another shrug. "Maybe I am. I'll ask my therapist. In the meantime, at least be polite to her. I've promised her some consultant fees."

"Sorry. I don't baby-sit."

"You must need someone to type your reports."

"What reports? When I find the Rubens, I'll hand it over to you. You'll give me the rest of my fee, and I'll head back to Budapest, where I actually *have* a redhead waiting for me."

"Why didn't you say so?"

"It's not relevant."

Arthur's leer was unmistakable. "Is this one special?"

"No."

"Are any of them?"

"I'm not looking for trophies or wives like you—only sex. It's pretty simple."

"Was it simple with Claire?" Innuendo melted through Arthur's words.

"Nothing was simple with Claire." Bobby's tone was cool. "You know that."

"By the way, I saw her last month at an opening in New York. She still turns heads."

"I haven't seen her in five years. I think I'll leave it that way."

"Unrequited love?" Arthur murmured.

"Christ, cut the crap. There was nothing unrequited about our relationship. We just wanted different things. Like you and your various wives."

"Amen to that. I'm not sure men and women were meant to cohabit."

"On that profound truism, I'll bid you good night. I want to be at the museum early." Bobby drained his glass of cognac and set it down on a Chippendale table so fine he suspected it came from the museum storage rooms.

Arthur rose with him and escorted him to the door of his Georgian mansion on Lake of the Isles. "You're sure you don't want to stay here?"

Bobby shook his head. "A friend lent me his house. I'll give you the phone numbers in the morning."

Bobby's car and driver were waiting on the boulevard, and before the town car reached the freeway, Bobby was fast asleep.

SIX

EVEN WHILE CASSIE DESPISED HERSELF FOR her insecurities and vowed to do some further reading on self-confidence and emotional calm, her bedroom floor was awash with discarded clothing before she finally settled on an absinthe-colored suit with a not-too-short skirt, although it wasn't too long, either. She had good legs—maybe even exceptional legs. That thought put her completely out of sorts. Dammit, she shouldn't even be considering male/female dynamics when she was intent on personal independence and gender-free poise.

She shouldn't be thinking about legs in any form whatsoever. She didn't have to dress up for Bobby Serre. So he was handsome and smart and intimate with the jet set and international beauties. She didn't have to impress him. This was simply an assignment that would earn her additional money. An assignment. That's all. Nothing personal. Absolutely nothing. And after what Jay had done to her, she was the last person in the world looking for something personal from a man. She'd actually sworn off men, at least until she could contemplate the blissful state of matrimony without rancor.

Although that might require a decade or so. Perhaps she'd have to rethink the merits of a rancorless state. Ten years was a long time to go without sex.

Understanding she had more pressing issues at the moment than her marriage gone bad, she quickly checked the time. Damn. Only a miracle would get her to the museum by eight. She hoped like hell 394 wasn't bogged down with traffic. Pulling on the skirt, she wiggled her hips, wondering if she'd put on weight or the skirt was really that short. Not that it mattered. There wasn't time to change.

Could she pretend it was going to rain and wear her trench coat?

A possible solution had she not sent her coat to the cleaners, she recalled a moment later.

Breathe in, breathe out, breathe in, breathe out, she silently coached herself, hopping on one foot, then the other while she slid on her really sweet purple heels with the open toes. Then, grabbing her car keys, she raced out of her bedroom, telling herself with what little calm she could muster that this wasn't a goddamned audience with the Queen.

394 was going to be without traffic.

God would provide.

And the nail she'd just broken wouldn't show if she clenched her fist.

BOBBY WORE TAN canvas hiking shorts, worn tennis shoes, and a plain white T-shirt, which immediately jarred her already faltering self-confidence as she burst into Arthur's office apologizing for being late. Quickly trying to recall the previous day's conversation, she wondered if a picnic had been mentioned without her noticing.

Arthur looked, as usual, as though he'd stepped from the cover of *GQ*. Reassuring in terms of picnics.

Both men shot a look at the clock.

That color suits her, Arthur thought.

She'd either forgotten to button the top button on her suit jacket or she was deliberately exposing her cleavage, Bobby noted. Either way, the view was fine.

Aware of his gaze, Cassie glanced down and, flushing an even deeper pink than that occasioned by her sprint from the car park, she quickly fastened the revealing neckline.

Arthur cleared his throat and swallowed once before speaking, thinking he'd have to discuss this strange new interest with his therapist. "I was about to show Bobby from where the Rubens was stolen. Bobby, this is Cassandra Hill, Cassandra, Bobby Serre. I'm not sure he's convinced he needs an assistant yet."

"Why don't we see." Bobby's voice was neutral.

"I'd appreciate the chance." He was cool and detached, and if she didn't need the money so badly, Cassie would have allowed him his indifference.

"I usually work alone."

"No need to make a decision now," Arthur quickly interposed, beginning to usher them out of his office. "Let's see if any evidence is left after the police ransacked the east wing."

When they reached the cluttered workroom where the Rubens had been in the process of being cleaned, Bobby walked around the room in silence while Arthur and Cassie watched. He stopped a dozen times to look at something neither one of them could see. He examined the easel where the painting had rested, lightly brushing his fingertips over the worn wood, stooping to lift a minute fragment of thread from under the easel base.

"How many people knew the Rubens was down for cleaning?"

"Probably everyone at the museum. It's one of our crown jewels."

"How many extras did you have in the building setting up the flower show?"

"A couple hundred or so."

"Any thoughts of canceling?"

"I'd like to, but the flowers are almost all in place, and rescheduling would entail some high replacement costs. Not to mention the spring show's a tradition at the museum."

"I'll need the names of everyone involved in the flower show—from the deliverymen to the arrangers."

"That'll take some time. We have sixty displays, all from different contributors." Arthur's cell phone rang. "Excuse me, I'm expecting a call. I'll just be a minute." Turning, he walked from the room.

"You get the names." Bobby nodded at Cassie.

"Now?"

"Later. Come here. Look at this." He stooped and pointed at the floor.

As Cassie approached, she surveyed the area he'd indicated and saw absolutely nothing. A bare wooden floor. Paint spattered. But it wasn't Ruben's paint. "Yes?" she said, hoping bland evasion would serve as an answer.

He looked up. "Tell me what you see."

Lord. It was a quiz. She frantically scanned the floor, thinking her consultant fees, her bills, and her future were at stake.

Bobby tamped down his libido. From this angle all he saw was tits and legs. Arthur was right. She was a piece of work. But he was decades past adolescent distractions, and when he spoke, his voice was neutral. "It's small and pink."

Not a good choice of words, he realized, when she was close enough to touch, when his brain was segueing small and pink into a totally inappropriate image. "That small bead there," he quickly amended, pointing again. "Do you see it now?"

She blew out a breath. "Yes."

He half smiled. "It's not an exam." Picking up the minute object, he came to his feet, his priorities back in order. "Take it." He held out his hand, the pink bead centered on his palm.

She hesitated for a moment, the thought of touching him suddenly unnerving. When it shouldn't be. When this was strictly business. When whether she touched his very large, tanned hand or not was incidental to her life.

"Maybe you could find an envelope to put it in," he prompted. The flush on her cheeks was damned provocative, along with all the rest of the provocative package from the top of her tousled curls to her painted toes in her spiky heels. But he purposely didn't make eye contact. He had no plans to stay a minute longer in Minneapolis than necessary.

As she raised her hand, he found himself anticipating her touch.

Telling himself not to be stupid, he plucked the bead from his palm and dropped it into her outstretched hand. "Now all we have to do is see if someone in Minneapolis is missing a bead and whether they have an interest in the Rubens," he quipped.

"You're kidding, right?"

"Probably." He shrugged. "But you never know. We'll check it out."

"Check out what?" Arthur inquired, reentering the workroom.

"Show him."

Cassie held out her hand.

"It's probably nothing," Bobby said. "I'll need the names of the flower and delivery people, though. Whenever you get the names, send them along. You've added extra security?"

With Arthur back in the room, Bobby found himself able to concentrate once again.

Arthur pursed his mouth. "Too late, but yes."

"When does the exhibit open?"

"Friday. Tomorrow, the trustees have an evening preview."

"I'll begin with the employee interviews."

"The police have already questioned many of them. My assistant doesn't have all the names of the temps yet, but she will soon."

"I'll take the list of regular employees first." Bobby looked at Cassie. "Bring the list to lunch. Palomino. One-thirty. Make reservations. I'm going to run a quick survey of the premises." With a last glance around the workroom, he walked out.

"You must have impressed him." Arthur's brows arched faintly. "He didn't want you onboard."

"It must have been my witty conversation."

"No doubt." Arthur wondered if the unbuttoned button had been deliberate.

Cassie recognized sexual innuendo when she heard it, but she didn't give a damn what Arthur thought so long as he paid her a consultant fee. "I'll get the list from Emma and go over the names before lunch."

SEVEN

CASSIE ARRIVED AT PALOMINO FIRST.

When Bobby walked in, he surveyed the room, caught sight of her, and turned to speak to the maître d'. The maître d', in turn, spoke to a waiter, who spoke to another waiter, who spoke to another, and a scurry of activity ensued as though Bobby Serre bore some intrinsic authority beneath his casual attire.

The other diners—mainly businesspeople—looked up at the commotion, trying to gauge the importance of someone dressed in shorts who commanded such overt truckling.

Seemingly unaware of the intense scrutiny from every diner in the room as he moved toward Cassie, Bobby smiled on reaching her. "I forgot to say I like corner tables." He nodded toward the staff moving another party from a corner table.

"You attract attention." Although tall, dark, handsome movie-star types tend to do that.

Bobby surveyed the room, and gazes shifted away. "Must be the shorts," he casually said, helping her up from her chair. Waving her before him, he followed her to the table that was quickly being reset. After pulling out her chair, he took a seat opposite her—one with his back to the wall. He glanced at the blinds, and a waiter jumped to shut out the sun.

She looked at him from under her lashes. "I've never been in the presence of royalty before."

"Drink?" Ignoring her comment, he crooked a finger at the hovering waiter.

She shook her head.

"Belvedere," he said to the young man gazing at him with the awestruck expression of a rock star fan. "Four ice cubes." He turned back to Cassie. "Don't you drink?"

"Sometimes."

"But not today?"

"I'm on my best behavior."

He quirked a brow.

"Arthur said you didn't want my help. I'm more polite sober."

"You need money, he said."

She nodded. "Although Arthur has trouble understanding the concept of financial need."

"He's led a privileged life."

"I'd say you have, too. The wait staff is practically bowing."

"I know the owner."

"Is she a woman?"

He almost smiled. "Your husband left you, I hear."

"Arthur just left his second wife. Perhaps it's a virus in town." She could avoid answering questions, too.

This time he did smile. "Are you in decline?"

Facetious or not, she knew what answer he wanted. "No, just poorer."

"Can you handle the work?"

"Of course."

"I don't like tears."

What man does? she wanted to say. "I'm fine, okay? My husband just turned out to be a jerk. Nothing serious."

"Good enough. You brought the list?" He took his drink from the waiter and set the offered menus on the table.

She tapped the papers beside her plate. She could do impersonal and businesslike—even efficient on occasion.

"Why did you marry him?" he suddenly asked.

"Do you really care?"

He shrugged. "Consider it your employee interview."

"I was naive and stupid." The last person she wanted to talk about was Jay. She couldn't afford to lose whatever slight inner poise she aspired to. "How about you? Are you married?" Didn't they say a good offense is the best defense?

"No."

"Ever been?" Blatant curiosity couldn't be entirely discounted.

"Why?"

"A yes, then. Did you get the house or did she?" She'd never met a James Bond type up close. She was allowed.

"We didn't have a house. I traveled. She traveled."

"What about the apartment, the toaster, the wedding album? I'm an expert on division of property."

"We had two apartments, so it was painless. She kept hers. I kept mine."

"You must have left her if it was painless." *All men are the same,* she thought with disgust. *James Bond types included.*

"It was mutual. Look, let's change the subject. We're not going to sleep together. We're just going to work together."

Her eyes narrowed. "Excuse me. Did I miss a segue?"

"Whenever women start asking you about your personal life . . ." He shrugged.

"You asked first."

"My mistake."

"Can I say 'screw you' and still keep my job?"

His mouth quirked into a grin. "Yes, but no thanks."

"It was a figure of speech."

His expression went bland. "Gotcha. Let's order and then take a look at that list of employees."

She forced herself to respond to his casualness with equanimity because a substantial sum of money was at stake, and she had no intention of sleeping with him anyway. But the indignity of being rejected before she could reject him was galling. With effort, she overcame her irritation by visualizing her checkbook balance growing, her bill pile diminishing, and her freezer filled to the brim with pints of Edna Mae's ice cream. Definitely a soothing image.

Glancing up from his menu, Bobby took note of Cassie's half-smile. He was tempted to ask why she was smiling. But he wasn't in town for long; he didn't *want* to be in town long. He asked instead, "Have you had the sea bass?"

Over lunch, while Bobby ate not only the sea bass, but a side of grilled rib eye, Cassie resentfully questioned the fairness of the world when he could eat like a linebacker and every leaf of lettuce she consumed potentially turned to cellulite. Not that she was precisely calorie-free in her choice of dessert. Maybe she wouldn't eat it all though—maybe she'd just taste a very little of the chocolate torte with raspberry ganache. And the small scoop of house-made vanilla ice cream that accompanied it was almost minuscule. Really. Not to mention the fact that chocolate was supremely healthful, she'd read.

Their conversation was restricted exclusively to the list of employee names. He asked questions about personalities, job duties, and lifestyles, and she answered with a brisk competence, offering up thumbnail sketches of the museum staff.

Finally setting aside the list, Bobby pushed away the remnants of his tiramisu and met Cassie's gaze. "Do you have any ideas on who may have stolen the Rubens?"

"I'd like to say Arthur. He's such a jerk. But he doesn't

need the money even a Rubens would fetch on the black market."

"How do the rest of the staff feel about Arthur?" He was suddenly looking at her differently.

"I didn't do it. Okay? Although, I admit, I did consider how the sale of the painting would set me up in style. And my dislike of Arthur is shared by the other staff members— their resentment only exceeded by their annoyance with his arrogance and stupidity."

"Everyone feels that way?"

He spoke softly, but his eyes gave her a sense of unease, as though he could see inside her brain. She scrambled to cover up her private observations on his movie-star good looks. "You'd be hard-pressed to find a single advocate for him on that list," she said, honesty tres simple in this case.

"I've known Arthur a long time."

"Oh, damn, you're friends. Although, if you know him well, his lack of staff support can't come as a complete surprise."

"We climb together. He's dependable—a necessary quality on an ice cap at fifteen thousand feet. But I'm aware of his shortcomings."

"How diplomatic."

"No one's perfect."

She thought of Bobby Serre leaving his wife. Men liked that platitude; it made them blameless.

"But we both know Arthur didn't take the painting." He leaned back in his chair, his scrutiny suddenly relaxed, as though she'd passed some internal litmus test. "We'll begin interviewing the staff tomorrow. You can serve as liaison."

"Meaning?"

"Smooth ruffled feathers."

"Definitely not my strong point." At his lifted brows she thought of her bills. "But I'm willing to learn."

"Good." He drained his espresso. "Meet me in the conference room tomorrow morning at seven-thirty. I'm an early riser." Aware of the sudden flaring shock in her gaze, he said, "Set your alarm. I want to get through as many interviews as possible tomorrow." His blue eyes took on a sudden coolness. "Don't be late. I hate excuses."

"Yes, sir."

His mouth lifted in a faint smile at her sarcasm. "Go to bed early."

"I'm a night person."

"You'll have to change."

"I do so enjoy having a man tell me what to do."

His gaze was amused. "I don't see any problem then."

She felt a completely incongruous sensual jolt as though some dominant/submissive sexual interchange had just occurred. "For you," she muttered, feeling the need to guard herself against sudden danger.

"For both of us, I hope." He smiled. "I've some phone calls to make right now. I'll see you in the morning."

Had his smile been flirtatious? And what was with that casual "both of us" reply? But he was gone a moment later, and she was left contemplating the faux Matisse mural on the wall. She'd misunderstood, of course. His smile hadn't been flirtatious, nor was there any innuendo in his remark. He was being polite, that's all. Her fleeting moment of lust must have been induced by the rich chocolate torte. Besides deterring cavities, chocolate had aphrodisiac properties. Right?

Taking a deep breath, she warned herself to get a grip. Obviously, it had been too long since she'd had sex. Not an excuse for what had happened, but a reason. Although there was no point in following this totally ridiculous train of thought.

Bobby Serre had said he wasn't interested.

EIGHT

ONCE MORE IN CONTROL OF HER FEELINGS—
the drive to the museum offered sufficient time to rationalize away any further aberrant emotions—Cassie
stopped to collect the list of temps from Arthur's assistant,
Emma. Bobby Serre hadn't asked her to, but then he hadn't
told her *not* to, and curious after their discussion of the staff
and robbery over lunch, she felt like drawing up a list of
possible suspects on her own. It was pretty clear he thought
someone inside the museum had copped the Rubens.

"I don't know if I should give you this," Emma equivo-
cated. "No one said anything to me."

"I'm helping Serre. I'm his liaison."

"I'll have to think about it." Emma had been a temp herself before deciding she could stand Arthur's rudeness—the
defeat of a dozen assistants before her. Over six feet tall,
built like a female Viking, Fridley's best volleyball player in
the intermural league didn't take any crap from Arthur.

"I'll introduce you to the great Bobby Serre if you give it
to me."

"Hmmm." Emma looked down at the list on her desk and then back at Cassie. "I can introduce myself. He'll be back."

"I could tell him something nice about you. I hear women who spend the night with him are always smiling in the morning."

"Hell, as if you and I stand a chance," Emma said with a grin, flicking the sheet of paper toward Cassie. "I don't think we've done any international modeling lately."

"I've sworn off men, anyway." There was no need to mention that Bobby Serre had already shot her down. Picking up the sheet of paper, Cassie quickly perused the score or so of names.

"A cheating husband is the pits."

"And I was too stupid to notice. Can you believe weekends visiting his parents? And evenings with coworkers on Minnetonka?"

"Hey—everyone wants to believe marriage is forever. You were into optimism and silver linings."

"More like castles in the air. I kept overlooking Jay's personality change when his company started making money. We'd had a pretty good marriage before that; we laughed a lot in the beginning, went places, did things. Had fun. Jay was a great date. He just started getting a big head. After that, he decided he wasn't in for the long haul."

Emma shrugged. "And there's always bimbos." She'd seen Tami once. "Men can't resist them."

"I expect there are men who can."

Emma wanted to say she could have told Cassie that Jay wasn't one of them the first time she'd met him and he'd looked at her in a totally inappropriate way. "You're way too nice. That's your problem."

"I don't know about that. I'm currently fantasizing about Jay's murder-that-looks-like-suicide."

"Good for you. I scared the shit out of my last boyfriend when I found out he was cheating on me."

"You've got six inches on me and biceps I'd die for. I can only scare Jay by threatening to tell Tami about his mother."

"Have you?"

"Not yet. But it kept him from pushing me to sell the house."

Emma raised her fist and grinned. "Female power."

"It seems to be working for you with Arthur."

"You bet. I can out-press him, and he knows it."

Vowing to dust off her weights, begin her workouts first thing tomorrow, and get on the female power track, Cassie thrust the sheet of paper into her hand-painted carryall with Marilyn Monroe's portrait outlined in sequins. "Thanks for the list."

"You ever need anyone—Jay, for instance—intimidated, you let me know."

Cassie smiled at the gratifying image. Not only did Emma stand eye to eye with her ex-husband, but Cassie was pretty certain she could out-press Jay as well. "I'll keep it in mind. I may need you if he threatens to take me to court over that last painting."

Emma winked. "You know my number."

The temp list was long—a reflection of Arthur's personality flaws. No one worked for him any length of time, which didn't say much for those on the staff who were, like herself, either committed to the museum or the city or perhaps more flawed than Arthur. This was an ongoing personal debate she'd not yet satisfactorily resolved.

But Cassie had an uncommon independence in her position, thanks to a grant from Isabelle Palmer specifically tailored to her expertise and person. Trusts and grants offered to museums could be dictated in general-use terms or for specific application—those applications often cited in the most definitive legalese. In Isabelle's case, her trust named Cassie as its sole curator so long as she chose to remain at the museum. Should she leave, the trust would be renegotiated—always a scary thought with possible heirs preferring to put their inheritance elsewhere. Bringing in Isabelle's fifty-million-dollar windfall had been a definite coup—even Arthur didn't step on Cassie's toes when it came to acquisitions for the Palmer collection. And the exhibit she'd prepared two years ago had garnered worldwide acclaim. *The Role of Women as Subject and Artist in Narrative Painting* had traveled to the Los Angeles County Museum, the Met, the Tate, and the D'Orsay. Cassie had felt as though Isabelle had overseen it with a smile on her face, a martini in her hand, and a dozen men friends surrounding her in her comfortable loggia on the Elysium Fields.

Back in her office, Cassie studied the temp names, profiling each one in a few short sentences, conscious now of what Bobby Serre would be looking for in terms of information. Did they need money? Did they have family obligations? Wives and children? Ex-wives and children? Contacts or family outside the city or outside the country? Drinking, drugs, gambling habits? Not that she was familiar with all their personal lives, but one learned a great deal in the coffee room over lunch or breaks. People bitched and grumbled. Everyone had some trauma in their lives. If you put enough people together in a room day after day, the soap opera of life eventually unfolded.

And perhaps she had a better nose than most for those personal idiosyncrasies, raised by a mother like hers who often categorized people by their teeth or hair. Her mother could also remember what someone wore twenty years ago and what she'd eaten at a dinner party in 1976 (and recite the recipe from memory). Her mother's gift for conversational recall was equally amazing. She could tell you what someone said to her in an airport in Cincinnati between flights when she was twelve.

From such a mother, Cassie had acquired an eye and ear for detail—a quality further refined by her field of expertise. She could pick out a Hapsburg or Bourbon nose in a portrait from any century, distinguish between countries of origin in a painted face, date any costume within a year or two, and recognize the hand of a particular artist in a brush stroke.

A shame she'd been blind to her husband's sudden interest in boating on Lake Minnetonka and long weekends in Biwabik.

For the remainder of the afternoon, Cassie concentrated on putting together her list of suspects, adding last those she knew outside the museum who were connected in some way to the institution. There were the occasional patrons who had become disenchanted with their treatment or offended when their tastes in art hadn't been supported. Even a few of the trustees fell within her wide net, although certainly none of them needed money. But she preferred erring on the side of excess. It was easy enough to scratch a name later. A shame Jay hadn't been interested in art. She would have loved to add him to the suspect list.

Call her vengeful.

She had reason.

As if on cue, her phone rang. When she picked it up, the unwelcome voice of her husband barked, "My lawyer says your lawyer is telling me I can't have that painting. What the fuck's wrong with you?"

"I paid for that painting on our honeymoon. You're not getting it." She'd bought the painting because she'd liked it. Jay didn't spend money on art. It should have been a clue about their compatibility.

"It's in the divorce settlement."

"Why don't we have the lawyers argue the point?"

"If you think I'm letting you have my favorite painting, you're crazy!"

The only reason Jay wanted the painting was because he knew she liked it almost as much as Edna Mae's ice cream. "My lawyer wanted me to take half your income for all the years of our marriage. Consider that before you complain about one damned painting."

"Over my dead body you would have gotten half my income!"

"Had I known there was such incentive . . ." she murmured.

"You always were a fucking bitch!"

"You should have considered that before you asked me to marry you." She set the receiver down very gently, inhaled deeply, counted to ten, counted to ten again, counted to ten a third time, then threw her paperweight across the room, where it bounced off the grass-cloth wall and landed with a thud on the sisal carpet.

The malachite turtle, upside down and rocking, seemed particularly analogous to her own impotent rage, and she wondered how long it took before an ex-husband no longer incited such fury.

Not much longer, she hoped, because she couldn't afford a therapist.

When the phone rang a minute later, she checked her caller ID in the event Jay was calling back. But her sister's number appeared on the screen. She picked up.

"Don't forget dinner tonight." Meg always sounded cheerful, a fact that on occasion made Cassie question her sister's grasp of reality.

"I thought it was on Wednesday."

"Today is Wednesday. And I invited Willie Peterson, too. I ran into her at Barnes and Noble. Her two-year-old and Luke were both at the children's hour."

"She has a two-year-old? When did she get married?"

"She didn't, but it's all for the best. She'll tell you about it tonight."

"What happened to Todd?"

"You'll have to come to dinner to find out."

"You sound like Mother. I would have come anyway."

"Really—after you've canceled on me three times?"

"I haven't been hungry lately."

"Since Jay left you mean. Did I find a way to lure you out or what?"

"I admit, I'm intrigued. I thought Todd was going to be the youngest vice president First National ever appointed and when they were married Willie was going to leave us all behind in her dust and send us postcards from exotic spas and golf courses around the world."

"She's still golfing. She won third place in the Women's U.S. Open. Dinner's at six-thirty. The kids can't wait. I'm making Mom's chicken pot pie."

"Why didn't you say so? I would have come without Willie."

"I just thought I'd make the evening irresistible."

"I don't suppose you're making homemade rolls."

"I suppose I might be."

Cassie laughed. "If you say you've made lemon sherbet and sugar cookies, too, I'll bring you a present."

"Something from Godiva would be nice."

"I'll be there early." Her grandmother's lemon sherbet recipe dated from the days when refrigerators had first entered the kitchens of America and was still made in little ice cube trays. It had the rich, sumptuous, lemony flavor of nostalgia and childhood well-being. "Dessert before dinner?"

"Of course. It's a family tradition."

*　*　*

WHEN HER PHONE rang a third time shortly after, Cassie glanced at the screen. Unknown caller. At least it wasn't Jay. His ego required his company name—Sibley Clubs—be prominently displayed. He wasn't shy.

"Do you have time for dinner?"

The voice was vaguely familiar.

"My brain's in overdrive sorting through names and—"

Bingo.

"If you could bring the list of temps to dinner, we could work for a few hours tonight."

"Sorry. I have plans."

"A date?"

"Does it matter?"

"Of course. If you're going on a date—"

"I'm going on a date." Bobby Serre's voice had been much too assured, as though women never said no to him.

"Meet me later then. Anytime. I'd like to go over the new names."

"Can't it wait until morning?"

"This project is eating into my vacation. All I need is an hour or so for you to give me some quick profiles. Maybe you could spare some time now."

She sighed, understanding instant gratification. It was right there at the top of her "Need to Improve to Reach Maturity" list. "I suppose I could give you a few minutes now."

"I'll be there in five."

"Where are you—outside?"

"Sort of. I'm on the loading dock."

WHILE CASSIE WAITED for Bobby to arrive, she quickly called her sister to explain that she'd be a half-hour late—giving her a swift rundown of her new lucrative liaison position. Before she could finish, Meg interrupted.

"Bring him along. I've never known a man who wasn't charmed by a home-cooked meal."

"I'm not interested in charming him."

"If you have to work with the guy, and if you're relying on his good graces to continue this lucrative employment, you might consider the usefulness of charm."

"You don't understand. Bobby Serre is the last person in the world who's susceptible to charm. He dates international models and jets around the world. And believe me, he doesn't eat chicken pot pie. I'll come to dinner alone."

"I happen to love chicken pot pie."

The deep voice came from the direction of her doorway, and when Cassie swivelled around, Bobby was leaning against the doorjamb, grinning.

"I'm not talking about you."

He gave her a like-hell-you're-not look that triggered a tremulous flutter where she didn't want to feel a flutter, where she hadn't felt a flutter for a very long time.

"Whatever—but I do love chicken pot pie," he said, smiling. "My grandmother made it."

"I heard that," her sister gleefully murmured in Cassie's ear. "Tell him he's welcome!"

"No!" A rush of color pinked Cassie's cheeks.

"What's for dessert?" Bobby nodded toward the phone.

"See. He's more sensible than you. It's only a family dinner, for God's sake," Meg hissed. "Tell him it's lemon sherbet." Her sister had been trying to fix her up almost before Jay left, apparently having been more enlightened about her philandering husband's extracurricular activities than she.

"Maybe you'd like to tell him yourself," Cassie muttered.

In two long strides, Bobby was beside her, the phone was slipped from her grasp, and Bobby was introducing himself to Meg.

Cassie glared at him as he hung up the phone after a

much-too-lengthy conversation that had unaccountably turned to Willie and her ex-fiancé. "What happened to 'let's keep this impersonal'?"

"I haven't had a home-cooked meal in ages. Be nice to me, and I'll see that Arthur gives you a raise."

"As if you could."

"You doubt me, ye of little faith?" he teased.

"I don't like the sound of this be-nice-to-me shit. You sound like Arthur at his most provoking. Haven't you guys heard of the Civil Rights Act?"

"Don't get technical. You help me, and I'll help you— that's all."

"Does this mutual aid society have to include dinner at my sister's house?"

"She invited me."

"She's too damned friendly."

"Apparently you've been staying home too much."

"She said that to you?"

"She's worried."

"Jeez." Cassie blew out a breath of disgust. "Look. I'm perfectly fine."

"You don't sound perfectly fine. You sound frustrated."

Her green eyes flashed. "If you dare imply like some patronizing male throwback to another century that—"

He put up both hands to stop her. "I really do like chicken pot pie and lemon sherbet. I'd also like to run through that list of temps with you. I'm not implying anything. But when I'm on the scent, like now, I don't sleep much until I've put together a notion of who and/or why a piece of art has been stolen. If all goes well, maybe we can finish this up in a few days."

The sound of the word *we* cooled her temper as though he was asking instead of telling. Her pulse rate began to subside. She could also hear the echo of Meg's words of warning. And he *had* said he could get her a raise. "Okay, okay."

"Great." Ignoring her sulky tone, he gestured toward the door. "My driver's downstairs."

He waited for her to grab her purse and stepped aside so she could come from behind her desk and walk by him.

"Pull the door shut, will you?" Cassie said as she walked out into the hall. "Is he waiting in the front or back?"

"Back. I came in through the loading dock."

She walked ahead of him to the stairway, which was all right with him because the view from behind was first rate—those long legs, great ass, and sway of her hips kept him focused. Not that he should be fixating. But it didn't hurt to look.

Cassie led the way because she was more comfortable when Bobby Serre wasn't too close. Maybe it was his cologne. Or his immense size. Maybe she'd been without a man too long. Whatever it was, it was impossible to ignore his damnable gorgeous presence, and she felt better with some distance between her and temptation.

She descended the steps quickly, Bobby a few paces behind, but as they neared the door to the loading dock, he moved forward. "I'll give you a hand down the stairs," he said.

"I'm fine." She'd prefer not touching him for reasons that didn't bear contemplation.

"There's no railing."

She shot him a look as she walked across the dock. "I'm fine, really."

Those spiky heels—he wasn't so sure. As she reached the top of the narrow cement stairway, he jumped from the dock to the ground and waited for her at the bottom of the stairs.

"That's unnecessary," she said with a small frown, taking the first step. "I've probably gone down these stairs a hundred times."

"Just in case," he said with a smile. Arthur was right. She was prickly.

She was just about to give him an I-told-you-so smile as she reached the ground when her right heel sank into the soft asphalt, she lurched, he caught her, and her I-told-you-so smile ended up on his throat.

She felt just like he thought she'd feel, soft where she should be and toned where she should be and sumptuous as hell. He shouldn't be thinking this when he had a job to do.

My God, he was all steel hard muscle like some Mr. Universe who worked out ten hours a day—which only added to his very long list of admirable attributes, none of which was available to her because he wasn't interested.

He'd only offered his hand to be polite.

She should have taken his hand like a mature adult and saved herself this horrendous embarrassment.

Blushing and stammering and making no sense at all, she tried to extricate herself from his arms.

She finally managed to put together words in a coherent sentence as he set her back on her feet. "I'm so sorry. Did I hurt you?"

"Nothing's hurt. Are you okay?"

"Except for being mortified, I'm fine."

"Good. How about taking my arm on this soft asphalt." He nodded to the car several yards away.

She had no choice short of looking like an idiot.

He put out his arm.

She placed her hand on his strong, tanned forearm covered with a light dusting of black hair.

He placed his hand over hers, because she might be more mortified if she fell again.

Just to be sure, she took care not to let her heels sink into the asphalt.

It was a long walk to the car.

Or it was a short walk to the car.

Depending on whether you were focused on embarrassment or pleasure.

It was just about impossible to embarrass Bobby—her scent, the occasional brush of her hip against his, the close proximity to her really lush boobs. Hell, he could have walked for another ten miles.

As was often the case with Cassie, she was ambiguous, her embarrassment still hovering on the fringes of her brain. But she wasn't averse to the titillation of feeling the scrumptious, hunky Bobby Serre under her hand and over her hand and against her hip. Like that.

As they approached the car, the driver jumped out, came around, and opened the back door.

"Where to?" he asked.

Effectively breaking the spell.

Meg is waiting, Cassie thought. *Life is waiting.*

Dinner at some stranger's house, Bobby thought, reminding himself why he was here.

And it wasn't for a piece of ass.

"I don't know the address," Bobby said, taking a step back so her hand fell away from his arm.

Cassie gave the driver the address, her voice as cool and collected as Bobby Serre's.

When she sat down in the backseat, she placed her purse on the seat between them.

He noticed.

But that was fine with him.

Everything was under control again.

NINE

THE DRIVER WAS EITHER AN OLD FRIEND OR
Bobby Serre made friends easily, because Joe from
Eden Prairie talked about hunting and fishing in Montana practically the entire way to Meg's house.

Bobby carried on a conversation with the driver deliberately, preferring to keep what was under control just that—under control. But he politely apologized as they moved up the front walk to Cassie's sister's faux farmhouse in a new sub-development of faux farmhouses with front porches, peaked roofs, and potential rose gardens and trees. "I'm from Montana, as you probably figured out, and Joe and I've been swapping stories. He likes to talk. Sorry."

"Not a problem." In fact she'd been relieved, not having to decide what to say and how to say it. His Montana background explained his hair and eyes, she reminded herself, suddenly recognizing the Native American heritage in his looks. As if his movie-star appeal needed any further romanticizing—a vision of dashing warriors in full battle regalia astride magnificent horses galloped into her consciousness. And the warrior leading the troop, of course, was—

"Are you okay?"

Jarred back to reality, she tried to sift through the tumble of excuses fighting for supremacy in her mind.

"She daydreams a lot."

Meg stood at the open door, smiling.

"I do not."

"I'm trying to be polite. He thought you'd dozed off." Stepping forward, she held out her hand. "I'm Meg. You must be Bobby. Thanks for helping Cassie earn some extra money. Jay really left her in this mess, not that it's any of your concern, but—anyway . . . thanks."

"What—am I invisible?" Cassie protested, preferring her personal life not be discussed with strangers.

Meg grinned. "I'm an older sister. I can be protective."

"Is that what you call embarrassing the hell out of me?"

"Divorce is unpleasant." Bobby shrugged. "Don't be embarrassed."

"See." Meg shot Cassie a grin. "Now come on in, you two," she said, as if they were actually a couple when they were so *not* a couple. Cassie flushed pink just thinking about the ridiculous presumption, that misconception apparently going unnoticed by her sister, who added, "I made a pitcher of lemon drops to take the edge off your busy day. You look tired, Cassie. She hasn't been sleeping well." Meg gave Bobby a smile. "But with you here, maybe things will be looking up."

"Do you mind?" Cassie expostulated, the flush deepening on her cheeks.

"I'm sorry. Can't I say you look tired when you do?" Meg replied, looking innocent. "Go make yourself comfortable on the sun porch, and relax."

Cassie was going to have to find a moment alone with her

sister and explain that Bobby Serre wasn't likely to respond to an unsubtle ten-ton Mack truck attempt at matchmaking when he'd remained seriously single even in the midst of a bevy of aspiring starlets and models. More important, the Bobby Serres of the world weren't her style. Although Jay had turned out to not be her style, either. Perhaps she need a dating consultant to steer her in the right direction.

As they entered the house, two towheaded children came charging down the hall, screaming, "Cassie! Cassie! Cassie!"

Dropping her purse and kicking off her heels, she stooped to meet them, braced for the impact. But she was smiling. Just seeing them made her instantly happy.

"What did you bring us?" they screamed in unison, wiggling in her embrace. "Where's our toy?"

"Mind your manners," their mother scolded.

"I came from work," Cassie said, not taking offense at the children's mercenary outlook. Her favorite aunts had always brought her neat presents. "I'll bring you something next time."

"How about these?" Bobby drew out a small brass compass and a flashlight pen from his shorts pocket.

Immediately deserted for the lure of shiny objects, Cassie and Meg watched the Serre charm captivate an age group normally considered outside the purview of international sex symbols. Two-year-old Luke and three-year-old Zoe stood wide-eyed and mesmerized as Bobby squatted down before them and showed them the mysteries of the compass and pen. He spoke in a soft, low tone; let them each manipulate the light and spinning dial; and explained in child-speak how to make both work before giving the children their prizes.

"I'm impressed," Meg said as her children ran away clutching their offerings. "I'll rescue them later."

"Don't bother. They're expendable. And thank you for

having me to dinner. I haven't had a home-cooked meal for a long time."

"We're just waiting on Willie. Oz is out of town."

Cassie met Bobby's searching glance. "Oswald is Meg's husband, but don't even consider calling him Oswald unless you can take on a three-hundred-pound ex-linebacker."

Bobby grinned. "Got it."

"Oz's mother was looking for some inheritance from a rich uncle," Meg explained. "When the uncle was seventy-five, he married a waitress who was young enough to be his granddaughter and left his money to her instead. A little like—"

"Don't you dare say it," Cassie warned.

"Okay, fine, go have a drink." Meg nodded toward the kitchen. "I'll check on dinner and the kids."

SLIPPING HER HEELS back on, Cassie led Bobby down the hall and into a sun porch that overlooked the backyard as well as the neighbor's backyards in the spanking-new housing development fashioned out of a former cornfield.

"Nice," Bobby said, taking in the view through the floor-to-ceiling windows.

"If you're the sociable type. Meg says you can see what the neighbors are eating when they sit on their patio. But Meg gets along with everyone—don't look at me like that. We can't all be extroverts."

"Or linebackers. I understand."

"You were a receiver, weren't you?" she said, moving toward the sweating pitcher of lemon drops atop a Lucite tray on an old wicker table Meg had refurbished.

"About a hundred years ago."

"Before you became the James Bond of the art world."

"Hardly. It's a job, that's all. One I happen to enjoy."

"Rumor of your particular style of enjoyment titillates a great many in the humdrum world of museum curators."

He grinned. "I didn't think you cared."

Picking up a martini glass, she glanced over her shoulder. "I don't. I've sworn off men for the next millennium."

He was surprised her words struck him as a personal challenge. It took a second or two to rein in his libido. "That's what a divorce can do to you," he blandly noted.

"Speaking from personal experience?" She poured the lemon drink into her glass.

"Not exactly."

"Stupid me. You're a man."

He could have explained that he and Claire should never have married, which made their divorce slightly less nasty. He could have explained that *slightly* was a relative word. He could have explained that he was pissed for a very long time when the inevitable had happened. Although he guessed Cassandra Hill wouldn't have cared to hear that his libido was immune to any of the emotional fallout. The sexy redhead with the killer legs who Arthur had saddled him with would have felt vindicated in her blanket condemnation of the male sex. And strangely, he wasn't in the mood to piss her off completely—the obvious reason for that making him vaguely uncomfortable.

Not that it mattered if he decided he wanted her.

A decidedly inauspicious thought under the circumstances—here in her sister's house. Although his libido seemed immune to providence as she bent over slightly to set the pitcher back down—displaying a fraction more of her long legs under her short skirt . . . giving him an instant hard-on.

Fortunately, childish screams echoed through the house just then, the high-pitched sound capable of quelling even his fired-up libido. When Cassie turned around with a drink in her hand, he was able to say in a relatively neutral voice, "If we're going to work together, we should probably avoid personal subjects."

"So I shouldn't mention that phrase, 'You seem happy to see me.'"

He grimaced. "Your skirt's too damned short."

Her brows rose. "Your lack of control is my fault?"

"What's your fault?" Meg entered the room carrying a tray of crab canapés.

"Nothing's my fault. I lead a faultless life," Cassie said with a smile as Bobby half turned to hide the bulge in his shorts and moved toward the drink table.

Meg lasered her sister with a reproving look. "Don't argue with him. He's nice to my kids."

"I'm not arguing. I never argue. I'm the least argumentative person on the face of the earth." Half pleased at Bobby Serre's reaction when he was more familiar with bedding international models, she avoided the alternate thought that perhaps any woman would do and allowed her vanity an unblushing moment of glory.

"How much have you had to drink?" her sister suspiciously inquired.

"Not enough." Lifting her glass to her mouth, Cassie emptied it down her throat, because beyond her fleeting moment of self-conceit, she was finding it difficult if not impossible to resist the image of Bobby Serre's hard-on when she hadn't had sex for a very, very, *very* long time. And what she had seen even at a glance was super *large*.

"Watch her for me," Meg ordered, setting the canapés on a side table and glancing at Bobby. "She can't hold her liquor."

Cassie swallowed. "Can to."

"Since when?"

"Since always." Why did she always revert to a childish vernacular in the presence of her sister?

"Hmpf." Meg nodded at Bobby. "See that she doesn't have more than two," she said, walking from the room.

A small silence fell.

Bobby turned around and lifted his drink in mocking salute. "As if. Right?"

"I don't need a keeper," Cassie muttered, carefully not looking south of his waist.

He noticed and almost said, *You can look. Everything's back to normal.* "Tell me about it," he said instead. "I have an older brother."

"You're kidding. Someone gives you orders?"

It took him a moment to answer because she'd moved to a wicker chair, sat down, and crossed her legs like Sharon Stone in *Basic Instinct* and his libido was right back up there in ramming speed. "He tries, but I don't see him much," he said in a carefully constrained tone, sitting down as well for obvious reasons. "He lives in Hawaii."

"Why?" After his talk about Montana, she'd recalled the working ranch there; it was part of his showy biography for public consumption.

Don't look at her legs. "He likes to surf."

A simple answer to a simple question, but way the hell out of her sphere of reference where glamorous lives were relegated to her TV screen. "Is he married?"

In that wary tone of voice men had when the word *married* came up in conversation, he answered, "He's married."

"Kids?"

"Four."

"Wow. So you're the brother without family values."

"I don't see *you* with kids."

"Don't go there."

"Sorry. Sore point?"

"One of many with my ex-husband who perceived the world as his own personal amusement park."

"While you were the stay-at-home, making-pies kind of wife?"

"Why are we having this conversation?" He could shove his sarcasm.

"You asked about my brother."

"So did you really find what's her name—the DeBeers widow's painting behind a sofa in Hertfordshire?"

He smiled faintly at her politic shift in conversation. "Yes. It was her favorite Rubens—the self-portrait with his first wife. The banditos dumped some of the other pieces in a ditch if you can believe it." He relaxed. Talking about art was a helluva lot safer than thinking about fucking her. "Most art thieves don't have much of a clue what they're doing—you know, hammer and crowbar guys, like those in Norway who stole *The Scream* and tried to sell it to two detectives from Scotland Yard. On the other hand, there are the occasional professionals like those who copped the Corot from the Louvre during prime visiting hours. That painting disappeared from view. Into some drug lord's hacienda, I suspect. Your top button's undone again." He gave himself points for not responding to that glimpse of cleavage.

"It's not on purpose, okay?" she quickly replied, re-closing the button. "It wasn't this morning, either. Arthur might have thought otherwise, and I wouldn't want you to be equally deluded. Clear?"

"As crystal."

"Good," she crisply said, rising from her chair. "And for your information, I can so hold my liquor, so don't give me any grief over another drink."

"I wouldn't think of it," he murmured, just as a voice from the doorway exclaimed, "Wow and double wow. Introduce me, Cassie."

"Willie Peterson, Bobby Serre. And stop panting, Willie. It's embarrassing."

"Is he yours? Do you allow poaching?" Willie asked, striding into the room like a suntanned example of intense strength training and a daily eighteen holes of golf.

"Go for it." Between Meg and Willie working Bobby Serre, it was going to be a very long evening. Cassie took note of the number of drinks left in the pitcher. She was probably going to need them.

Bobby had come to his feet, and Willie put out her hand as she reached him. "Tell me you golf, and I'll know I've died and gone to heaven."

"Sorry," Bobby said with a grin, taking her hand. "Only when I absolutely have to."

"You probably do other things really well though," Willie purred.

He laughed and smoothly slipped his hand free. "Meg tells me you were in the money at the Women's Open. Congratulations."

"Mommy, I want dompass, too!" a peevish toddler proclaimed, running into the room. "Duke has dompass! Won't give me none!"

Willie turned to her son, Cole. "Look, sweetie," she said, pulling her keys from her purse and holding them out to him. "You can have these instead."

A pouty toddler face was instantly transformed. Taking the offered key ring with a wide smile, Cole immediately jammed the attached whistle into his mouth and proceeded to blow so hard his little face turned red.

"Darling, *please*—take it outside!" Willie shouted above the earsplitting shrillness. "Show it to Luke and Zoe!"

Cassie's ears were still ringing as the outside door slammed on Willie's son. "What a darling little boy," Cassie said with a smile, hoping her eardrums weren't permanently damaged.

"He looks like Todd, doesn't he?"

"The perfect image." Too polite to ask why he looked like

Todd when Willie was single, Cassie said instead, "He has your high spirits, though." Social lies weren't really lies at all, but a means of avoiding rude statements.

"Isn't he just perfect," Willie cooed with that inexplicable blindness of parenthood.

"Too perfect for words." Was she smooth or what? "How about a drink?"

Over drinks Willie explained the particulars of her win at the Women's Open before Meg came to fetch them for dinner—the children having been corralled and seated at the table.

Meg had one of those childproof dining room sets with a solid maple table and heavier-than-usual Windsor chairs that wouldn't tip no matter what acrobatics three rambunctious toddlers attempted. Conversation at dinner was almost nonexistent unless constant haranguing and remonstrances to "sit still and eat or you won't get dessert" counted. Which only worked for the briefest period of time before Meg caved and decided lemon sherbert and sugar cookies would serve as the primary food groups that night.

"Why don't the children eat outside on the picnic table?" Willie suggested so calmly Cassie wondered if she was partially deaf and blind. "Cole just loves picnics. I'll help you settle them down, Meg."

A sudden silence descended once the dining room cleared, the debris from three children's meals the only evidence a toddler tornado had passed through.

Cassie lifted her brows. "I'll bet you're sorry now you wanted chicken pot pie."

"Kids don't bother me." Bobby reached for another roll. "You haven't seen my brother's brood. Pass the butter, will you?"

"Are you brain-dead? Cole apparently has never heard

the word *no,* and Luke and Zoe were close to dancing on the table."

"At least they didn't throw their food." He was buttering his roll with a detached air of calm. "Count your blessings."

"You know children who throw food?"

"Oh, yeah. Watching four nephews under ten can get dicey at times."

"Jeez, I'm losing my James Bond image here."

"Just as well," he murmured, forking up some chicken pot pie. "I lead a pretty normal life."

"Except for the villas in Europe, the starlets, and the parties on the Riviera."

He looked up, his fork poised near his mouth. "I guess."

"Which means you don't lead a normal life at all."

He didn't answer for the time it took to chew and swallow. "Depends on what's normal," he said mildly.

"Shopping for groceries, eating at McDonald's, mowing the lawn."

"Do you mow the lawn?"

"I've been known to mow a lawn."

He smiled. "Rider or push mower?"

"Okay, I admit, the kid down the block mows the lawn."

"I have a rider out West—but then I have a pretty big yard."

"And you actually mow your lawn?" she challenged.

"When I'm home, I do."

For some reason she didn't want to hear it; she would have preferred the larger-than-life Bobby Serre she could dismiss as unattainable. She didn't want him to be too normal and maybe within reach if she was standing on a really high ladder. It made it harder to talk herself out of noticing how good he looked and how pleasant he seemed and how she'd probably be the ten thousandth female who wanted to sleep with him this week. She'd better stop drinking because she hadn't seriously thought of sleeping with anyone since Jay had served her divorce papers.

Unfortunately, the troublesome voice inside her head took that opportunity to point out without any sense of propriety that perhaps she'd finally passed the stage of grieving over her marriage and was ready to move on to the next stage. You know, the one where men like Bobby Serre could really serve a useful purpose—in terms of getting on with her life. In like, moving on.

In like, trading her anger and resentment for a good lay.

"If you're not going to eat your roll, do you mind if I do?"

Actually, I do, she thought, coming back to the scene of destruction on her sister's dining room table. She minded that he could eat seven rolls and three chicken pot pies and two servings of mayonnaise-laden cole slaw and not have an extra ounce of body fat on his buff body. "Not at all," she lied, handing over her roll because she wasn't about to expose her insecurities and lustful thoughts by actually speaking the truth.

Although, in her slightly mellow frame of mind after two lemon drops and a glass of wine, she allowed herself the pleasurable sensation of feeling lust for the first time after months of celibacy. She wasn't quite certain if it was the lemon drops and the glass of wine or the gloriously handsome man smiling at her across the table or whether she'd finally run out of outrage. But there it was—LUST—in (eight-point) caps. Definitely not good, her voice of reason reminded her, throwing off the warm, cozy blanket of alcohol-induced mellowness. Remember, he said he wasn't interested.

SO FOR CHRIST'S SAKE, DON'T EMBARRASS YOURSELF.

Instantly sobered by the terrifying image of public rejection, Cassie smoothed the napkin in her lap, sat up a little straighter, and said in a voice so neutral she could have been the female spokesperson for the nuclear energy industry explaining on the six o'clock news that no danger existed despite the recent meltdown at a nearby facility, "I picked up the list of temps from Emma this afternoon and started to make notes for you."

He did a double take but recovered smoothly and continued tearing her roll in two. "Good. I appreciate your initiative. Fill me in on the various personalities on the way home."

"Don't go home until you've had dessert," Meg declared, coming back into the dining room with two servings of sherbet—apparently in her best company mood, serving dessert last. Setting down the dishes, she began clearing the children's mess.

"Let me help you," Bobby offered, rising to his feet.

"Nonsense. Tell him he doesn't have to help, Cassie."

Cassie met his gaze.

"I don't mind," he said. "Really."

Not about to argue with a man who was willing to clear the table, Cassie said, "Bring the sugar cookies when you come back."

"You could help, Cassie," her sister said, giving her one of those significant looks vacillating between reproof and unspoken advice that was impossible to interpret under the best of circumstances—meaning in a more sober state than her current one.

"No need," Bobby said, arranging numerous plates on his forearms like a practiced waiter. "I've got them."

"I wish I had *him*," Willie whispered, sliding into her seat beside Cassie. "Where the hell did you find that glorious hunka, hunka love? If I wasn't going on tour again next week, I'd fight you for him."

"Save your energy. He's spoken for by several Miss Worlds and sundry starlets, and he's only in town for a brief time to find the missing Rubens. He's also well aware of his accomplishments and appeal, believe me. So for all the above reasons"—and for a more pertinent, he's-not-interested reason she chose not to mention—"I'm staying way clear."

"You're crazy. Enjoy him while he's here. Life's short."

"I doubt he's interested." A half-truth, but what the hell, one had to consider one's vanity, and he'd been pretty plain at lunch that he didn't want to screw the hired help.

"Of course he's interested. He looked at you a hundred times during dinner. I was sitting across from you. I saw."

"You're hallucinating. This man amuses himself with jet-set women."

"So? There's no jet-set women here tonight."

Cassie shook her head. "I have to work with him. Sex muddles things up." *As if anyway,* she thought.

"What do you have to lose?" Willie said, as though reading Cassie's thoughts.

"My pride."

"That's crap. This is the twenty-first century, sweetie, where women are going to finally level the playing field. If you want him, take him. Female power rules. Give it a try."

Sure, right after I travel Buddha's trail to enlightenment, Cassie thought. "Maybe I will," she lied, not about to argue with Willie's sense of entitlement.

"Way to go, babe. Let me know what he's like in bed."

"Sure." It was getting easier to lie by the minute.

"That's why I didn't marry Todd," Willie said, as if Cassie had asked. "He wasn't good in bed, *and* he wanted me to stay home, like really stay at home. Can you believe the selfish bastard when he knew I'd been dreaming for years about being good enough to make the cut in pro golf? He threw a fit when I wouldn't marry him, but it was him or golf—no contest there."

"Is he . . . well—parenting at all?"

"When he's not too busy making his way in the banking world."

The sneer in her voice didn't give much room for a pleasant rejoinder. "It's probably for the best," Cassie said, as though she was a lexicon of lies and platitudes tonight. God almighty, was there a happy marriage in her circle of acquaintances? She couldn't think of one. Which didn't say much for her friends. Except for Meg, of course, and Egon, the prints curator. She almost exhaled in relief, thinking of the two couples' mutual adoration as though they were her lifeline to a more harmonious world of loving kindness and compassion.

"Absolutely. Cole's happy. He travels with me. And I love playing golf."

"You always were slated for stardom, Willie. Everyone knew it." Even as a child, Willie had been single-minded in pursuit of her dream. "I envy you that all-out commitment."

"You're doing what you've always wanted to do."

"That's true." And if she could only strangle Arthur, her job would be ideal.

"To dreams." Willie lifted her wineglass and winked. "And Bobby Serre in your bed."

Cassie clinked wine glasses and smiled. "To dreams at least."

"One out of two—what the hell."

"Amen to that."

And they giggled like they'd been doing since they'd become friends in the first grade.

"You want some action, meet me on tour sometime." Willie grinned. "I can assure you complete anonymity if you want it."

"Anonymity for what?" Meg asked, just like an older sister wanting to know everything.

And like a younger sister familiar with evasion, Cassie said, "Willie's telling me how to avoid the paparazzi."

"Right. And don't ask me to tell you what Mom said about Aunt Lizzie." Meg placed a large plate of sugar cookies on the table. "Coffee anyone?"

"Aunt Lizzie never does anything."

"Once in a while she does."

"I'm not biting."

"Fine. Coffee, Bobby?"

Bobby had been standing in the kitchen doorway with a half-smile on his face, taking in the not unfamiliar sibling scrimmage. "Yes, please."

"Sugar? Cream?"

He shook his head.

"Your sherbert's melting."

As he sat down at the table, Cassie glanced up from under her lashes and smiled. "Meg gives orders to everyone."

"Not a problem. The food was great."

He ate every drop of dessert, took seconds, ate three cookies, drank his coffee, and answered Willie's and Meg's questions about his life with a well-mannered courtesy that gave away very little. Not that either woman was deterred, continuing their interrogation nonstop until Cassie finally said, "It's getting late. We'd better go," to save him from the line of questioning that appeared to be leading to his past marriage.

Thank yous and good-byes were exchanged, the children came in to wave from the front porch, and as they settled into the leather upholstered interior of the town car, Cassie made sure she sat in the farthest corner of the seat, as distant from the alluring Bobby Serre as possible. After all Willie's talk of good-in-bed men, she was feeling the need for caution.

"Thanks for letting me tag along. I enjoyed myself." Bobby smiled. "And you didn't have to save me."

"I didn't want you embarrassed."

"I'm good at avoiding that subject." He grinned. "Practice. Now tell me if any of the names on the temp list look intriguing."

She appreciated his focus on business, but a niggling little resentment took exception to his indifference. Not that she expected to compete with starlets, she rationalized, but still. The tiniest little bit of interest wouldn't be remiss. The thought inexplicably jarred her brain, and she suddenly realized she was actually looking at a man without resentment. Was that progress or what? She glanced over to test her newly functioning male awareness antennae only to find the magnet for her awakened sensibilities asleep.

But he wasn't.

He was pretending because her scent filled his senses, her nearness was like a mega-watt charge to his libido, and the small distance separating them was insufficient if his carnal impulses were to take over and call the shots. Better to feign sleep than to make a move on her that he'd be sorry for the second after he climaxed. *Think with your head, not your dick,* he kept reminding himself. *She'll be home soon and out of the car, so chill out. You'll be able to face her in the morning without making excuses.*

He pretended not to hear her give directions to Joe; he pretended not to feel her eyes on him. He seriously tried to curb his rising erection, although his libido had had a mind of its own too long to comply to some newfound morality. He heard her suck in her breath, knew why, and felt himself swell even larger. Which precipitated a small, suffocated gasp from his companion that wasn't particularly helpful to his unfamiliar and perhaps dubious virtue. That word, *virtue,* perversely flooded his mind with decidedly unvirtuous images, his visual catalogue of artistic erotica voluminous. Definitely not helpful.

He opened his eyes and turned to her. "Look, you're very

beautiful, but I'm trying to be sensible." *That's the way. Get a grip. Discuss this like an adult.* "So don't move, and I won't move, and when I see you at the museum tomorrow morning, everything will be just fine. Okay?"

She nodded because she couldn't find the breath to speak with her pulse rate peaking somewhere in the stratosphere. After he'd said she was beautiful, she wasn't really sure what else he'd said . . . something about the museum.

"Don't move. I mean it." His words were taut with restraint. She'd half turned when he'd spoken, and that damned button on her suit jacket was unbuttoned again. Christ. The fabric strained across her breasts, the neckline was wrenched askew, and it took every ounce of willpower he possessed to keep from reaching out and sliding his finger down her tantalizing cleavage.

"I won't." But it was tempting in the darkness of the backseat, the atmosphere charged, a sexy male body close enough to touch. She felt as though she were isolated in darkness, Bobby Serre enough of a stranger to make no permanent demands, the sexual heat he generated so shockingly urgent she was inclined to throw caution to the wind. But she understood that morning would come and with it the awkwardness and gaucherie of having to work together—afterward.

"It's for the best," he muttered, speaking in the same low undertone inaudible to Joe.

"I know." Her voice was the merest wisp of sound.

"One has to be practical." Each word was tightly curbed.

"Agreed."

He shot her an impatient look. "This might be easier if you were your usual argumentative self."

"I don't feel like arguing."

"What do you feel like doing?"

"You know."

"Tell me." The freight train was moving.

"I'd rather not."

"I didn't know you were prudish."

"You don't know anything about me."

"What if I wanted to find out?"

"I thought you wanted to be sensible."

"Screw sensible."

"Or then again . . ."

"Screw you," he whispered, lifting his hand, brushing the mounded fullness of one breast, slipping his finger downward into her shadowed cleavage.

"That would be very nice," she murmured, her body instinctively opening of its own accord at his unhurried exploration.

"Perfect," he whispered, sliding his finger under the scalloped edge of her lacy bra, touching her nipple.

Perfect in more ways than one, she thought, aglow with lust.

He gently squeezed her nipple, and she gasped, a streak of pure flame racing downward to her pulsing core. It took her a moment to catch her breath and then she murmured, "Do that again," without grace or humility, without caring about not giving orders to a more or less perfect stranger.

He slid another button free on her suit jacket and dipped his head.

"No, no—wait!" She grabbed his hair.

He glanced up. "For?"

She flicked her gaze toward the front of the car.

Minnesota, he thought, *the temperate, circumspect heartland—except for Arthur perhaps*—and reaching out, he slid shut the glass divider. "Better?"

"Not really."

He smiled. "Now what?"

"This isn't going to be—you know"—she hesitated, her hands dropped from his head and she made a small wrinkly nosed moue—"very private—or comfortable."

Privacy didn't concern him. Any limo driver knew enough to be discreet. And the backseat looked plenty wide enough to him; when his cock was this hard comfort wasn't high on his list. On the other hand, he knew the long-term advantages of good manners and tact. Particularly when the evening was young, and Cassie Hill was hot. "Should we just neck?" he said, his voice teasing. "That's harmless enough."

"I don't know," she whispered, indecision in every syllable. Nothing was harmless in her current state of wild, desperate longing.

Something is happening here, he thought, feeling curiously involved, not solely gauging the performance necessary for consummation. But malelike or Bobby Serre—like, he dismissed the notion that he could be stirred by a woman in any but the most obvious ways. "One kiss," he whispered. "How can it hurt?" And bending his head, he lightly brushed her mouth with his.

She surprised him and herself as well with an impetuous, flame-hot response, pulling his head down to meet her lips, forcing his mouth open, kissing him hard, hard, hard.

The scent of her washed over him, invaded his nostrils, reminded him of hot sex and hotter orgasms, and, seizing her shoulders, he dragged her into his arms and kissed her back with a fierce, pent-up fury that would have been impossible to rationalize had he been so inclined. Which he wasn't, being pressed backward on the seat as he was by the feverish, highly aroused Miss Hill, her enormous breasts damned near falling out of her clothes.

Golden opportunity, he was thinking instead.

Her previous issues of privacy and comfort had apparently been dismissed because she was lying atop him, kissing his mouth, ravenous and needy.

And he had what she needed.

As impatient as she, perhaps more so for he rarely had to wait this long for a woman he wanted, his response was equally direct and avaricious, their kiss not so much a kiss as a greedy, gluttonous prelude to what they both wanted.

"Here and now—your house or mine," he murmured, turning his mouth aside just enough to utter the words.

"Mine," she panted, sprawled atop him, his legs spread wide, sliding her tongue so deeply into his mouth he felt the spiking jolt clear down to his toes. His erection was rock hard, her weight pressing against the rigid length, her hips moving faintly back and forth as if he needed further stimulation.

He took her face in his hands and forced her upward slightly. "It better not be much farther." It was the closest he'd come to being impolite, but she either had to stop rubbing against his cock or her house had to be in the next block.

"You have to wait."

"I don't have to do anything."

"Yes, you do."

He half smiled against her mouth. "Besides that."

"Good. Because I haven't had sex for months."

His erection surged higher at such tantalizing news. "I'm not sure you should be telling me that.

"Oh, God," she moaned. "I'm going to frighten you off."

"You're kidding, right?"

She didn't quite meet his gaze. "You hear stories about men being intimidated by—"

"Women who want sex? I doubt it."

"Oh, good." She blew out a breath. "I mean the way I'm feeling right now, I'd be really disappointed if—"

"Don't worry," he murmured, lifting her away and sitting up as the car came to a stop. "I'm not going anywhere."

She smiled. "Except, I hope—"

"Wherever you want me to go. Okay?"

"Thanks." There really must be fairies who made your wishes come true.

"On the contrary, thank *you*," he said with a grin and, leaning forward, he slid open the glass divider.

TEN

BOBBY EXPLAINED TO JOE THAT HE WOULDNT be needing him anymore tonight; he'd call him in the morning. Then he more or less bodily lifted Cassie out of the car, swung her up into his arms, and kicked the car door shut.

"The neighbors are looking," she hissed as the town car pulled away. "Put me down."

"You worry too much. It's dark. No one can see."

"You still shouldn't. You'll strain something and my night will be ruined."

"The only thing I might strain tonight won't be a problem for you, believe me. Now how do we get in?"

Cassie's house was a low, sprawling Tudor cottage facing Minnehaha Creek, the street side framed by a cottage garden that she'd labored over for the entire five years of her marriage. "Down that path." She pointed at what appeared to be a riotous display of daffodils and tulips.

"What path?"

"Put me down, and I'll show you."

"What if I don't want to?" The feel of her in his arms was a strange combination of aggressive sensual receptors and rare tenderness.

"Would you like to lie on my bed or what?"

"At the moment a bed isn't an absolute necessity."

"It is for me."

"Demanding, aren't you?" he said with a grin.

She winked at him. "Wait and see."

"Now *there's* reason to hurry." He placed her on her feet.

"This way," she said, taking his hand and moving toward what appeared to be a mass of dark tulips. But just short of the bed, a gravel path was revealed that wound through the scented spring garden and arrived at a small entrance portico.

Pushing the door open, she said, "Ta da," with a wave of her arm and beckoned him in.

"You don't lock your door?"

"Not usually. Nobody can find the door anyway. Would you like a drink?"

"No."

She smiled. "Would you like me?"

"Yes," he softly said, but he didn't move.

"There's no one here." Did she detect a faint unease? "We're quite alone."

His sexual frenzy had suddenly cooled. Maybe it was the starkly empty room beyond the entrance hall that reminded him of her divorce and ex-husband. Of the reason she was working with him. Of all the potential problems.

"Don't you dare change your mind."

Struck by her heated tone and the oddity of his even hesitating for a heartbeat at a time like this, he quickly reverted to type and smiled. "No way I'm going to change my mind. Where to?"

She held out her hand and he took it in his, the warm softness reminding him of all the other warmth and softness he wished to explore, obliterating any remnant of uncertainty. "I told myself I wasn't going to do this—but couldn't resist. I hope you don't mind?"

"I gave myself the same lecture." She grinned. "So much for cautionary tales."

"I've never been cautious. I don't know why I thought I could be with you."

"Arthur was a deterrent for me. Oh, dear, I've gone and ruined it."

Ignoring the sudden jolt of conscience, Bobby lifted his brows faintly. "Let's not talk about Arthur."

She grinned. "Ever?"

"That might be easier for me than you."

"Or maybe we could just not talk at all . . ."

His flashing smile warmed the entire room, perhaps the universe, she thought; and his physical beauty aside, she understood why he never lacked for female company. Wordlessly, she drew him along, taking him through her cavernous living room, past the vacant dining room, skirting the kitchen decorated with her card table and chair, and led him down the hall past closed bedroom doors until they reached her bedroom that overlooked the terraced backyard and creek.

Moonlight poured in the windows, illuminating the large room, spotlighting her canopied bed in a silvery light like a perfectly arranged stage set. Her pale yellow coverlet seemed to glow, and the spiral bedposts soaring upward to the lacy canopy were gilded in moon beams.

"Sorry about the mess on the floor." Her discarded clothes were impossible to miss.

"Mirrors," he said, as if she'd not spoken, his gaze on the wall of mirrors fronting her closets.

Men could be so focused, her inadequate housekeeping skills ignored. And for once in her life she embraced the concept.

He'd moved into the room, his broad shouldered form silhouetted against the light from the windows. God's gift to women here in her bedroom. For her. "Undress for me," she said.

Perhaps Willie's talk of female power had provoked her request. Or maybe sexually deprived for so long, she simply wanted to contemplate a beautiful, male body. More likely she was responding to Bobby Serre with unprecedented lust like every other woman who set eyes on him.

It took a millisecond to overcome his resistance to the peremptory note in her voice and another millisecond for his brain to race through the cause-and-effect-equals-reward equation before he reached behind his neck and, turning around, jerked his T-shirt over his head. Kicking off his sandals, he pulled down the zipper on his shorts, stripped off his shorts and boxers, and stood before her in all his glory, tanned, lean, muscled, and ready for sex.

Cassie's breath caught in her throat. There were aphrodisiacs and aphrodisiacs and the whole beautiful package with—that . . . it, that enormous, really huge, upthrust erection was breathtaking. Swiftly sliding off her jacket, she shimmied her skirt upward, too aroused to take the time to unzip and discard her skirt, wanting her panty hose off *now,* this instant, for immediate access to what was sure to bring her incredible pleasure.

Selfish?

You betcha.

Single-minded.

After seven and a half months of celibacy, no actual thought process was required.

He was walking toward her. Ohmygod it was coming closer. She was going to hyperventilate. She was going to faint. She was going to come just looking at it.

"Hey." A low calm voice. "Relax."

His hands covered hers, the rough warmth of his palms spilling over on her hips, the spiking pleasure she felt out of all proportion to the casual point of skin-on-skin contact. "I'm not sure I can wait," she breathed, desire a hard, steady throbbing inside her.

"Then we won't," he murmured, kneeling before her, his hands sliding down her legs, pulling her panty hose down. "Up," he gently urged, lifting one foot, slipping her shoe and stocking off. "The other," he said, repeating the procedure, then sliding the backs of his hands inside her thighs, he eased his forefingers along the cleft of her cunt, opening the pouty lips and, bending his head, tongued her pulsing clit.

She gasped, softly moaned, slid her fingers through his silky black hair, and held on for dear life because he knew exactly—as in the hottest spot in the universe exactly— where his tongue should go and stay. He knew it better than she knew it herself, and she'd had years of practice.

Which really made her wonder what he could do with the giant rest of him when he was so good at this. Which made her wetter than she already was and made her vulva swell even more so he had to search a little harder for her primary pleasure center. But he wasn't an ace bounty hunter for nothing. She was really, really glad she'd thrown caution to the wind. She was even more glad when she climaxed a second later.

When she opened her eyes after a time, looked around and remembered where she was, she smiled down at him. "Thanks. Really. Sincerely. From the bottom of my heart."

"No problem."

His hands slipped away from her hips, and she realized he'd been holding her up.

"Either you're spectacularly good or I needed that more than I thought."

"You said it's been a while," he modestly said, coming to

his feet. "Why don't you sit down," he added, lifting her onto the side of the bed. He grinned. "Just in case."

"I suppose women faint on you all the time."

"Not really."

"So I'm the only pathetic one."

"Or maybe you're the only go-for-broke, hotter-than-hot one."

"You're smooth," she said.

He shook his head. "Just waiting."

"For your turn?"

He half smiled, his dark brows lifting in the most charming diffidence. "If your schedule allows."

"If you can repeat what you just did to me, you might end up my sex slave, although that would mean I'd have to go grocery shopping to keep up your strength."

"Or we could have food delivered."

She grinned. "Apparently you're not averse to being a sex slave."

"Depends on the woman." He tipped his head. "So?"

His calm expectation was a self-confirming sort of candor. Without vanity or arrogance. Unlike—she ripped the image of Jay from her mind. "So let me get the rest of my clothes off," she said, coming back to the reality she preferred, sliding off the bed.

"Turn around. I'll give you a hand."

Strange how his voice soothed her, touched her senses, did the most curious things to her libido that had been out of commission for months. The tenor was almost hypnotic, velvety, a tantric massage of her mind.

And when she turned around, he unzipped her skirt, slid it down her hips, let it drop to the floor, and, holding her at her waist, lifted her away. Setting her down, he unhooked her bra, and slid it down her arms with an unaffected naturalness. "Nice," he murmured, his gaze on the mirror before them. Reaching around, he cupped her heavy breasts in his palms. "Really nice . . ." He gently lifted her breasts, raising them slightly, her soft flesh forced upward into high, ostentatious mounds.

She could see him, too, his tall, broad-shouldered form behind her, a half smile on his handsome face, his hands, fingers splayed, large like the rest of him. His size was tantalizing, provocative; she shivered in anticipation.

"We'll have to warm you up," he murmured, misinterpreting her shiver, brushing her nipples with his index fingers, watching her nipples spring to life. He gently stroked the rosy crests, his touch gossamer light, a lazy indolence to his actions as though he were capable of waiting.

When she wasn't so sure. His erection was pressed into her back, his hips moving faintly so she could feel the entire length and breadth and delectable tensile strength velvety and warm against her skin. He was so incredibly large, larger than she'd ever seen—or felt. A frisson of excitement flared through her senses. Would he fit? Or wouldn't he?

Her body was prime, he thought, and silicone free . . . almost a novelty in his world. Like a Titian nude come to life, she was curvaceous and lush, with gorgeous tits and sinuous hips and the most breathtaking legs that went on and on and on until they reached the wettest, tightest little cunt he'd seen in a long time. Why any husband would look for greener pastures was beyond him. But he was grateful. Really grateful.

"Turn around for me, Hot Legs," he whispered, wanting those legs wrapped around his back and hanging on tight, wanting to feel himself slide into her welcoming cunt and bury himself hilt deep.

The pet name uttered in that soft, husky murmur shimmered through her senses, his voice curiously possessive, his unruffled calm additionally intriguing—like he'd done this once or twice before and was good at it.

He eased her around, gentlemanly and polite, as though they weren't naked and virtual strangers. As though he'd been here before—or maybe not here but other places like this. "I've been wanting to do this all day," he murmured, cupping her breast. And bending his head, he took her nipple into his mouth with enough pressure to send instant messaging of the flame-hot variety to the heated core of her body. She moaned softly, pressing her thighs together to contain the rush of pleasure, hot desire washing over her in a lustful deluge while he sucked lightly and then not so lightly, licked and teased—making her wetter and wetter still.

"Now the other one," he whispered, his breath warm on her flesh, turning his attention to her other breast. "I wouldn't want you to feel deprived." He brushed the tip with his tongue and looked up at her from under the fringe of his lashes. "Lucky I came along."

Lucky didn't begin to describe what she was feeling. She was frantic for him, for it, for consummation. Slippery wet, aching for the feel of him, not inclined to wait, she reached out and captured the object of her lust, her hand closing around his erection—or almost closing . . . he was too large. But she measured the glorious size, her grip moving up and down his turgid length, the pressure gentle at first and then less so, her hips undulating as her body warmed to fever pitch, as her sleek cunt throbbed in eagerness.

Her soft breasts spilled over his palms. He could practically taste her longing, her little erratic whimpers sweet in his ears as he savored her sweetness. He debated letting her come again. Her lower body was writhing in that convulsive, on-the-brink way, and her eyes were half shut. He wasn't sure she was in any condition to wait. But a mirror glimpse of her luscious pink tush swaying to some inner, needy rhythm abruptly changed his mind.

He wasn't so unselfish.

He wanted to bury his cock in that delectable cunt—real soon.

Dropping his hands, he stood upright.

Instantly bereft, she whimpered, her little breathy sounds adjunct to the wanton rhythm of her hips.

"I'm not going anywhere," he whispered. But eyes shut, she seemed not to have heard. "Hey," he softly said. "Look at me."

Her eyes opened slowly, like they had to be levered up.

"Talk to me." He wasn't sure she was in the same time zone.

Her green eyes suddenly took on a clear and rational lucidity. "I sure hope you're not saving this." She slid a fingertip over the engorged head of his penis. "That would be really disappointing."

Apparently she was capable of rapid transitions. He smiled. "It's yours whenever you want it."

"About ten minutes ago would be fine."

"Where would you like it?"

"Anywhere at all so long as I don't have to wait."

His dark brows rose faintly.

"Actually the bed would do nicely," she said, not sure it was query, censure, or temper behind that cool look. "Do I have to apologize?"

She was quick. He *had* been considering various options when she'd said anywhere at all in that particular tone of voice. "No, you don't have to apologize." In his current state of arousal, he wasn't about get into any actual conversation. "Why don't you get up on the bed, and we'll deal with your time issues."

She grinned. "Remind me to send Arthur a thank you note for sending you my way."

"With Arthur's penchant for gossip, I'll have to think about that." He smiled and nodded toward her high bed. "Do you need a hand up?"

"How veddy English," she said, as she moved toward her bed. "Will we be playing horse and rider?"

"We'll play whatever you want."

That simple sentence said in that low, velvety voice was enough to make her reconsider all those S&M fantasies in, say, *The Story of O.* Maybe with him they'd actually work. Then again, she hated pain—even a hangnail required a pain-killer. "Let's keep it simple," she quickly said, climbing up on her bed, thinking perhaps she'd been a bit too suggestive, not quite sure what went on in a high-priced bounty hunter's world.

He'd caught the tremor of unease in her voice. "I'm not into games. But it's up to you."

She met his gaze. "No games, please. I mean it." After all, she barely knew him, and God knows what went on in Budapest or wherever he'd come from. On second thought, she reflected, watching him approach, every overwrought nerve in her body focused on his beautiful upthrust erection, maybe she could be just the tiniest bit open to new experiences. Provided no whips were involved.

But on reaching the bed, he stretched out beside her, put his hands behind his head, and gave her a bland look. "What's your middle name?"

Jeez, where did that come from? "Why?"

"You seem nervous. I thought maybe we should get to know each other better."

"Besides my recent orgasm you mean?"

He ignored her mockery. "What are you anxious about?"

He was naked. He wasn't carrying a weapon. What did

she have to lose? "I suppose I don't know what you expect—what with starlets and models, and probably the sex and drugs and limos that go with it."

He shrugged. "You set the pace, then. I'm easy."

He hadn't denied his rock-star lifestyle. But she was in charge. Good. Perfect. That was safe enough. On the other hand, once a man reaches a certain stage, they don't always think too clearly. "Can you vouch for him?" She pointed at his erection. "He doesn't look easy. He doesn't even look like anyone's in charge."

"He's under control."

"Wow. Can you do that Chinese pillow book stuff where you don't come for like hours?"

He smiled. "No."

Maybe he really was normal despite his unruffled calm and world-class equipment. Maybe living with the rich and famous whom everyone knew were into kinky stuff hadn't rubbed off on him. Maybe she was crazy to even have reservations with that prize-winning cock just waiting to meet her clit. As it turned out, it wasn't a long debate, what with him having something she wanted *really, really badly.* "My middle name's Hollyhock. Holly for short. Don't ask. Pleased to meet you." She held out her hand.

"My middle names are Andre, Charles, Clovis. My father insisted. A pleasure to meet you." And taking her hand, he hauled her on top of him and gave her a roguish smile. "Did I pass muster?"

"You had a few things going for you," she said with a lift of her brows. "You're not really a Bobby, are you?"

He shook his head. "It's Robert—French pronunciation."

"Very European."

"I guess. But I'm mostly Bobby Serre. All the other stuff is family shit."

"Don't talk to me about family shit. As you saw firsthand tonight, my sister is always telling me what to do."

He grinned. "Does that mean I can't be boss if I want?"

"Maybe next time," she said. "After I find out what a man with four names is like—"

"In bed?"

"Sort of." She smiled. "Look, I'm a small-town girl." But lordy, lordy, he was hard and muscled, sexy and hot, and the hardest, most spectacular part was pressed into her stomach and turning her on like crazy.

"Fine. We'll take it slow and easy. Missionary position. No surprises. Kind of like a get-acquainted afternoon tea."

She laughed. "Does that require any special dress?"

He looked up at her from under his dark lashes, amusement in his gaze. "Maybe you can dress up for me later if everything's satisfactory. If the tea's not too hot and the cucumber sandwiches are to your liking."

She knew what cucumber she was in the market for, but she wasn't about to voice anything so hokey.

"So are we on for tea?"

It was the sexiest look she'd ever seen. "I'd love it."

He rolled her under him with an effortless grace and lay between her legs, braced on his elbows, his dark, ruffled hair framing his face, the most beautiful smile on his lips. "Slow and easy now." And he nudged her thighs wider. "You can stop me any time."

Her green eyes were tropical sun hot. "I don't think that will be necessary," she gently said and, raising her legs, she twined them around his hips and raised her pelvis in the most fantastic, supple way so the head of his cock met her slick cunt and then her legs tightened on his back. It was one of those no-hands kinds of entry—smooth as silk and riveting.

She was slippery wet, sweetly eager, and apparently agile as hell as if he needed any more incentive to do what he was doing. As if he hadn't been thinking about doing this since he'd met her.

Ohmygod, he was *Huge,* but accomplished as well—invading her by slow degrees, her flesh yielding little by little, his enormous cock filling her and *Filling* her, the hot, slippery friction, the aching pressure of his penetration racheting up all her frenzied nerve endings, making her desperate for more. When he finally reached the deepest depth, when he whispered, "Are you okay?" and then pressed just a short distance more, she could only nod, carnal pleasure overwhelming her brain.

Relieved she'd responded because he wasn't altogether sure he could stop what he was doing if she wasn't, he stayed where he was.

She didn't move. She barely breathed, delirium bombarding her senses for what seemed endless, glorious moments.

Gauging her response, he politely waited and then waited some more until his libido—never one to settle for sensational feeling when overload was possible—initiated a languid withdrawal as prelude to another downstroke.

She said, "No," real emphatically, which suited him just fine because he was already moving back in, and, before long, they were matching up their personal criteria for thrust and withdrawal in a fierce, ardent flux and flow.

They were like good dancers, both intuitively meeting the other's rhythm, anticipating the other's movements, gliding one tempestuous step at a time to the sublime and, in their case, thunderous conclusion. Cassie screamed when she came, which might have startled Bobby if he'd not been intent on keeping his head from exploding.

Jesus Christ, he thought, rolling off her a few moments later and sprawling on his back. His body was still strumming, his brain trying to sort the superlatives tumbling through his mind from his breathing commands. Although, one thing he knew for sure—he was going to stay for a few more of those mind-blowing orgasms.

Cassie was floating on a pink cloud about ten feet above the ground, thinking Bobby Serre's splendid cock was right up there with the wonders of the world. And if she played her cards right, she just might get another chance to check it out and have another of those Richter-scale orgasms.

"That was nice," she said on a slow exhalation, her smile candy sweet and obliging because she had plans. "Really, really nice."

He winked at her. "Yeah, nice." Or maybe a hundred times better than nice.

"You're sweating."

"So are you." He grinned. "I'm also trying to catch my breath."

"You're really good, but I suppose you know that."

"*You're* pretty damn irresistible."

"Am I really?" Who could blame her for asking after five years with Jay?

"Definitely." He blew out a breath. "In fact, I'm thinking about sending Arthur a thank you note."

"You're teasing."

He lightly touched her tousled curls. "Not about being thankful I'm not."

"Does that mean—that is . . . would you mind—I suppose I shouldn't ask again so soon, but—" she hesitated, blushing a rosy pink.

Pushing up on his elbows, he glanced down at his rising erection. "I think we're good to go."

"Am I lucky or what?" she breathed.

"That makes two of us," he murmured, thinking that was the most artless display of eagerness he'd ever seen. And rolling over, he kissed her gently. "Now tell me what you want and we'll see what we can do . . ."

And Cassie Hill, who had been without a man in her bed for a very long time, had the good fortune to find Bobby Serre, who knew better than most how to give pleasure to a woman.

Greedy after being celibate so long, perhaps subject as well to Bobby's world-renown allure, Cassie basked in the luxury of carnal sensation, pure and simple. As the night wore on, she would apologize from time to time for her ravenous appetite only to say short minutes later in the most enticing way, "Do you mind . . ." or "If you don't mind . . ." or "Would you please . . ."

He didn't mind, of course. In fact, he kept thinking this is about as good as it gets, and he would smile and reassure her and say, "Come here and give me a kiss, Hot Legs, and tell me what you need."

It was always the same, her tastes simple. Another orgasm.

But Bobby had a wild streak, so they progressed from the missionary position pretty quickly. Cassie turned out to have an inventive talent herself.

It was one of those fly-me-to-the-moon nights.

Unforgettable and sublime.

ELEVEN

THE ALARM WENT OFF, AND CASSIE CAME awake, positive she'd not set any alarm, more positive she wanted to stay right where she was—in bed. She shut her eyes again.

"I made coffee."

"Ummm . . ."

"I left Arthur a message saying we were checking some leads. But I want to interview the staff today. Ten minutes. Okay? It's almost eleven."

Her eyes snapped open, and she stared at Bobby. He had different clothes on, but he looked as good as ever. Perhaps forever perfect after last night. "How long have you been up?" she murmured, trying to shake herself awake.

"A few hours. I went home and changed. I brought back some breakfast rolls."

"Rolls?" She was starved. Sex did that to her.

"They're from Wendy's. Your favorites, Emma said."

"You told her!"

"I told her I was picking you up at home this morning

and we were making a few overseas calls. That's all. No one knows."

"Meaning?" Even though she didn't want anyone at work to know she'd slept with Bobby Serre, she didn't know how to take his comment. How much didn't he want anyone to know? And how humiliating was that?

"Don't get pissed. I had a really great time last night. Starting with dinner at your sister's and ending with our bath at four this morning. But if you don't mind, I'd prefer not broadcasting the events of last night—particularly to Arthur. I have my reasons, and you probably have yours."

"What are yours?" So she was irrational. Sue her.

"Arthur's a voyeur and a gossip. I don't know about you, but I'd prefer not being on his breaking news."

"He'll be absolutely disgusting about it, too," Cassie muttered. "And I don't need any more of his leering than I already have to suffer."

"He likes you." Amusement underlay his words.

"Yeah, right. Lucky me. But not enough to give me a raise."

"I'll take care of that before I go."

He said it matter of factly—about the raise and leaving, reminding her that the real world was separate from last night's fantasy world. "Who do we interview first?" she said, like a grown-up would. Like she understood the rules. Like rule number one was that sex was just sex. It had no relevance to your real life.

"I thought we'd begin with the guards. They're the obvious disconnect in security. Perhaps too-long coffee breaks or lunches contributed to the theft. Not that they're going to admit it. We'll have to find out."

"You've done this a hundred times before, I suppose," she said, throwing the covers back and sliding her legs over the side of the bed.

For a flashing moment, Bobby debated putting off the interviews for a day, her lush body revving up his libido. "Put on some clothes," he gruffly said.

She *harrumphed,* not altogether satisfied with this separation of sex and real life, not to mention being told what to do when she was *thirty-two* years old. "Yes, sir, anything else, sir? A shave, haircut, your pants pressed?"

"Please, would you be kind enough to dress," he said, his tone ultra-polite. "I'm going through withdrawal this morning, and just looking at you makes me shaky."

That was much better, very much more flattering and soothing to the ego. She felt all warm and fuzzy—perhaps a personality flaw, accepting flattery so readily. No doubt some would call her gullible. On second thought, perhaps she was self-serving as well, she thought, the prime example of virile manhood standing before her in clean shorts and a T-shirt exerting a kind of animal magnetism impossible to ignore. "Why don't we both come just once," she murmured. "In order to quench the shakiness."

He grinned. "Is once possible for you?"

"Don't blame me for your flawless sense of place."

He laughed. "Get dressed, and we'll quit early instead."

"How early?"

"Early enough for you to come a dozen times before dinner."

"You say the nicest things." Thank you God—the fantasy world was just on hold.

"I know. Now get ready. I'll pour your coffee." And he escaped from the bedroom before he totally lost control.

"You didn't eat any," she said as she came into the kitchen and glanced at the full box of little frosted rolls on the counter.

"I stopped for steak and eggs." He supposed if he tore off her skirt and blouse and wrapped her long *bare* legs—a fact he immediately noticed as in easy access noticed—in those strappy green shoes around him he'd more or less shoot the day in terms of getting any work done. Which was sure to generate repercussions from Arthur. Should he ask her to wear slacks and a big jacket? How weird would that sound?

"Try one," she said, tearing off a gooey roll. "They're really good."

Watching her catch the dripping icing with her tongue brought back graphic memories of last night, and backing up a step, he tried to distance himself from temptation. "I don't know if this is going to work," he said on a low exhalation.

"What?"

She was lounging against the counter, about to take a bite of pastry, her mouth half-open. The irresponsible part of his brain thought, *Lift her up on the counter and spread her legs. Or better yet, just have her bend over.* He swallowed hard, decided he couldn't be around her if he intended to get any work done, and spoke quickly before he lost his concentration. "We'll get more done if I do the interviews and you take over the phone calls to my contacts."

"My French is rusty," she said through a mouthful of sweet roll. "My German will only get me a cab, and my Spanish only works at Taco Bell."

"I'll give you the list for the States—the East and West Coasts mostly, Miami in particular. A fair amount of art is passing through there." His brain was switching over to work mode at the thought of Jorge in Miami. Thank God.

"Tell me what to say. I'm new at detective work."

"It's easy enough. You're calling for me . . . I'll give you some reference phrases that will vet you. See what they know about the Rubens. Then I'll pick you up at your office, say, about four."

"Or I could meet you around the corner if that doesn't sound too juvenile. I'd prefer putting Arthur off the scent."

"Fine. We'll meet somewhere."

"Do I have time for another roll?"

He smiled. "It might test my self-control."

"Am I sexy?" She was allowed; divorce could shake even the most overweening ego.

"Do fish swim?"

How sweet. Self-validation. "Do we really have to wait until this afternoon—I mean how long would it take if we—?"

"In the mood I'm in," he brusquely said, "decades. I'll wait for you in the car."

She watched him stride away, female power welling up inside her in a tidal wave, happy as a clam to have found her groove again, sure of one thing at least in terms of sexual allure. She had it, he wanted it, and, with luck, it might take a month to find the Rubens. Thirty days, thirty nights, six hundred plus orgasms for her even if he decided to sleep at night.

Maybe Willie had been right.

Maybe "If you want him, take him" would become her new mantra.

Maybe she'd enjoy Bobby Serre's sexual expertise to the max.

Because life was short, the meek did not inherit the earth, and perhaps those who hesitated really did lose.

But more important, last night had made her a serious sexual addict.

Luckily, she knew where to get her fix.

TWELVE

THEY WERE BOTH TRYING VERY HARD TO ACT mature in the car, keeping their distance, their conversation exclusively on the art theft.

Cassie gave herself high marks for self-control. She only looked at his crotch twice.

Bobby mostly looked forward or out the window. His self-control was almost nonexistent.

But they made it to the museum without embarrassing themselves in front of Joe and quickly went their separate ways before they could change their minds.

CASSIE HAD NO more than settled behind her desk than Arthur appeared, looking smug.

"You look perky," he said, standing in her doorway.

"If I looked perky, I'd kill myself, Arthur. Do you actually want something?" She was feeling smug herself, what with her raise practically ensured, what with her own personal lobbyist working for her.

Arthur's eyes narrowed like they did whenever a subordinate didn't lapse into full sycophantic mode. "You're late."

"Mr. Serre and I made some overseas calls this morning," she lied.

"I'm doing you a favor on these consultant fees, Cassandra. I expect a modicum of gratitude," he huffily said, his nostrils flaring. "And respect for our office hours."

"I'm grateful, of course." Trying to gauge the degree of servility required against her newfound female power, she settled on a half smile and a neutral comment. "I worked late last night on this assignment."

It was a mistake to mention last night; she knew it the moment the words left her mouth.

His smug look returned, Arthur moved into her office and sat down on her Mies chair in front of her desk. "Tell me about last night."

Inwardly groaning, Cassie slid the paper on which she'd written Bobby Serre's name entwined with hearts a dozen times—really it was just her impulsive, newly awakened hormones guiding her pen—under the folder of contact names while racking her brain for an appropriate reply. What had Bobby told him? Had Arthur even talked to him this morning? Jesus, she felt like a teenager lying to her parents about having sex when she didn't know the cover story. "We went to my sister's for dinner and reviewed the names from the temp list afterward."

"We? Afterward?"

If Arthur had a mustache to twirl, he'd be right in character, his leer almost comical. "Mr. Serre and I. Afterward at my sister's house—in her den . . . where the children aren't allowed." She was beginning to warm up to her story.

"And?"

Jesus, Arthur looked like an expectant voyeur. "I filled him in on everyone on the temp list who might remotely

figure as a suspect. Mr. Serre is very businesslike. He said he
was hoping to find the painting quickly and return to wherever he was . . . Europe somewhere," she added with what
she thought was a fine display of casual acting.

"Budapest," he said. "Hmpf," he added, looking disappointed. "Bobby said as much."

Soul mates—now she knew what the phrase meant.
There was no other explanation for their identical lies. Not
to mention their incredible, really outstanding rapport in
bed, which wasn't always bed, of course, but she didn't want
to think about that now with pervert Arthur watching her
like a hawk, waiting for her to slip up. "I have a long list of
calls to make," she said, hoping he'd take the hint, making
the mistake of lifting up the folder before recalling what lay
beneath.

"What's that?" Arthur snapped, seizing the sheet of paper inscribed with her undeniable folly. "My, my," he murmured, perusing her infatuated scribbles, a nasty smile
forming on his face. "What do we have here?"

"He looks like a movie star. Okay?" She shrugged. "It's
just some silly nonsense. He can't even remember my name.
He calls me Miranda." Please, God, let him believe her.

"I could put in a good word for you," Arthur said with a
reptilian smile.

"I'd rather you didn't. I'm not interested in any more rejection."

"Women take divorce more seriously than men," he said
with his inimitable and selfishly male view of the world.
"Are you still missing Jay?"

She would have liked to take issue with his platitude but
decided this was one of those times when silence was golden.
As for his question about Jay, unless *missing* meant doing
bodily harm, she wouldn't be able to answer that one, either,
without lying through her teeth. "It can be sad," she said,

deciding on an all-purpose, one-size-fits-all generic response. Should she try to squeeze out a tear in hopes of distracting him?

As she was attempting to generate some eye moisture, the sound of approaching footsteps broke the silence, and a moment later, the very last person she wished to see stood in the doorway of her office looking like the exact tall, dark, and handsome movie star she'd previously alluded to.

"Come in, come in," Arthur boomed as though he were a shill for a carnival show.

It was really terrifying to see the shining expectation on Arthur's face. Was he one of those viewers who watched reality TV to see who had to eat cockroaches or who would be axed from the program because they were hated the most? Were his serial marriages an indication of a constant need for perverse stimulation? Did his custom-made suits hide the soul of a little old lady who thrived on gossip and personal disasters?

Casting a quick, imploring look at Bobby as Arthur waved him in, she was answered with a fleeting lift of dark brows.

Obviously a query she was currently unable to answer.

"Come in, sit down. Cassandra and I were discussing the case," Arthur said. "Among other things," he added with a waggish chuckle. "It appears you have an admirer." He handed Bobby the sheet of paper.

"I told Arthur it was just some silliness," Cassie quickly interposed. "I'm embarrassed, naturally." Which was God's own truth. "We scarcely know each other." A patent lie in contrast.

Bobby glanced at the paper, then set it on Cassie's desk. "You have too much time on your hands, Arthur. Don't you have some donors to shake down?"

Arthur smiled. "I thought it was charming."

"Good for you." He turned to Cassie. "I've brought some additional phone numbers for you to call." Leaning on her desk, he jotted a few lines on the tablet he carried, tore off the top sheet, and handed it to her. "There's a couple code words by each name. Make sure you use them. If you'll excuse me, Arthur, unlike you, I have work to do." Turning away, he walked from the room.

But he half turned at the door and winked at her.

She tried not to blush.

She desperately tried.

Without luck.

"He took it well, I thought," Arthur casually said, too wrapped up in his own twisted delusions to notice Cassie's pink cheeks.

"Thanks for embarrassing me. Especially when I have to work with Mr. Serre. You shouldn't have shown that to him."

Arthur's smile was bland. "Bobby's familiar with women throwing themselves at him. You're not the first, and you won't be the last. In fact, he has a lady waiting for him in Budapest. I'm sure that's why he's in a hurry to get back," he briskly added, coming to his feet. "Keep me updated on the case. You should have taken my advice and had your hair cut. Bobby might have given you a second look."

Cassie dug her nails into her palms to keep from leaping up and punching him out, a reaction she couldn't afford with the stack of bills on her card table waiting to be paid. Only when Arthur disappeared from sight did she allow her fingers to unflex.

Prick.

She hoped there really was justice in the world and then Arthur might someday, somewhere get what he so richly deserved. Unfortunately, his current princely life didn't portend well for that vain hope.

He was living large while the Mother Teresas of the planet prayed for better times.

It made one seriously reconsider the concept of justice.

THIRTEEN

SHE SHUT AND LOCKED HER DOOR AFTER that, defense against any further surprises.

If someone wanted to come in, they could knock. Then give the password.

And if she was in a really good mood, she might let them it. Which was the real reason she'd selected this office at the very end of the corridor with the exit door twenty feet away.

She wasn't kidding last night; she really wasn't the hostess type.

Sliding down in her chair, she contemplated her embarrassment. How should she act when next she saw Bobby? Although he'd been way cool before Arthur, surely he must have been startled by such juvenile scribbling. In hindsight, she couldn't imagine what had come over her. She hadn't resorted to any of that hearts-and-flowers crap since the ninth grade when she was enamored of Nick Cicero, who was a year older and had a Harley.

It was really humiliating.

Should she apologize?

Make some lame excuse?

Tell him she had PMS?

That excused everything, didn't it? It was one of those across-the-board, I-momentarily-lost-my-mind excuses.

Although she really wished she hadn't written *sexy* and underlined it four times. She'd even give up chocolate for a week if she could take that one back.

The phone rang.

Willie's name and number appeared on her caller ID.

Leave a message, she thought. She wasn't up to exposing her humiliation just yet, and if she picked up the phone, the next thing she knew she'd be spilling her guts.

Three rings later, voicemail took over.

There was no point in obsessing about something she couldn't possibly change. Even praying—always her last, desperate measure in times of crisis—wouldn't change a thing. She'd make the phone calls she was supposed to make, pretend this was a normal day, and try to forget her mortifying lapse in judgment.

Picking up the sheet of paper Bobby had brought in, she began reading through the added names. The list was handwritten in a partially printed, small, loose script—a name, phone number, city, and code word. Miami, New York, Chicago, Miami, Tampa, and then she gasped. On the last line was written Cassie Hill. SEXY. C U @ 4. And the word *SEXY* was underlined four times!

It almost felt like she was in the ninth grade again and Nick Cicero had asked her to take a ride on his Harley.

Hell, no. It felt better. Because she would get more than a ride on a motorcycle tonight. She would get to ride something really spectacular.

She had to tell someone. It wasn't every day she was the recipient of a really sweet, romantic gesture. In fact, it had been so long she was partially absolved of her descent into teenage name-writing angst. Wasn't she?

And when she explained everything to Willie, Willie said, "Of course you are. Sex does that to you. Fabulous sex at least. It makes you giddy and lightheaded and incapable of clear thinking. Isn't it great?"

She understood. "Yeah," Cassie said in a soft, dreamy sort of way. "Greater than great. Greater than the pyramids and Mt. Everest and chocolate cake."

"Greater than shoe shopping."

Cassie hesitated, and they both laughed.

"Seriously," she said a moment later, "for Bobby Serre, I'd give up shoe shopping for a week."

"Then I envy the hell out of you."

"For what it's worth," Cassie murmured. "I don't have any illusions."

"Hey, carpe diem, sweetie. There are no guarantees in this world."

"I know. He's unbelievable, that's all. I'll have to take notes so I don't forget once he's gone."

"That's what memories are for. The warm fuzzies of the brain. So I probably won't be seeing you before I leave if you're busy in bed," Willie cheerfully noted.

"When do you go?"

"Day after tomorrow. Keep me posted. My mom always has my number."

"I'll give you a call when he's gone, and you can console me on losing world-class sex."

"I'll do better than that. I'll line you up with some on the circuit."

"If I ever switch into a party-girl mode, I'll take you up on that."

"In the meantime, enjoy yourself."

"I intend to."

"So have you thought about Jay lately?"

"Jay who?"

Willie chuckled. "Way to go, babe. Call me."

Liv was in a meeting when Cassie tried calling her. Good news was meant to be shared. But she didn't leave a message; she would have sounded too over the top.

Energized or perhaps punch drunk with elation, Cassie set to work, starting at the top of the folder list, eventually moving to the added names, surprised at how easy it was after the second or third call. The contacts were generally art dealers, gallery owners, occasionally someone with accents less cultured who probably operated on the fringes of the law. Not that dealers and gallery owners were necessarily law-abiding. A lot of them weren't. With almost every country refusing to allow the export of national treasures, the line between legitimate and illegal imports was often no more than the stamp affixed to a crate by a bribed customs official. The courts were clogged with cases that dragged on for years between countries attempting to regain art works stolen from archaeological sites and tombs. Greece had been trying to recover the Elgin marbles taken from the Acropolis for nearly a century.

The small Rubens nude, in contrast, would be almost too easy to transport out of the country. It was small, not well known, originally in the artist's private collection, then lost for two centuries, as was so often the case with the rare erotica of major artists—that subgenre falling under the censure of various moral factions. Her greatest fear was that someone might destroy it. Over the centuries, that fate had befallen many paintings considered too salacious.

The Rubens, in fact, was a portrait of the artist's first wife, whom he loved deeply, the depiction of her young, nubile body portrayed with exquisite tenderness. Rubens and Isabella had been young when they married, and that utter devotion of youth not yet tainted by worldly cynicism was poignantly revealed in the painting. When Isabella died, Rubens was never the same. He became a businessman painter, a sophisticate, an occasional diplomat for the reigning monarchs of his time. He even married again, but not for love.

She always teared up looking at that painting.

She punched in another telephone number, glad to be doing her part in the search for the painting.

Only two more left on the list.

FOURTEEN

 SHE WAS JUST PUTTING AWAY THE FOLDER, mission accomplished, when the phone rang and someone knocked on her door—simultaneously.

She glanced at the caller ID. Liv.

"Who's there?" she called out.

"Your driver."

Her body came alive, her senses started dancing the tango, the phone kept ringing, and the door swung open without her moving from her desk.

"Are you some Houdini–Doug Henning clone?"

Bobby held up a small pick, a professional-looking instrument that further widened her eyes, tamed down the tango dances, and reminded her how little she knew him.

He nodded in the direction of her phone. "Answer it. I'll wait."

Shutting the door behind him, he relocked it and, because she hadn't moved, made a gesture with his hand to his ear.

Suppressing all the curious speculation rattling around in her brain, she picked up the phone.

"It's about time. I was about to leave a message."

"Can I call you back?"

"Is someone there?"

"Sort of."

"Is it Meg?" Bobby asked, sitting down in her single chair, sliding down into a comfortable sprawl.

Cassie shook her head.

"Who's that?"

"No one."

Bobby grinned.

"You're holding out on me."

"I'll call you later."

"Is he good-looking? Are you having sex with him? Do I know him?"

"Jeez, Liv. I'm at work."

"So?"

"So I'll call you back."

"You could have talked to her," Bobby said as she hung up. "Do you want me to leave and come back in ten minutes so you can divulge all your secrets?"

"I have no secrets. My life is an open book."

"Liar."

"Half-open, then."

"Shut to Arthur."

"Okay, I have secrets. I'll talk to Liv later, though, because I'd rather talk to you."

"That works out. Let's go."

She glanced at the clock. "You're early. It's not four yet."

"I couldn't wait."

The way he said it got the tango dancers back on the floor. Until she remembered Arthur and frowned. "Arthur said I had to observe office hours."

"I'll take care of that. Do you want to leave first or should I? And where do you want to meet?"

She just loved that "I'll take care of that" certainty—like he could smooth out all the bumps in her road of life. And after having gone through so many months of crap with Jay, she was in the mood for someone else to take care of everything. Call her a throwback to the past, call her schizoid, too, with her lust for female power a new and vigorous license to enjoy. What the hell—call her romantic . . . which thought prompted her to consider some explanation for her hearts and flowers doodles. Men didn't view romance with the same benign regard as women. "Just for the record, I'm really sorry about scribbling your name and stuff. I'm blaming PMS."

"Don't worry about it. I was thinking about tattooing your name on my ass."

Cassie shut her eyes and held up her hand. "Don't let me lose that sweet, tender image."

"I'm just saying it was weird for me, too. So we're even. Now, let's get the hell out of here. Joe's parked out back. Tell me where to pick you up."

"Maybe I should say I have other plans." She lifted one brow. "*The Rules* book doesn't allow for such last-minute invitations."

"Did I say it was an invitation? You're working for me, babe," he said with a wink. "Arthur's paying you the big bucks to make my life a little easier."

"And as an added job benefit, my life is—how should I put it—fuller?"

His grin matched hers. "Now I really don't want to wait. Where do I pick you up?"

"How about on the corner behind the parking ramp?"

"Five to ten minutes?"

The phone rang, she glanced at her caller ID—Jorge's Gallery—and motioned it was for him before picking up. "Cassandra Hill, here," she said. "Would you like to speak to Mr. Serre?"

Leaning over, she handed the receiver to Bobby, then rose to get her purse and Marilyn Monroe tote bag from the hook on the wall. As Bobby discussed not only the Rubens but another painting that sounded like a Titian that had been missing, she returned with her purse and bag, set them on her desk, and leaned against it, listening. If the *Isabella d'Este in Red* had really surfaced, that was huge news. Painted by Titian from life, it had been sold by her heirs to Charles I of England. A few months after the king's execution in 1649, an act of parliament ordered the sale of the former royal family's possessions. In the ensuing Commonwealth Sale, the portrait of Isabella d'Este passed to Charles I's silk draper in lieu of money owed him. After that, it had disappeared.

Smiling, Bobby reached out and ran his palm up her leg, pushing her purple silk tweed skirt upward.

She brushed his hand aside and rearranged her skirt.

Rising, he leaned over the desk, jabbed the speaker button, set the receiver back in the cradle, sat down again, and pulled Cassie onto his lap without missing a word of conversation. "Miss Hill is listening, too, Jorge, so watch your language. Go on. I can't believe the portrait's real." He eased her skirt up, forced her thighs open against her silent protest, one hand holding her firmly in place and only smiled when she mouthed an emphatic no. "The last authenticated owner of that Titian was Geeres in London in, what—1650? And now it's in Romania?"

"*Was* in Romania. The state security chief was gunned down in a restaurant six months ago, his collection looted, and the *Isabella d'Este in Red* is now reportedly in Bulgaria."

"And no one knows how the security honcho came by it?" Bobby slipped his finger inside her panties, traced her wet cleft with a light stroke, then slid his finger upward, burying it in her cunt palm deep, muffling her gasp with his mouth.

"Not at the moment." Jorge spoke with a faint accent—Cuban, upper class. "I was approached by some Turkish contacts in Munich. They're the ones looking for a buyer."

"Do your Turks know it's been missing for centuries?" Bobby was gently stroking her clit, up and down, around and around.

"I don't think so, but they know it's a Titian and valuable. I don't suppose you have time to come and look at it with me?"

"I'm a little busy right now," Bobby said, sliding in a second finger, forcing her pulsing tissue wider, inciting a little suffocated gasp. "If it can wait until I find this Rubens, I'll come."

Cassie was panting, her hips moving faintly, her own style of coming approaching lift-off with Bobby's deft fingers massaging her liquid cunt in slow, gentle strokes, his delicate pressure on precisely the right spots—like that . . . and ohmygod—that, and she wasn't going to be able to wait even with Jorge in hearing range.

"It's all right," Bobby whispered, his mouth pressed against her ear, as if he knew, as if he could tell, as if he understood this would be the opportune time to cover her mouth with his . . . right, right *now*. She came in a convulsive rush, her scream vibrating down his throat.

"Am I interrupting something?" Jorge inquired, his voice polite as though he might have arrived early at a party.

"No," Bobby said, lightly kissing Cassie. "We're about done here. I am surprised though," he went on as though he were capable of multi-tasking with the best of the multi-tasking record holders, "that nothing's come up on the radar on the Rubens. It's the kind of painting some billionaire would like in his girlfriend's bedroom. Resale is normally fast."

"It is strange. But there's not a whisper on the East Coast.

I checked with everyone I know. My man at Butterfield's in LA says he has a blank screen out there, too."

"Ditto where I am." Bobby's brows flickered in transient query as Cassie slid off his lap and kneeled between his legs.

"Any usual suspects there?"

"I interviewed the guards today and most of the staff." Bobby smiled as she unzipped his shorts. "This museum's not what you'd call high security, but none of the guards appear to be involved." He shifted slightly in the chair as she drew out his erection. "Just a gut feeling." As her mouth closed over his engorged crest, he went still.

"You're usually right. At least you have been in the past. I'll keep you posted on this end. And you let me know when you can travel to Bulgaria, Sofia probably. I doubt the Titian is out in the country. You still there?"

"I'll call you," Bobby said, on a soft exhalation, sliding his fingers through Cassie's hair. "Hang up for me will you?"

Jorge chuckled. "Got your hands full?"

And then the phone line went dead, the steady buzzing on the speaker disregarded by the two occupants of the office.

For Bobby, sensation definitely overrode auditory receptors as Cassie ran her tongue up the length of his erection, then down again in a slow descent, then up again, as she cupped his balls with one hand and held him firmly at the base of his penis with the other. All his nerve endings were on full alert, waiting for her to wrap her lips around his cock again, waiting for her to take him in.

She looked up, her lips a hair's-breadth from touching the swollen head. "Ready?" she whispered.

His grip tightened, forcing her head downward, and no one had to be a mind reader to get the idea.

She drew him in by slow degrees, sucking, licking, resisting the pressure of his hands with surprising strength, setting the pace . . . slowing him down, making him wait for that moment when his cock came to rest against the back of her throat.

Sudden pleasure flooded his body, melted his bones, the phrase *prisoner of love* lit up in neon in his brain.

That neon pulsed in a highly charged straight-line path to the throbbing core of Cassie's avaricious body as well.

And suddenly who exactly was captive or captor was up for debate.

Bobby's eyes were shut, his head thrown back, his grip no longer harsh.

He was holding the fount of pleasure in his hands.

Liquid desire oozed down Cassie's thighs, as though touching him, tasting him, measuring the length of him with her tongue triggered an insatiable need. He was a fever in her brain, an irrepressibly carnal urge.

She was starved for him.

Or maybe just for sex.

But that brief moment of denial was quickly beaten down by the no-nonsense voice inside her head—as in no contest. It was him.

The exquisite measured cadence of her rhythm, the sensual flux and flow, the choice image of his cock sliding in and out of her mouth, his neanderthal impulse at the sight of her submissive kneeling pose giving him head torched his already flame-hot senses. He groaned deep in his throat as her mouth moved up and down, as his cock slid in and out, his fingers flexing at the very depth of each down stroke, and he offered up thanks to whatever charitable gods were in the vicinity that Cassie's husband had had the bad taste to find himself a girlfriend. He would have been pissed had he come here and found Cassie Hill married and faithful. He would have thought his luck had run out.

As it was, his luck was prime, his orgasm was racing for the finish line, and all he could think of was the glorious prospect of unremitting, gluttonous sex with the beautiful, hot-blooded redhead sucking his cock.

A second later, she was swallowing his come, he was trying to find enough air to draw into his heaving lungs, and the continuous beep of the open phone line was suddenly loud and clear.

Cassie lifted her head.

Bending over, he kissed her mouth dry.

"You're polite," she murmured, wiping her mouth with the back of her hand.

His dark brows flickered. "It's the least I could do to repay you."

She grinned. "Same here . . . although—I mean—if you don't think me too demanding . . ." She glanced down at his rising erection.

"He's listening," Bobby said, his libidinous dick already anticipating the end of her sentence. "Come here." Lifting her to her feet, he shoved up her skirt, pulled down her panties, waited for her to lift each foot, then tossed the scrap of green lace panties on her desk. "This is fucking unbelievable," he whispered, holding her around the waist to steady her as she settled down on his cock. "I'm figuring we'll just fuck until we pass out."

"Or Arthur knocks on the door."

He looked at her from under his dark lashes. "Don't rain on my parade."

"Don't talk." She kicked off her heels.

He laughed. "Yes, ma'am." Flexing his hips, he thrust upward hard, his hands still on her waist.

She couldn't move.

He knew it.

She could only absorb the powerful upsurge—with gratitude and a breathy little sigh and the most welcoming of cunts.

"Let me know when you've had enough," he whispered, a warning of sorts in his present ramming speed mentality.

She didn't seem to hear him. She was moving her hips and slippery cunt to feel him better.

His cock surged higher, his fingers flexed around her waist, and he powered up to meet her rhythm.

It was a frantic, pumping rush to orgasm, galvanic, tempestuous, as if they'd not just come—a curious, shared selfishness of purpose. Panting, flushed, their hearts pounding, they climaxed only moments later with impenitent exultation.

"We need a bed," he gasped.

"And privacy," she breathed.

"And some tissue," he muttered. "This is going to be messy."

"Don't move." Leaning back with a suppleness owed exclusively to sexually heated muscle tone rather to any exercise regimen, she reached for her purse.

A packet of tissue was soon unearthed, he helped her gingerly rise from his lap without dripping on his khaki shorts, and they both wiped themselves dry.

"Now I need some food," she said, straightening her skirt and blouse.

"Tell me what and where. And I'm thinking screw Arthur. We should be able to walk out together as long as I keep my hands to myself."

"We *are* working together." She slipped on her strappy green shoes.

He looked up from zipping his fly. "Nice work."

"You, too. Thanks. I should last for an hour or so. No pressure," she added with a grin.

"No pressure, believe me."

"I'm not too demanding?"

"I'll let you know if you are."

"Would you really?"

"It's not going to happen." His smile was serene. "Guaranteed. Your house or mine? A restaurant first or take-out?"

"My house. My clothes are there."

"We'll stop at my place then, and I'll get a change of clothes for the morning."

She smiled. "You're really easy to be with."

He smiled back. "I like what I'm doing."

FIFTEEN

BOBBY'S CELL PHONE WENT OFF AS THEY walked into Cassie's house, and the minute he began talking she knew it was Arthur. Anxiety started tripping through her brain.

Bobby smiled and shook his head, telling her to relax.

And then he proceeded to converse with Arthur as though he was alone with all the time in the world.

After he hung up, he said, "Sorry for talking so long, but I didn't want him to pick up any clues. He asked me over for a drink."

"Do you have to go?"

"Kinda. But come with me. We could still be working—it's not very late."

"God no. I'm not as blasé as you. He'd tell in a minute."

"Come with me in the car then. I won't stay long. I like knowing you're waiting; it eases my addiction."

"As if."

"As for sure. You're my drug of choice."

"You just have a primed libido."

"Well, that, too, but come with. One drink and I'll be back in the car."

"When do you have to go?"

"Not for a half-hour." He grinned. "Plenty of time."

"Perfect," she said, really meaning it. "And I'll go if I can have take-out. I'll eat in the car while you're with Arthur."

"And then I'll eat in the car when I come back out." His smile was wicked.

"Only if you're talking about food with Joe a foot away."

"Joe's busy tonight, and I thought we were staying in." He shrugged. "We'll take a cab."

"If my car wasn't still at work . . ."

"It doesn't matter. Call a cab. Tell him a half-hour." His smile was indulgent. "Will that be enough time to humor you momentarily?"

She grinned. "A first course, anyway."

He was thinking more—appetizer. He had plans for a full-scale meal orgy later that night.

SIXTEEN

THEY WERE SWEATING SO MUCH WHEN THEY got into the cab and gave the driver directions, he took one look and said, "It's not a good idea to run this time of day. The sun's too hot."

"That's what I told her," Bobby said, shooting Cassie a grin. "But she's gotta have her own way."

"It ain't healthy, lady."

"He only complains afterward. He can outrun me any day." Her gaze was amused. "Can't you, darling?"

"I guess if I die of a heart attack, it's a good way to go."

The cabbie was watching them in his rearview mirror and suddenly understood. "You're not married."

"Not yet," Bobby said, putting his arm around Cassie.

"I recommend it. Been married thirty years, four kids, and two grandkids. I still like goin' home at night."

"What do you say, darling? Want to fly to Las Vegas?"

"Right after I fly to the moon."

"I'll ask you again after you've eaten. She's touchy when

she's hungry," Bobby said to the cabbie with a *mano a mano* quirk of his brows. "You know women."

"Damn right. I've got three girls and a wife. It don't pay to talk to any of them until they've had breakfast. No offense, lady."

Cassie wasn't really listening. After Bobby had joked about flying to Las Vegas, her brain had gone into full fantasy mode. She could already picture her Vera Wang gown, dozens of white roses and lilacs, Dom Pérignon, and, naturally, a ten-carat ring. She was switching the venue from Las Vegas, though, visualizing Florence this time of year. One of those small neighborhood Renaissance churches with the fifty-foot ceilings would be nice—someplace intimate for the ceremony. Not that she actually contemplated anything so outré as marriage after knowing Bobby for two days, after knowing his reputation, after only recently escaping the misery of divorce. But in her current cheerful mood, she was disposed to crazy flights of fancy where Bobby Serre figured large. *Large,* of course, the glorious operative word.

It was sheer bliss to bask in the afterglow of mind-blowing sex. It was heavenly, and while the men segued into the usual fishing stories *de rigueur* in Minnesota once the fishing season opened, she only half listened, more inclined to exist in her rare, Zenlike state of grace—not that she actually understood Zen. But she'd recall a wise phrase on occasion from those little instruction books she bought where you could flip through page after page of feel-good, inspiring verses, and the one currently looping through her mind said it all:

Things to do today: Exhale, inhale, exhale. *Ahhhh.*

Which was exactly what she was doing, thank you very much, or actually thank Bobby Serre very much. He deserved a medal or whatever Zen Buddhists gave as rewards. Sex with him was really divine—very healing and clarifying, like a good massage and a facial. Or divine like finding the most fabulous outfit for 70 percent off—one of those little miracles of life. Or extra divine like eating the perfect egg-salad sandwich with tiny bits of onion and relish, tons of mayonnaise and fresh rye bread that you're supposed to eat with mindful and respectful attention. Just thinking about it made her hungry. "Stop at the deli on Forty-Seventh and Chicago," she abruptly said.

She would reflect on the healing powers of sex while eating her egg-salad sandwich.

A short time later, they were back in the cab with two large bags of food, enough really to feed a family—or in this case, Bobby Serre's remarkable appetite. It was astonishing—okay, irritating as well, but only mildly so in her new tranquility—how much he could eat. Not that she hadn't chosen three desserts. But consider how impossible it was to be prudent with the lights in those refrigerator cases glistening off the shiny chocolate frostings and puffs of whipped cream atop various fruit tarts and cheesecakes. Only a saint could resist such temptation.

In the remaining thirty blocks to Arthur's, Bobby ate a serving of lasagna to tide him over, and Cassie savored her egg-salad sandwich in an aura of contentment and smiles.

"One drink and I'll be back," Bobby said as they pulled up to Arthur's grand Georgian pile on the lake boulevard.

"I gotta park down the block," the cabbie said. "The cops tow here."

Cassie's heart did one of those happy flip-flops. The thought of sitting outside Arthur's house had been patently nerve-racking.

Bobby leaned over and gave her a kiss. "See you soon."

The man had all the moves, she thought, her lips tingling faintly from his kiss, her wanton little cunt doing a flutter of delight in anticipation. He was small-town sweet and big-city smooth. There was no discounting his flawless looks, either. She wanted him about as much as she wanted the double-fudge chocolate cake just waiting for her in that little gold-trimmed box.

How nice. She could have them both tonight.

And barring Arthur having Superman vision, she was safe and sound in this cab until Bobby returned.

A jazz station was playing on the radio, as though in perfect conjunction with her lazy, blissful mood. Sliding into a corner of the backseat, she put her legs up, leaned back, and indulged in her deli smorgasbord, intent on trying a few bites of everything.

SEVENTEEN

"YOU DIDN'T HAVE TO DRESS FOR ME," Bobby drawled, giving Arthur the once-over in his tux.

"It's the members' preview tonight. I assumed you didn't want to go."

"Rightly assumed." One drink, definitely. His luck was holding.

"Jessica has a conflicting charity event," Arthur explained as he ushered Bobby into the coolness of the screened porch. "We'll have you over for dinner before you go. You'll like her. She's a . . . delight."

Bobby had been tempted to insert the word *young* in Arthur's brief pause, but he restrained his impulse. Each of Arthur's wives was younger than the last. Hopefully this was the final one or the police might be involved next time.

"Jessica's a first-rate tennis player, too. Sit. I'll get us a drink."

Arthur prided himself on his tennis game. "Shared interests," Bobby pleasantly said. "Isn't that what holds a marriage together?"

"My preference is great blow jobs," Arthur said with a lecherous smile.

Some things never changed, Bobby thought, Arthur's locker-room mentality undiminished over the years. "Whatever turns you on," Bobby murmured.

"Vodka, gin, cognac?" Arthur stood before a drink table.

"Vodka, three ice cubes."

"Speaking of blow jobs, Cassandra appears willing. Although I never took her for such an unblushing romantic; more the type who would eat you alive, I thought."

"I wouldn't know." Bobby kept his voice even with effort, the words *blow job* and *Cassandra* recalling recent activities that quickened the blood flow to his cock. Not a good idea with Arthur's lurid imagination and eagle eye. "I prefer keeping our association businesslike. It saves problems in the long run."

"One learns, right? You've had your share of women wanting you to stay, I suspect." Arthur flicked a glance over his shoulder. "Or so the stories go."

"I lead a quiet life. Despite the gossip. Montana or Budapest, mostly."

"Except for Cannes during the festival," Arthur said, walking over and handing Bobby his drink.

"Once or twice," Bobby modestly replied. "Usually on business."

Arthur sat down opposite him. "High-priced artwork down there, no doubt."

"Quite a bit."

"Cheers." Arthur lifted his glass. "To a quick recovery of the Rubens."

Bobby raised his glass. "It doesn't look like professionals at least. Although that's good and bad."

"Meaning?"

"With professionals, the word's out on the street quickly.

A recovery price is negotiated, and voilà. You have your painting back. Art theft is the number-three enterprise in the world behind drug trafficking and weapons trafficking. Seven billion a year. You want this to be a professional job."

"If it isn't, then what?" Arthur asked, not that he wasn't aware in general of the illegal traffic in art, but he'd never personally dealt with it.

"With amateurs, one never knows the motivation. Does some wacko want to put it in his porno-lined closet and look at it at night? Is it some game of wits where simply accomplishing the lift is the rush and the painting is incidental—and unfortunately, often tossed?" Bobby added with a faint scowl. "Is it revenge for some slight? Those, too, don't see the light of day often. The perpetrators don't want money; they want vengeance." Bobby half lifted his glass. "Is there anyone you can think of who might wish to harm you or the museum?"

Arthur shrugged. "I can't think of anyone."

Knowing what he knew from Cassie, Bobby marveled at such obtuseness. "I'm about halfway through the staff interviews. Your guards weren't derelict so much as untrained; your security needs to be upgraded. I'll give you a printout that should be useful. As for the rest of the curators and temps, there's still a possibility one of them might be involved, but"—he lifted one shoulder—"it's rare."

"I have faith in you. You're the best. So tell me about your little redhead waiting in Budapest."

Arthur wasn't really interested in the theft. He'd spent a lifetime delegating authority, his idea of a director's role was that of benign sovereign. Servants and bureaucrats did whatever work was required. His nose for gossip, however, was insatiable.

"There's nothing to tell. I met her skiing last winter. She happened to be in Budapest the same time as I and—"

"Happened?" Arthur archly remarked.

"In a manner of speaking." He wasn't about to say he'd come home one night and found her in his bed.

"What does she look like? What does she do?"

"She's beautiful. She models for the Milan shows. She parties when she's not in Milan. Nothing out of the ordinary."

"You dog, you."

"I work most of the time, Arthur," Bobby mildly said. "My leisure time is minimal."

"But that redhead's still there waiting for you in Budapest," Arthur said with arched brows. "Sometimes I envy you your amusements. Young cunt everywhere, no museum board looking over your shoulder, no alimony," he added with a grumble.

"If you have kids you have to pay for them. You can't complain about that."

Arthur sighed. "I know. And they're good kids, but it's costing me a fortune."

Luckily you have one, Bobby wanted to say. "There's always a trade-off with family."

"Is that why you're single and footloose?"

"There's no particular reason. It just happened that way."

"Claire's not remarried. Is that happenstance, too?"

"I haven't a clue."

"Honestly—you never talk to her?"

"I've been busy."

"There's a rumor she might get the costume directorship at the Met."

"I heard. She'd be good."

"No regrets?"

"It was over a long time ago. Let's leave it at that."

His voice had turned curt, and even Arthur, who wasn't known for his perception, took note and quickly said, "I hope none of my family connections get in the way of the investigation. I do talk to Claire on occasion. She and Sarah went to Bennington together as you probably know; she's godmother to Flora." He shrugged faintly. "Everyone knows everyone in this business."

"Don't worry. Your friends don't have to be my friends." Bobby set down his glass. He didn't want to talk about Claire. What used to be good in their marriage had gone sour. He wasn't sure why. But he'd wanted out when it did. And apparently, so did Claire.

"Another drink?"

"No thanks. I have some paperwork to go over tonight."

"With Cassandra?"

He couldn't help it, Bobby thought. *Arthur was an incorrigible voyeur.* "No. Alone. Thanks for the drink. I'll see you tomorrow."

"I hope Cassandra won't be a problem for you. Say the word, and I'll cut her loose."

"It's not a problem. She's useful for some of the legwork. And she needs the money, you said. I wouldn't want to be a prick."

"It's your call. If you don't want her, just say the word."

"I'll let you know if I change my mind."

"Just a reminder," Arthur said, escorting him to the door. "The flower show starts tomorrow. The museum will be mobbed, in case it matters."

"It shouldn't matter. I'm going to check on some of the temps . . . and your exes, if you don't mind—or even if you do. It's routine."

"Be my guest, but you're wasting your time. Paige and Sarah wouldn't have a clue how to pull off a heist. Nor the desire."

"I'm sure you're right, but I'll check them off my list."

"Make sure you tell them I'm not harassing them, or my lawyer will get a call."

"I'll be polite as hell. I'll bring Miss Hill with me so the call appears completely benign. They must know her."

"They've met her once or twice, I'm sure. Emma has Paige and Sarah's addresses," his gaze narrowed, "for which homes I'm paying handsomely."

"I'm sure they're appreciative," Bobby politely noted. No way was he going to sympathize with Arthur's inclination to serial marriages and divorces. The man was old enough to know better. "I'll talk to you tomorrow."

Two minutes later, Bobby was loping down the sidewalk, the yellow cab shining like a vision of nirvana at the end of the block—the distraction he needed only seconds away.

Quashing the unwanted memories Arthur's questions about his late marriage had dredged up, he thought instead of the lush woman waiting for him and the sure-to-be-gratifying night ahead.

AS BOBBY SLID into the backseat of the cab, Arthur was running through his speed dial directory. D, D, D, Dumont. He punched talk.

"I'll bet you have no idea who's in town," he said a moment later.

"What happened to 'Hello, how are you,' Arthur?" Claire Dumont murmured, having a very good idea why he called. She knew Arthur's penchant for meddling. She also knew who he'd call when his Rubens was stolen.

"Take a guess."

"The president."

"Of what?" Arthur was on a first-name basis with numerous presidents of universities and foundations.

"Our country, Arthur. I hear he was in Minneapolis recently."

"No. Guess again."

"Bobby Serre," she said, because Arthur would go on forever and she was already late for a cocktail party.

"How did you know?" he exclaimed.

"Anyone with half a brain would call Bobby to find their stolen artwork. Now I have a question for you. Why are you calling to tell me this?"

"I just thought you'd like to know."

"And?"

"Bobby doesn't like to talk about your divorce. I thought you'd like to know that, too. I tried to get him to talk. He wouldn't."

"He doesn't like to talk about anything, Arthur. I blame his Montana upbringing where men are men and women take second place to horses."

"Do I detect a note of bitterness?"

"Of course, you idiot. Who wouldn't want to be married to Bobby Serre?"

"He gave me the impression the divorce was mutual."

"That's interesting. I was the one who came back to New York from London to find him gone. Not gone on an investigation, but gone gone." She hadn't thought he'd meant it in London, but he had.

"Who filed for divorce?"

"Really, Arthur, does it matter?" She wasn't about to say she did on the advice of her lawyer and numerous friends who understood the monetary specifics of divorce. Nor was she about to tell Arthur that Bobby had begun to suspect her friendship with a museum trustee might have been more than platonic. She would never admit it, of course. What was a few times at the Carlyle? Certainly not memorable.

"You could come to visit. Who knows? Maybe Bobby's changed his mind."

"Then he can get in touch with me."

"Give Sarah a call. She'd be delighted to see you."

"Such persistence, Arthur. What's in it for you?"

"Can't I be concerned for a friend?"

There was no point in saying something rude. "Why don't I think about it," Claire politely said instead. "I really have to go now. A car is waiting for me downstairs. I'm expected at the Hammersmiths' for cocktails tonight. You remember them."

"Of course. Say hello to Richard for me. And think about what I said. You never know."

"Ciao, Arthur. Good luck with the recovery of the Rubens." And she hung up before he said something more about fixing her up with Bobby Serre. Really, Arthur was such an insatiable busybody. She always pictured him dressed in heliotrope satin exchanging tittle tattle in Prinny's inner circle during the Regency. He would have fit in perfectly.

But Arthur's words kept replaying in her mind on the ride to the Hammersmiths'——the thought that Bobby might be harboring some feelings for her intriguing. After several cocktails and a glaring dearth of eligible men at the Hammersmiths', she was feeling even more intrigued. What did she have to lose? Didn't she have a free voucher that allowed her to fly anytime? Wasn't she at loose ends with most everyone in her department at the Dusseldorf conference? Couldn't she take off a day or so and visit Sarah and her goddaughter Flora?

Of course she could.

EIGHTEEN

 A SECOND NIGHT OF NONSTOP SEX WAS beginning to take its toll on Cassie's and Bobby's energy levels, and they slept in Friday morning.

The phone rang at seven.

"Don't answer it," Bobby muttered.

"I have to."

He opened one eye. "No, you don't," he said and pulled her close.

Her voicemail kicked in, and they both drifted back to sleep.

The second and third time her phone rang neither even heard it, as though their brains had been given justifiable reason to overlook the sound.

When they finally came awake, it was ten o'clock on one of those glorious spring mornings of sunshine, singing birds, and balmy temperatures.

"You know what we have to do first?" Bobby murmured, kissing her cheeks and eyes and nose and lips, tasting her with a smile. "Grocery shop."

"Second," she whispered, relatively sure she'd become a nymphomaniac in the space of three short days, but unconcerned about therapy until she had another orgasm. "If you don't mind."

"If you don't mind if we make this a short work day because Fridays are my favorite fuck-off days."

"I love Fridays, too. We could sit outside in the sun this afternoon and drink champagne."

"Or we could sit inside and look at the sun through the windows and drink champagne. Then the neighbors wouldn't notice your lack of clothes."

"You better stop right there, or Arthur won't get a lick of work out of me today."

"We'll pace ourselves. A little work, a little fun. A little fun, a little fun."

She grinned. "Because it's Friday."

"You betcha. So tell me what you want, Miss Hill, because I'm on the clock this morning, and you won't be able to have your way with me past eleven. You and I have an interview about one, and I want some groceries in your empty refrigerator."

"I do so hate to rush my way through sex."

"You could have fooled me."

"Are you complaining?"

He laughed. "Not likely. Come here, babe. Earn your consultant fees."

She would have decked anyone else for such a chauvinist remark, but she was more than ready to earn her fees or whatever else he wanted to call it. She hadn't felt so good since—let's face it—since forever. "What do I have to do to earn my consultant fees?" she purred, teasing him in flirtatious play, her libido kicking in as though a few hours of sleep had been more than enough to restoke the fires. "I've never been a consultant before . . ."

Understanding a little game had begun, he smoothly said, "It's easy. You just have to do what I tell you." He came up into a sitting position and leaned back against the headboard. "I'm sure you'll do fine."

"I've heard you can be demanding." He hadn't missed a beat, but then he never did. Play or not, games or real, he was smooth.

"You heard wrong," he said with a faint smile. "Come, tell me why you want the position."

"I need the money." Sitting cross-legged beside him, she piled her tousled hair atop her head in a blatantly seductive gesture. "Arthur doesn't pay me enough."

"Why don't we remedy that," he softly said, contemplating the rise of her luscious breasts, his dick taking note as well.

"How nice of you," she said in a breathy, little-girl voice employed by movie sex kittens to get what they wanted. And what she wanted was in clear view and getting larger by the second. She dropped her hands and met his gaze. "I really appreciate your help."

As her hair tumbled onto her shoulders and her heavy breasts settled into place with a tantalizing quiver, it took him a moment to refocus his thoughts because she was asking. Not that he wasn't interested, but speed didn't have the same appeal to him as it did to her. And he liked her game. "Did Arthur tell you I'm researching Romano's erotica? I hope that's not a problem."

She looked startled for a moment, and he gave her high points for improvisation. "Are you embarrassed?"

"No, sir—well . . . perhaps a little."

"You're blushing." Her feigned innocence was hotter than hot.

"I've seen his work, of course, but I don't usually discuss it with—"

"A stranger?"

She looked down and nodded.

My God, his libido was loving this—her false virtue a real turn-on. "I doubt we'll be strangers long."

Her lashes fluttered upward, and she smiled. "I'd like that."

"Good. Now, tell me what you think of Romano's sketchbook. We'll begin with that."

"I find it intriguing," she said sweetly, her gaze flickering downward from time to time as though she didn't know where to look. "He portrays so many curious positions."

"Sexual positions, you mean."

"Yes," she whispered, twisting her fingers together as though talking about sex was disconcerting.

But he knew better. Her nipples were taut and hard, the flush of arousal pinking her skin. "Which is your favorite?"

"I liked"—she looked down again, her hair tumbling over her forehead—"several of them."

Her voice was almost inaudible, her blushing pose so damnably arousing he was tempted to fuck her right now. But then he'd miss the rest of the game.

"Show me your favorite one."

"I couldn't." Her gaze didn't quite meet his. "Really."

"There's no one here. Don't be bashful."

She looked at him then down again. "I shouldn't . . ."

"Do you find the centaurs intriguing? Look at me. Do you?"

Her gaze came up slowly as though she was complying reluctantly. "I don't know—I mean—yes . . . in some ways I do."

"You like to look at their huge cocks and balls?"

"Sometimes, yes. They're—the women seem frightened."

"Are you frightened by a huge cock?"

"I'm not sure"—her gaze briefly rested on his rampant erection—"perhaps not entirely."

Or not at all, he thought. "Have you ever thought about a centaur or a faun forcing you to have sex?"

She didn't immediately answer. "Yes," she finally said, her voice the merest whisper.

"And the men in the Romano sketchbook. Did you like them?"

"They were very attractive."

"Because they had massive erections?"

"I couldn't say . . . I mean—perhaps in some ways I found that agreeable."

"Then you'll enjoy our project. We'll be analyzing Romano's oeuvre and comparing it to Picasso's later sketches."

"I prefer Romano's."

"Because they're highly representational. Is that what appeals to you?"

"I'm not sure. Yes, actually, it is," she admitted.

"So you like to look at big cocks. Do they arouse you?"

"Very much." She glanced at his erection again.

"Show me a female pose from Romano." His voice took on a new brusqueness.

"Would this be considered part of my job duties?"

"Initially. There would be others later."

"Such as?"

"Why don't we see how you do on this first."

She was so ready for sex little rivulets of pearly fluid were trickling down her thighs, her vagina was flexing in tiny pulsating spasms, her senses riding high on the sex-spree bandwagon.

"I'm waiting." His voice was gruff.

"If you insist," she said with constraint as though she were compelled, when during the night past she had been more likely to make unbridled demands than he. "Do you remember this pose?" Sliding her hands forward on the bed, she came up on her hands and knees and glanced back over her shoulder at him. "Although the sketch had two men and one woman."

"Would you like me to find someone else?" His voice had dropped half an octave.

Causing her slight, but genuine alarm. "No, no— please . . . I meant it only in—"

"Play? Does thinking about two men and one woman make you wetter?" But he didn't wait for an answer because he had other things on his mind. He was already positioning himself behind her, the heated intonation of his words drifting over her back, the head of his penis nudging her cleft. "See if this is big enough," he murmured, beginning to enter her, his hands on her waist holding her immobile. He drove in deeper. "Let me know . . ."

She screamed in ecstasy as he plunged forward, as his enormous cock stretched her and filled her, every vaginal cell shuddering in rapture, her addicted senses overstimulated but already shamelessly racing for climax. Because— there . . . *now* . . . he was fully submerged. She could feel the peaking rapture scorch through her senses. It was astonishing how easily she could reach orgasm with him. She could practically come in seconds. Like . . . sort of . . . right—

"Wait," he said, glancing in the mirror. "Look."

She didn't hear him or ignored him, thrusting backward, grinding against his erection, wanting what she wanted, reaching for her addictive fix.

He smiled.

Because she was coming now and he wasn't.

Which meant next time she could look.

* * *

AS IT TURNED out, Bobby was off the clock later than eleven, which meant the business of the day was forced into a tightly compressed time frame.

A slightly harder adjustment for Cassie when she was in her addicted-to-love phase. But Bobby coaxed and sweet-talked and made promises that brought a smile to her face. And finally brought her out of bed.

He went grocery shopping alone while Cassie soaked in the tub and dreamed of an entire weekend free of museum work.

Bobby had promised, and she was holding him to it.

She didn't question her startling assertiveness with a man she had only met a few days ago.

She figured her newfound propensity for female power must be a by-product of the practically nonstop sex. It only made sense. What with her hormones on a rampage and the full moon and that female goddess thing and all.

NINETEEN

AFTER A LUNCH THAT BOBBY PREPARED FROM the groceries he'd purchased; after Cassie had said with awe at least a hundred times, "Where did you learn to cook like that?"; after they'd finished the last drop of butterscotch pudding with whipped cream and the final morsel of chicken fried steak and real handcut french fries; Cassie called Emma for Paige and Sarah's addresses.

"You're home, I see," Emma said. "We haven't seen Bobby Serre today, either. Could that be a coincidence, or is my female intuition working overtime?"

"Neither. I just happen to be working at home," Cassie lied, not about to go into detail about the type of work she'd been doing, although just the thought of her brief consultancy on Romano's sketchbook brought a smile to her face. "I don't know where Bobby Serre is."

Unfortunately, Bobby called out from the bathroom, "Where's the shampoo?" at that inopportune moment, his voice loud enough to carry into the bedroom and over the phone lines.

"You lucky girl, you," Emma murmured.

After answering Bobby, Cassie anxiously said to Emma, "Don't you dare say a word. I mean it. Arthur would be impossible if he knew. And that's not just me talking."

"Don't worry. As if Arthur has to know anything. Your secret is safe. Now, you go, girl, and all best wishes for the future from me and all your friends at this fine institution. Not that I won't expect a blow-by-blow some day in the far, far distant future."

"Thanks, Emma. You're a dear."

"So is he hung?"

"I really couldn't say."

"He's standing there?"

"Sort of," Cassie lied *again,* her red-hot sex life turning her into a lying nymphomaniac, but she just couldn't bring herself to actually discuss the length of his really spectacular you-know-what to a work colleague.

"Then we'll talk business. One item of a less cheerful nature, your ex phoned yesterday. He couldn't scream at you on your voicemail, and he sounded deeply frustrated. Something about suing your ass if you don't turn over some painting."

"Jeez. Sorry he bothered you."

"Not a problem. I told him you'd gone to Paris for a conference and wouldn't be back for two weeks."

"You're a doll."

"I know. I also told him you were staying there with an old friend—Georges Bellecoure—you know, the one Jay dislikes 'cuz he's gorgeous and rich."

"Wow. Thanks. I owe you big time for that one."

"I just thought you might like some peace and quiet while you're doing your consultant thingy. I wouldn't want you to lose your groove because your ex has anger-management problems."

"How did you know—and I ask only because I may have to consider that everyone else knows as well . . . which means the news might have reached Arthur."

"I hadn't seen you since Wednesday—and the illustrious Mr. Serre only briefly. You always show up for work barring hurricanes and acts of God, so vulgar mind that I have—I went with the obvious."

"Do you think others noticed?"

"Nah. Everyone's chasing around with the flower show and the theft, and you're so pure as the driven snow—who would suspect?"

"I'm not like that."

"I know and you know, but look, honey, you've been standin' by your no-good man for a long time. Most wives would have been warming someone else's sheets by now . . . that's all. Don't give it another thought. Everything's copacetic. Go on with your detective stuff and have a good time. By the way, if you're going to see Paige and Sarah, they're usually at Sarah's on Friday afternoon. They have a play group together."

"Do you keep track of everyone?"

"Not by choice with them, but I've been delegated their fix-it-up chappy for some ungodly reason. They call me for every plumbing and yard man problem they have, as well as school tuition payments, summer camp schedules, and lists of nannies."

"You're kidding!"

"I wish I were. Sweet as they may be, and Arthur certainly has an eye for pretty little blondes precisely five years apart in age because he has a short attention span, they are not take-charge kind of women. Which works for Arthur, who's looking for a docile wife who tells him he's perfect. So in a way, they're a little naive—actually a whole lot naive.

Which begs the question, why are you and the man in your bathroom going to see them?"

"He says it's just routine. A matter of checking on everyone."

"Tell him he can interview me anytime—in my bedroom, preferably."

Cassie smiled. "I'll let him know. And we're not calling ahead, so don't mention we're coming should you talk to them. He prefers people not have planned responses. Not that Paige or Sarah need any, I'm sure. And thanks, Emma, for your understanding."

"You deserve it, kid. Let me know if you need anything else. Gotta go. The Sun King is walking through—" and the phone went dead.

"Who was that?" Bobbie asked as he came out of the bathroom rubbing his hair with a towel.

"Emma. She knows. She also said you can interview her in her bedroom."

"I figured she knew. The look she gave me yesterday was like the ones my mom gave me when I was a kid and lying through my teeth to her. She's sharp."

"She has to be, working for Arthur. Actually, she's the only assistant to last more than a few weeks. She's on a record two years and counting."

"It helps that she can wrestle Arthur to the ground."

"And he knows it. They have an uneasy truce."

"Why are you dressed?" he asked, coming to a sudden stop and frowning slightly.

"I thought I'd better."

He sighed. "Yeah, I guess."

"Once we interview them, we're done for the day, right?"

"Right."

"Then what would you like to do?"

"Need you ask?"

"I was being polite. I thought you might like to see a movie or play golf or go for a bike ride—" her sentence trailed off.

"I'd like to go for a ride all right."

She smiled. "You're such a dear."

TWENTY

SARAH'S HOUSE WAS A COMFORTABLE BRICK bungalow in an upscale suburb with a swimming pool in the backyard, two white SUVs parked in the drive, and a border of red tulips lining the sidewalk to the blue front door. Large potted hydrangeas decorated both sides of the curved stoop, and the welcome sign hanging from the ornate door knocker was painted with singing warblers.

It was Midwest frictionless charm.

Right down to the white ribbon around the neck of the larger-than-life-size bronze bunny rabbit stationed to the left of the door.

They rang the doorbell, heard a trilling "I'll get it," and waited for the door to open.

"Cassandra! Bobby! What a surprise!"

"Forgive us for not calling," Cassie said, "but we were in the neighborhood, so we thought we'd stop by. We're interviewing everyone who's connected with the museum," she smiled, "no matter how remotely."

"I hope you don't mind answering a few questions," Bobby politely added. "They're purely routine."

"Of course. Come in. Excuse the children everywhere. Paige and I have play day here on Friday afternoons. Paige! Come see who's here!"

As they were ushered into a large, sunny room at the back of the house that opened on to a yard filled with every imaginable playground toy, Paige came in from the adjoining kitchen. "Hello. What a surprise." All Arthur's wives had met Bobby and Cassie at some time or other.

"My words exactly," Sarah declared. "They're here to interview us about the theft at the museum—just routine, Bobby says."

"We're interviewing everyone, including trustees and docents." Bobby shrugged. "We have to at least go through the motions of talking to everyone."

"Have you talked to Frank Hauser yet?" Sarah asked. "That should be a stitch. Do you remember when he started to lecture us on manners because we weren't wearing white gloves at the cocktail reception?" She smiled at Paige. "He's sure the world is going to hell in a handbasket because proper etiquette is no longer a priority. Aaron, honey, don't climb so high! Aaron, stop this instant! Aaron, if you don't stop you won't get any ice-cream sandwiches!"

The preschooler paused.

"I mean it, Aaron. Everyone else will have Blue Bunny ice-cream sandwiches except you!"

The young boy dressed in toddler Patagonia began descending the jungle-gym ladder.

"Thank you, sweetheart. Your mommy will be pleased. Sorry," Sarah apologized. "Some of the children are fearless. Do sit down. Would you like coffee, tea, lemonade, or cranapple Juicy Juice?"

"We're fine," Bobby said.

Cassie was thinking she could use a stiff drink with all the potential accidents waiting to happen on the playground outside—six young children crawling, climbing, and hanging in precarious positions on the Disney Land–size apparatus. That little girl dressed in pink from head to toe looked like she was losing her grip on the monkey bars. Oops. Lucky they had soft sand underneath.

Bobby was moving several small trucks from the couch and motioning Cassie over. He said in a semi-official way, "If you'd take notes," and handed her the tablet he carried. Unfortunately, his request in that low, deep murmur reminded her of the very sexy Romano fantasy of recent memory, which hampered her ability to concentrate for a minute. "Do you need a pen?" he asked when she didn't move.

She saw the pen he held out to her, forced her brain to rewind and process what he'd said, locked away the tantalizing fantasy behind imaginary closed doors, and took the pen. But he was still looking at her strangely, as were Paige and Sarah, and she wondered if something was unbuttoned. "Thank you very much," she added, trying to appear normal and quickly sat down, sneaking a quick glance at her blouse buttons just in case.

Everything was in place, fortunately. She inched sideways on the colorful Provencal print couch, hoping to put sufficient distance between her and the combustible fuel to her libidinous tinder—namely one much too handsome and well-endowed Bobby Serre.

Bobby was talking about the theft in general terms, putting the two women at ease, explaining what questions he would be asking and why. But the interview turned into a puppets-on-a-string scenario with Paige and Sarah spending most of the time jumping up to avert some childish disaster, sitting again only to hop up once more to run to the door and deliver a barrage of warnings and chiding that seemed to have little or no effect on their charges.

After ten minutes of spasmodic, disjointed replies, Bobby had gleaned that no, they hadn't been to the museum lately, neither of them were involved in any of the museum functions any longer, they had no idea what the stolen Rubens looked like—"Is that the one with the man on the white horse?" Sarah had asked—and in terms of understanding anything about the museum alarm system, he'd drawn blank looks when he brought up the subject. Almost too blank, he thought, considering Arthur's casual attitude toward security. But then again, maybe the women were just slightly fearful at being interrogated.

When it came to Arthur, he kept his questions as polite as possible.

"How is your relationship with Arthur?" he inquired.

"We don't have one," Paige replied, but her voice was temperate.

"Not since Jessica," Sarah added, her words rushed together, her personality less constrained than Paige.

"Why is that?"

The women looked at each other and then Paige answered, "She wants him for herself, I suppose. It's only natural. We understand."

Of the two women, the older Paige seemed to have been designated their spokesperson. "Have you had words with Jessica?" Bobby asked.

"No."

"Except for the picnic," Sarah blurted out.

She received a critical glance from her friend.

"It was an unfortunate misunderstanding," Paige explained. "We were under the impression the children had been invited to the picnic."

"But Jessica said they weren't," Sarah said with a little sniff. "Can you imagine?"

"She doesn't have children." Paige half smiled. "She can't be expected to understand a child's sensitivities. Flora and Seth were disappointed."

"But we took them to the zoo instead, and they had a really good time," Sarah offered with a smile. "So everything worked out just fine."

"It's difficult for Arthur," Paige politely noted. "As you can expect."

"Do you have any disagreements with Arthur—money, visitation, custody issues?"

"No, not really," Paige answered.

"There was the wall-to-wall carpeting," Sarah said in her breathy semi-explosive way.

Paige stepped in smoothly. "Arthur explained the stock market was down. His dividends had been affected."

"Jessica got new carpeting," Sarah muttered.

"And the children had their trip to Disney World, don't forget," Paige declared, giving her friend a pat on the hand. "Arthur does his best."

"Yes, Arthur's a very conscientious provider," Sarah added, looking to Paige for approval at her well-mannered remark.

"Arthur *can* be demanding," Bobby observed. "And perhaps not as diplomatic as he could be. Has he been difficult in that regard?"

"No, not at all. Arthur is always polite to us. And now the poor man has this robbery to deal with. We both sympathize, don't we?" Another pat on Sarah's hand.

"It must be awful for Arthur to be involved in something so sinister," Sarah murmured.

"It almost makes one fearful of one's children's safety," Paige interposed. "The world is changing. Didn't I say that,

Sarah?" She looked at her friend. "And it's not changing for the better."

"I don't even like to turn on the news anymore," Sarah remarked. "There's so much violence. I'm glad they're showing the *Mr. Rogers* reruns. He was such a kind man."

"A perfect role model for young children. Matilda!" Paige screamed. "Don't you dare hit Flora with that whiffle bat! You'll have a long time-out if you do, and I'll tell your mother you were very naughty!"

They all watched the little girl reluctantly lower the sponge bat, stick her tongue out at Flora instead, then lob the soft bat in Aaron's direction.

"I'm telling!" Aaron shouted. "She hit me! Tilda hit me! You won't get no ice cream! I'm gonna tell!"

"If you'll excuse us a minute," Sarah said, coming to her feet.

"The children need a little conversation about playing together nicely," Paige observed, rising from her chair.

"I think we're about done here anyway," Bobby said, standing up. "You've been a great help."

Page smiled. "It's the least we can do for Arthur."

Sarah giggled, quickly muffled it, and smiled as well. "We're more than happy to be of help."

"Any way we can," Paige added. "I hope you find the painting soon."

"We're all hoping for that," Bobby said.

As THEY WALKED away from the house, Cassie said, "Those two are so weird, they should be on *Jerry Springer.* 'I'm best friends with my husband's ex-wife.' "

Bobby blew out a breath. "That was definitely weird. Were they wired or what? They could barely sit still."

"It was just the kids and play day. I'd go crazy with so

many kids to watch. They do seem genuinely fond of each other, though. Did you see how they sometimes finished each other's sentences?"

"Weirder yet. Could you tell how they felt about Arthur? I was getting some conflicting vibes in their tone of voice or their expressions when his name came up. Like they didn't really mean what they were saying."

"Why would they like him? They're polite, that's all. He's paying for everything; they'd better watch what they say or get a job."

"Maybe that's it. A restrained dislike."

"Give them points for the restrained part. He's a first-class prick."

"I suppose," Bobby murmured, shrugging away an undefinable inconsistency, telling himself anything would seem strange when you were talking to two ex-wives who not only had shared a husband but looked so much alike they could be sisters. "If I didn't know better, I'd say Sarah and Paige were related. They look alike; they even dress alike." The women had worn slacks and camp shirts in coordinated shades of melon and aquamarine.

"Arthur's eye for women is confined to petite blondes."

"Not necessarily." Bobby grinned. "He likes you."

"Don't say that. It gives me the creeps. The last thing I need is creepy Arthur staring at me in a way I don't want him staring, if you know what—" Cassie's voice trailed off as Bobby came to a sudden stop midway down the sidewalk, his gaze on the passenger getting out of a cab.

The woman was tall and slender, her short black hair cropped in a freshly tousled hairdo, her glamorous face the kind that stared out at you from magazine covers. Her long, tan designer raincoat swung away as she stood upright, revealing the longest legs, shortest skirt, and most perfect breasts under a pale cashmere sweater that Cassie had ever seen.

Shit. The cover model was waving at them. Correction. At Bobby, 'cuz if she'd met a woman like that, she would definitely have remembered her.

"Bobby! My God! What are you doing here?" the woman from some modeling agency exclaimed. "Don't say you've come to meet me," she lightly added, smiling like some ingenue starlet as she moved toward them with a graceful model's walk, the traveling bag in her hand a sleek, expensive leather.

Why did glamorous people always dress in muted tans and neutrals that seem to proclaim their elevated station without saying a word? Suddenly, Cassie felt *de trop* in her favorite chartreuse slacks and tangerine T-shirt. Not to mention jealous because Bobby Serre was standing there staring like he'd seen a real, bonafide angel descend from a cloud.

"How long has it been, darling?" the gorgeous woman asked, smiling faintly. "I'd say too long. Give me a hug." And she dropped her at least two-thousand-dollar bag—more, if that was real crocodile and not stamped—and held out her arms.

Bobby hesitated marginally before giving her a hug, stepping away after only the briefest moment—but not before the woman smiled at Cassie over Bobby's shoulder. Her smug smile said, "You don't have a chance."

"Cassie Hill, Claire Dumont. Claire, Cassie."

"And who are you?" Claire inquired, her gaze critiquing.

"Cassie's a curator helping me check out clues on the Rubens theft. You probably heard about the robbery. We're interviewing a cast of thousands, including Sarah and Paige."

"They didn't tell you I was coming in, did they?" Claire said with what could only be defined as a breathy coo. "I told them not to. I wanted to surprise you."

"Why?" His voice was wary.

And that made Cassie super wary.

"Just for fun."

"Is that so?" A distinct constraint colored his words.

"Don't panic, darling. I'm godmother to Sarah's youngest. You wouldn't know that, I suppose, because she's only . . . well . . . not very old." Claire had no idea how old Flora was.

"Arthur mentioned it."

Claire touched his cheek. "No need to get all grim, sweetheart. I'm not stalking you. It's little Flora's birthday. I was invited." She turned to Cassie. "I'm Bobby's ex-wife. We weren't married long, but we had a very *long* engagement, didn't we darling, traveling the world—Peru and Florence, Istanbul, Paris, St. Petersburg in the summer. You can't say it wasn't fun."

"It was nice seeing you, Claire. Enjoy your birthday party."

"You're trying to brush me off," she said, with a lilting laugh. "Have it your way, dear, but we'll talk again before I go." She waved her fingers in a casual flutter, picked up her bag, and moved toward the house.

For a fraction of a second, Bobby remained motionless. Then he exhaled softly. "I need a drink."

If he needed a drink after seeing his ex-wife, Cassie needed at least two and counting.

That woman was flawless.

Damn, damn, damn, she silently swore. Not that she had any long-range plans for Bobby Serre, but her short-range plans would fly out the window if gorgeous Claire decided to take him into *her* bed.

There was no doubt in her mind her recently revived and currently hotter-than-hot sex life was at risk.

Claire Dumont wasn't in town just for a birthday party.

TWENTY-ONE

SOME TIME LATER, THE THREE WOMEN WERE having drinks in the rare silence of play day, the children having been quieted with Blue Bunny ice-cream sandwiches and a DVD of *Finding Nemo*.

"He looks as good as ever, doesn't he?" Sarah brightly observed, smiling at her college roommate over her lemonade-laced vodka.

"Better." Claire's smile was self-assured.

"Better than your polo player?"

"Augustin was so committed to the game." Claire lifted her cashmere-covered shoulders in the merest of shrugs. "I don't know why he thought I'd travel with him."

"Maybe because you did for a season," Paige pointed out. She'd come to know Claire through Sarah and had followed Claire's polo player romance with interest.

"I couldn't possibly continue doing that." Claire lifted her glass of single malt scotch, neat, and squinted at it against the sun streaming in through the windows. "Anyway, it's over, and I've decided Bobby and I really didn't put enough effort into our marriage. I blame myself for being so involved in work." She was offering the edited account of her motives. Good judgment deterred her from saying she might have made a mistake by having an extramarital affair. Pride restrained her from pointing out she'd been unable to find a suitable replacement since her divorce.

"I'm not sure Bobby's marriage material." Sarah arched her brows. "From what I hear, he's very much a bachelor. He might not be interested in working at a marriage."

"We'll see." A certain degree of confidence and certainty weighted Claire's words. Bobby had been surprised to see her, but she'd detected something else as well. An imperceptible interest? He hadn't been indifferent. Of that she was sure. "In any case, I'm pleased Arthur called to tell me Bobby was in town. How much simpler to bump into him here than in Montana or Budapest."

Sarah gave her a conspiratorial grin. "You mean you can't suddenly appear at his ranch fifty miles from the nearest town by accident."

"Or run into him at his villa outside Budapest," Claire remarked with a lifted brow.

"So what are your plans?" Paige inquired with a smile. "Give us the juicy details."

"Marry him again, of course."

Sarah giggled with delight, an arch conspiratress at heart. When she'd inveigled her way into Arthur's bed, it had been the greatest fun. Not that she didn't feel a little guilty about it now that she and Paige were best friends. But everything had worked out for the best. And maybe it would for Claire, too. "Tell us how we can help," she declared.

"I'm not quite sure. I haven't had time to calculate my best course of action. I just heard about Bobby from Arthur last night."

"How long can you stay?" Sarah was leaning forward

slightly in her excitement. "I just love a seduction," she added with a grin.

"I'll stay as long as it takes. But I'm really hopeful. Bobby and I always got along very, very well."

"In bed, you mean."

Claire's violet eyes sparkled. "With Bobby, that's the only way that matters. Speaking of hedonistic pleasures, have either of you found anyone of interest?"

"Nothing permanent." Sarah smiled. "But then, Arthur's alimony has to be considered."

"There's no point in getting married and losing that, I suppose."

"It wouldn't be practical," Paige noted. "And the children don't need any more disruption in their lives. We date on occasion, but—"

"Aren't really seriously looking," Sarah finished.

"Do you actually get along with Arthur?" Claire knew him and his rudeness, temper, roving eye, and complete lack of concern for anyone but himself.

"We manage," Paige carefully said.

"But his wife is a grade-A bitch," Sarah irritably declared. "And we don't manage all that well with Arthur, either. Paige is just being diplomatic. We don't have to be diplomatic with Claire, Paige. She knows what a shit Arthur can be, especially about money. But he's nothing compared to his mean-spirited wife. She never wants him to see the children, and if he does, she's right there at his side. And if either of us ever calls the house and she answers the phone, she always says he's not at home. Bitch. We've been thinking about taking a little revenge—you know, embarrass him and his spiteful wife. Make him sweat."

"Sarah's just resentful because Arthur told us we've been spending too much money lately," Paige murmured. "Aren't you, Sarah?" she added, firmly. "We've been going over our quota, and he's been grumbling."

"I suppose you're right," Sarah reluctantly muttered. "I'm just mad. Still, it would be nice to ruin Arthur's life a little." She smiled at Claire. "Haven't you wanted to get back at someone sometime in your life?"

"Absolutely. Or *get* someone," Claire added with a wink. "Like, for instance, Bobby Serre. And planning a seduction is even sweeter than planning a revenge. What do you say? I'm going to need some help."

"This is going to be so much fun," Sarah exclaimed. "I think we need another round of drinks to spark our creative juices."

"Why not?" Claire replied, although just seeing Bobby again had sparked whatever needed sparking already.

He looked as good as ever. Maybe better.

TWENTY-TWO

A WHOLE LOT OF HIGH-VOLTAGE SPARKING of another kind was going on at the moment on a houseboat on the St. Croix with a view of the river—had anyone been inclined to notice. The boat lent to Bobby by a friend was very large, powered by twin diesel engines, and crewed by two men who knew how to be invisible. The bedroom was located on a flying deck twenty feet above the water, the bed large enough to sleep six. Or accommodate six more accurately, because Bobby's newly divorced financial trader friend was making up for lost time and into group sex.

That particular form of amusement had never been Bobby's style, and when Cassie had remarked on the size of the bed, he'd only said, "I think it came with the boat."

They spent Friday and Saturday there, their only excursions ashore to nearby restaurants, a kind of single-minded search for sensation taking up the remainder of their time.

Cassie was thinking she might as well enjoy Bobby Serre while she could, the specter of his ex-wife a disconcerting unease flitting around in the nether regions of her mind.

He seemed distracted at times, as though he wasn't quite sure who he was with. She thought about taking issue and decided that would be counterproductive in terms of her pleasure.

Which was why she was here.

Which was why her body had morphed into total insatiable mode, desire strumming through her senses full speed ahead.

It was nice here with him.

It was better than nice.

It was a definite gold-medal adult-entertainment sport.

And she was a winner any way you looked at it.

WHILE CASSIE WAS luxuriating in a very agreeable halcyon bliss, try as Bobby could, fuck as much as he could, that damnable image of Claire getting out of that cab was glued to the back of his retinas. Jesus Christ, she was the last person he wanted to see. The absolute last. Especially after the dreams he'd been having just before he left Budapest, the ones with them saying good-bye that last day in London, their room at the Savoy with the fabulous view of the Thames trashed from all the heavy objects Claire had thrown at him. Him gimlet-eyed and grim about his suspicions, her with tears streaming down her face, saying he was wrong, she was sorry. Him saying he didn't care if she was sorry or not after she'd nearly killed him with that bronze sculpture.

They might have had their good times, but they fought like cats and dogs. Claire was always on the make, and he'd decided that gray day in London that seemed to suit his sour mood, that he didn't care to spend his life fighting with and wondering about his wife.

He'd walked out that day and never looked back.

Life was too fucking short.

And now he was having goddamned flashbacks and—worse—some kind of nostalgia for a past that didn't deserve nostalgia.

But damn, she'd looked good today.

You couldn't fault her beauty even if she had a vile temper and ambiguous ethics about fidelity. He certainly hadn't been a poster boy for abstinence, either before or after his marriage. Maybe things just happened. Maybe she had her reasons.

But regardless of what Claire may or may not have done, what he may or may not think about it, he was having a helluva time shaking her image from his mind.

He'd heard about the polo player. Who the hell hadn't? It had been all over the U.S. and international gossip columns, their pictures everywhere when Augustin had taken his team to the championships last year.

Could it be he was jealous?

Did she intrigue him because some challenger had entered the scene?

Or was his reaction purely physical and perfectly normal?

"Hey."

He looked down. "I'm here."

"Just checking."

He smiled. "Sorry."

Her gaze was amused. "No problem. Even when you're on automatic pilot, you're good. Ex-wife?"

"How did you know?" But he abruptly rolled off her, stared up at the ceiling, and sighed.

"You always react to an ex," she said, easing up on the pillows. "In my case, homicide comes to mind, but hey, it's an emotion."

"Mine isn't too far off."

"Bad memories?"

He glanced over at her. "I guess."

"Divorce isn't unique." She smiled. "In fact, it's common if you don't mind being common."

"Do you want to see a movie?"

"No."

He laughed. "My voice of reason. Are you hungry?"

"Always."

"Let's walk to that restaurant on the river this time. I need to clear my head."

"It's seventy-five and sunny."

"There must be a breeze somewhere."

"I could distract you with my scintillating conversation."

He rolled back over and pulled her into his arms. "Distract me with a kiss instead."

"After we eat. I'm hungry."

"Before."

"After."

He was stronger and perhaps more persuasive when it came to matters of having sex.

Or maybe Cassie was in the mood to be easily persuaded.

The walked to the restaurant . . . afterward.

TWENTY-THREE

ON SUNDAY MORNING, MUCH TOO EARLY FOR good manners, Bobby's cell phone rang.

It was Arthur, with an invitation expressed in his usual fashion—as an order.

His daughter Flora's birthday party. Sarah's house. One o'clock. Casual dress.

Bobby flipped his phone shut with a grimace. "Why me?"

"Because your ex-wife wants you there."

His gaze snapped in Cassie's direction. "If that's the case, I need a body shield. You come with me."

"And incur Arthur's wrath? God, no. No one invited me."

"I'll call him."

"Don't you dare!"

But he was already punching in the phone number, and when she lunged for the phone, he rolled out of bed and walked out on the balcony stark naked.

She wasn't about to go outside nude as well—in sight of all the other boaters in the marina—but before she could grab Bobby's robe, he was coming back inside, his smile portending her doom. "Arthur would love to have you attend. In fact, I quote, 'Bring Cassandra along. She has great tits.'"

"Now I'm definitely not going." She lay back against the pillows.

"Fine, stay here. I don't think I feel like having sex anymore." He sat down on a chair across the room and stretched out in a sprawl.

"That's blackmail!"

"We'll just stay a half-hour, give the little tyke a present, say hello to Arthur and the rest of them, and get the hell out of there."

"That's not fair. I hardly know any of them."

"You know Arthur, and you've met his wives."

"What if I don't go?"

He shrugged. "It's your decision."

"That's cruel and unusual," she said with a pout.

"So is my having to see Claire with Arthur watching every move."

Now that was an ambiguous statement possible to read either way. Did he not want to see Claire—which would be a definite *yippee!*—or did he just not want to see her in Arthur's presence—a less-cheerful supposition.

"Come *on*," he coaxed. "Do me a favor."

He sounded more like an impatient little boy than an international sex symbol, making her melt inside when she should have remained resolute and determined. She sighed, silently chided herself for being a pushover, and asked, "What will you do for me if I go?"

"Anything you want."

"Anything?"

He laughed. "Just so long as no animals are involved."

"Okay."

He sat up. "No negotiation?"

"I trust you. You said anything." She smiled. "I'm real

happy with an expansive concept like that. We have to stop at my place for clothes, though." She glanced at the clock shaped like a ship's wheel and stretched lazily. "Which gives us a couple hours for a start on that 'anything.'"

"Did we agree to some time limits on this?"

Her smile was pure sunshine. "Not as I recall."

Lounging back in the chair, he spread his legs and looked at her from under his dark lashes. "Then you come here, babe," he murmured. "I'm not doing all the work."

She should hold firm and make him come to her.

After all, he was the one who had offered her anything.

Why should she have to make concessions?

But he lifted his hand, crooked his index finger, and looked at her like he might eat her alive if she did what she was told.

There was really no point in being obstructive when one's pleasure was at stake. To be obstinate just on principle was not only immature but impractical with his erection luring her like some pagan virility symbol. "Ask me again," she said, as a conciliatory concession to her newly acquired female power.

He ran his finger up the astonishing length. "Pretty please."

So call her easy.

Against that very sizeable temptation, what was a girl to do?

She went and not even reluctantly, although she supposed she should have shown a modicum of restraint. Maybe tomorrow. Or next week.

He lifted her on his lap when she reached him and kissed her for a very long time. It was really sweet and nice and remarkably considerate if she hadn't been focused on more selfish ends. She debated exactly how to broach the subject.

Finally, pushing away a little, she said, "I really need more."

He not only seemed to know what she meant by more, but he didn't take offense. He immediately stood up—with her in his arms . . . how strong and cool is that—and carried her to the bed. He lay down—again with her still in his arms . . . really she would have to start lifting weights so she could have that lithe, effortless power.

He was sprawled on his back, his eyes half shut. "Why don't we say this is your turn. I need a rest."

What exactly did "your turn" mean? Did he require something in particular, or could she indulge herself first? It was really astonishing how selfish she'd become about needing orgasms when she'd almost forgotten what they were until Bobby Serre arrived in town. "Do you have anything special in mind?" Even as she asked, she was dearly hoping he didn't. She didn't want to look ungrateful and certainly he'd been super-indulgent, but the truth was—

"Why don't you use me."

Was he the most wonderful man in the world or what? Or perhaps he was clairvoyant. Either way, she had what she wanted. And she really didn't have time for debate anyway, what with Arthur's command performance at Sarah's looming.

Climbing over him as he lay quiescent, she sat on his thighs. His erection was splendid. He was eminently, superlatively useable. Really, his testosterone levels must be out of this world.

He smiled faintly. "Everything all right?"

How casual he was about sex, about nonstop sex. No wonder he ate like a horse. "It will be soon," she said, thinking if casual worked for him it could work for her. And rising slightly, she levered his stiff cock up, guided the swollen head to her insatiable G-spot and C-spot and a dozen other clamoring spots, and slowly eased back down.

Her blissful sigh matched the blissful sensations inundating her brain and body and glowing nerve endings. In fact, she felt so good, she didn't know whether she wanted to move or not. Maybe she'd try a stationary orgasm.

But then he moved in a restrained yet forceful way.

She immediately felt even better.

Then he opened his eyes fully and grinned. "Want some help?"

"I want anything you have," she purred, when she rarely purred, when she hardly ever had reason to purr. Until Bobby Serre had entered her life.

He proceeded to give her everything he had in the most delightful way—several times and several different ways—until the ship's wheel clock ruined everything by ringing the hour. He looked up, blew out a breath, and murmured, "Time out, babe. Duty calls."

"But what about me?" she almost wailed, not even caring he might think her the most selfish of women.

"You've got my IOU. I'm good for it. It won't take long," he gently said.

"Do I have to go?"

He gave her a look even she couldn't misinterpret. "I'd say I've been holding up my end of the bargain. It's your turn. Now get your clothes on or I'll carry you out of here naked."

That tone of voice—crisp and commanding. She didn't argue.

TWENTY-FOUR·

THEY TOOK A CAB FROM THE HOUSEBOAT TO the museum ramp, where they rescued Cassie's car rather than bother Joe on the weekend. From there they drove to Cassie's house so she could change from her Friday clothes—not that she'd needed many clothes that weekend—a circumstance of much personal satisfaction to them both.

After rummaging through her closet, Cassie decided on a cropped black twill jacket, Tsubi jeans, and bright yellow wedgie sandals for the birthday party, while Bobby wore his usual uniform of khaki shorts and a T-shirt.

She drove because Bobby's long legs didn't fit comfortably on the driver's side of her small Ford Focus. Taking a short detour to Creative Kid's Stuff, they chose a gift for Flora—a small baby doll with a suitcase full of clothes. The store specialized in educational toys, but both Cassie and Bobby agreed that they'd preferred *toy* toys when they were young and went with the doll.

As they approached Sarah's house on the tree-lined street,

Bobby slumped lower in the seat—or marginally lower. His side of the car was maxed out for leg room. "Why the hell are we doing this?" he muttered.

Cassie smiled. "I don't know about you, but I know why *I'm* doing this."

He scowled. "Cute."

"And face it, Arthur expects compliance."

"Not from me."

"Then why are you here?" she asked, when she should have never, never, never been so stupid. When she should have pretended his ex-wife didn't exist. When she should have turned around and driven away at his first equivocal question and worried about Arthur later.

"Pull over. Give me a minute."

Great, now he was going to do the nostalgia playback, mentally running through all the glorious times he'd shared with Claire and get all sentimental, and she was going to be driving home alone because she didn't have sense enough to keep her mouth shut. Damn. It was a crying shame. However temporary his presence in her life, the amazing sex was going to be damned hard to give up.

He was staring straight ahead, his gaze unblinking, his broad-shouldered, powerful body filling that side of the car. Five seconds passed, ten, and another ten, then he inhaled, glanced at her, and smiled tightly. "Let's go."

A rush of questions filled her mind: What was he thinking? Was he thinking of Claire? Of course he was thinking of Claire. Could he have been contemplating something about Arthur instead—yeah, right—get real. God—how should she act when they went inside? What was expected of her? Look, she was just assisting in his detective work, she answered herself. Nothing was expected of her but gopher work.

Fine. Good. She just had to walk inside, find some quiet

corner to hide in, and wait until the great Bobby Serre was ready to leave.

It didn't matter if he had an ex-wife who looked like some goddamned supermodel. It didn't matter if he was carrying a ten-foot-high torch for her. It didn't even matter that Arthur and his two, and maybe three, wives were going to all be under the same roof. Just pretend everything is normal. Pretend you're onstage in some weird off-Broadway play with totally dysfunctional characters in the cast, and once the shipwreck of a play is over, you can get back in your car and drive away.

Hopefully not alone.

For sure, hopefully, not with Arthur—her sudden scary flip of mind so frightening she momentarily questioned her sanity. Arthur—*ugh!* Even if she could afford a therapist, she would never, ever mention so aberrant a thought. Something must have short-circuited in her brain for a second. Lack of sleep this weekend. That was it. An explanation she could live with. Relax.

Okay, so the play is over, she's back in her car, and when she looks over, Bobby Serre is smiling at her.

Like that.

"Jeez, you *do* daydream. I'm going to tell your sister she's right."

They were parked alongside the curb by some miracle of subconscious reflexes like when you talked on your cell phone all the way home and had absolutely no memory of having driven twenty miles in rush-hour traffic.

"I'm not daydreaming. I'm concentrating on parking."

"Then you might want to move up," he murmured. "There's a tree blocking my door."

That's what came from blatant lying. You had a real good chance of being caught. "Sorry, I was busy checking the traffic on the street," she said, lying again because, on a day like today, or at least at a time like this when she was facing various possible disasters, lying was the only option to telling the truth and looking completely insane.

Because she certainly couldn't mention that his ex-wife was giving her hives when there wasn't a reason in the world why she should care or he should care that she cared, when their relationship was essentially carnal and sure to be short-lived.

"Are you going to move up, or will you be going in alone?"

"Sorry." She couldn't even think of a suitable lie this time, and silently putting the car in gear, eased forward enough so the passenger door opened.

He got out quickly, she noticed, as if afraid she might keep him prisoner against his will. Or so her paranoia surmised. The rational part of her brain, functioning less well in these stressful circumstances, suggested she get out of the car and deal with the what-ifs and uncertainties at some later date. Preferably when she had all her faculties operating once again.

Opening the back door, Bobby took out the present and gave her a searching glance. "Ready?"

She nodded much like a convict about to ascend the scaffold might, stiffly, with a big lump in her throat, and really cold feet.

He held out his hand, which eased the constriction in her throat, and his sudden smile did much to warm her heart and feet. Walking over, she took his hand.

He grinned. "What say—into the jaws of hell?"

"Your marriage must have been as good as mine."

"Don't forget the certainty of Arthur's inquisition."

"I'm only giving name, rank, and serial number. Actually, I'm planning on hiding until you're ready to leave."

His mouth quirked. "Coward."

"Uh-uh. Prudent. I'm guessing I don't have a lot of friends in there."

IF NOT PRESCIENT, Cassie was capable of shrewd deductive reasoning. Sure enough, the moment they walked in the house and Sarah accepted their gift, Claire glided over as though she were a human hovercraft and took Bobby away. Ducking under Arthur's beady radar, Cassie made her getaway to the bathroom farthest from the party activities.

"Come say hello to Arthur," Claire said, taking Bobby's hand and drawing him toward the study. "Jessica is hiding from Arthur's exes."

"One big happy family, I see."

"If you only knew, darling." She smiled up at him. "The dynamics remind me of that Christmas in Bath when Georgie and his new wife and ex-wife were celebrating the holidays in residence at his little restored vicarage."

"Don't remind me." The tension had been something fierce, although everyone tried to be polite for the sake of the children.

"Ah, there you are," Claire called out as they entered the study lined with bookshelves displaying Sarah's collection of first editions and Daum glass.

"Have you ever seen so many little useless objects?" Jessica said with a dismissive wave of her hand. "Such clutter."

"It's certainly not my style," Claire smoothly replied. "Have you met Bobby Serre?"

"I've certainly heard a lot about him," Arthur's youngish wife murmured, smiling up at Bobby. "How nice to finally meet you. Arthur tells me you're going to save the museum from ruin."

"Nothing so dramatic," he replied, thinking Arthur had outdone himself with Jessica's engagement diamond. It was blinding. "The Rubens will turn up. And Arthur will be back in business soon."

"Didn't I tell you? You see that assurance." Arthur smiled at his wife and then turned to Bobby. "I told the trustees you were on the job, my boy, and all will be well."

"These usually work out one way or another," Bobby blandly said.

"Because Bobby is the best," Claire cooed, leaning into his arm. "He always has been."

"You two seem to be getting along," Arthur slyly said.

"Don't we look good together?" Claire flirtatiously purred.

"A matched pair without a doubt." Arthur's gaze narrowed. "And you certainly have things in common."

"I suppose we have one or two things," Claire playfully noted. "Do you remember that little villa along the Bosporus and that summer in St. Petersburg when we walked along the Neva every night and the sun never set?"

"I remember," Bobby said, besieged by memories, the feel and scent of Claire familiar.

"Have you been in St. Petersburg during their white nights?" Claire asked Jessica. "It's quite spectacular."

"We were there last June. Arthur was a dear and bought me some wonderful furs."

"You can't beat their prices," Arthur acknowledged. "Sable at half price. You can't pass that up."

"Arthur, dear," Jessica said, pointing at her Rolex. "Gwen's expecting us. It's one of those affairs you can't get out of," she explained.

"We have a charity event." Arthur half smiled. "Is it birds or tennis?"

"The arboretum. They need so many things," Jessica murmured.

As though anyone believed the arboretum couldn't wait a few hours.

"It was a pleasure to meet you," Bobby said, smiling at Arthur's newest wife, a younger facsimile of his exes. Although this one might have been a couple inches taller.

"If you'll excuse us," Arthur murmured, "we'll say good-bye to the birthday girl and be on our way."

"The new wife lasted a full twenty minutes," Claire said under her breath as their companions moved away.

"Arthur has his hands full." It was an observation only; Arthur could take care of himself.

"He likes new toys."

"I understand. What I don't understand is why he can't tell the difference between a toy and a wife?"

"The children, I suppose."

"You're right. But Jessica now. He could have waited."

"Maybe he's in love."

Bobby shot her a dubious look. "You jest."

"It happens. For instance, as I recall, you were rather amorous at one time. Remember how you couldn't wait that time in Paris and we made use of that janitor's closet at the Louvre?"

He could have said that wasn't precisely love, but smiled politely instead and said, "I remember."

"And the Medici Gallery in Florence. You were one randy young stud. I don't think we made it through more than one gallery when—" she glanced up as a caterer entered the study with a tray of hors d'oeuvres. "Get out!" she snapped. "Can't you see we're talking?"

The sharp-as-a-blade tone reminded him of other times when he'd heard that barbed edge. Of the hundreds of times he'd heard it. Claire could never treat a chamber maid or a waitress or waiter with courtesy.

"Darling, you *have* to come to New York and stay with me," she said, switching to a soft, cajoling tone. "We'll have such fun. Remember how much fun we used to have in bed?" She tightened her hold on his arm. "Come. I insist."

He shook his head. "I'm working."

"Pooh. How long can it take to find a painting in this quaint little town?"

He shrugged. "Hard to tell."

"Promise you'll come as soon as you're done then." Her tone was sultry and low, her breast rubbing against his arm.

"I can't."

She made a little moue. "Of course you can."

"Jorge is waiting for me after this. He has a job in Bulgaria."

She wrinkled her nose. "That trashy little man. I'm surprised you still do business with him."

"He's a friend," Bobby said cooly.

"Don't get all touchy and sulky, darling," she murmured, moving around to face him so her body was brushing up against him. "If you like Jorges, I like Jorge. Just tell me *when* you can come and see me."

"I'll let you know." He thought of Cassie, who didn't play games like this, who said what she meant with refreshing candor, who was hiding out somewhere waiting for Arthur to leave. "Look, I have to find Cassandra. She's secreted away somewhere waiting for Arthur to leave."

"I'll go with you," Claire casually said, not about to give up on the man she'd come so far to see. "She seems sweet— with a Midwestern kind of naturalness. I'm always reminded of rosy-cheeked farm girls when I'm in town."

Bobby gave her a faintly incredulous look. Cassie was about as far from a farm girl as the *Venus de Milo*.

"What? You don't agree?"

He shrugged. "It doesn't matter."

"What does matter is if she's been helpful to you. Has she?" Claire watched his face closely.

"Yes. She knows the museum," Bobby neutrally replied, surveying the rooms on either side as they moved down the hall.

"Married, single?"

"Divorced."

"Ah."

"Meaning?" He slanted a look at her and didn't like what he saw.

"I imagine she's being helpful in more ways than one, then."

"Look, Claire, just leave her alone. She's a nice kid." Cassie wasn't in the great room where they were handing out birthday cake. He'd check out the bedrooms.

"I can see that. Don't worry about me, darling. I'm nice to everyone."

"I don't really need an escort," he pointedly said.

"You needn't be rude. I haven't seen you in years."

"Fine. But mind your manners."

"Of course, darling. If you like this woman I'll be nice as can be to her."

"Jesus. Give me a break."

One bedroom, two, three, and four. Nothing. Which left the bathrooms. He decided to check the farthest one first, Claire keeping up a pointless conversation about their old friends as they moved through the house.

CASSIE HAD STAYED in the bathroom so long, she'd memorized all the prescriptions in the medicine cabinet, read the two magazines that rested on the edge of the tub, and counted the tiles by twos and threes, perfecting her memory of the three sequences that had become rusty over the years.

"Cassie, are you in there?"

It was Bobby's voice. Relief washed over her. "Is it safe?" she cried.

"It's safe. Arthur's gone. Come out."

What he failed to say was that he wasn't alone, and when she opened the door and saw him standing there with Claire clinging to his arm, she almost screamed.

It was the shock, really . . . that was all.

And she managed to stifle her scream—sort of.

If he could have, he would have shaken off Claire, who had suddenly grabbed him as the bathroom door began to open. "The coast is clear," he said. "Come have some birthday cake, and we'll say good-bye."

The coast didn't look real clear to her. From where she was standing, the coast looked way the hell too full.

Of ex-wives for one thing.

And smiley ex-wife's faces for another.

She was screwed.

But Cassie composed her tumultuous, unfriendly thoughts, put a smile on her face—although it couldn't compare to the genuine one before her—and said, "Great. Cake. I can hardly wait."

SHE HAD NO choice. She had to follow the happy couple back into the great room where cake was being dispensed by the caterer. She had to keep her fake smile in place while sitting on the Provencal print couch eating the pink cake with pink frosting and drinking her pink champagne. She had to keep smiling even when Bobby disappeared, pulled outside by some male guest who was talking loudly about a putting green and she found herself alone in a room full of strangers. Sarah and Paige were outside with the children, overseeing the hired clown who was doing magic tricks for the benefit of the under-fives. *Perfect,* she thought. *This is the way I want to spend my Sunday afternoon.* She couldn't even get her flute refilled because the waiters had disappeared.

The only very small consolation was the pink cake, which was very good. In her current disgruntled mood, she didn't even care if it was three thousand calories. She required a lift to her spirits even if it was only a sugar rush. *Please, God, get me out of here,* she thought, *or if that's not possible, have a waiter bring me more champagne.*

She was willing to be flexible with the almighty.

But instead of the hand of God or a waiter, Claire appeared so suddenly, Cassie considered some divine intervention of the satanic kind might have been at play.

She'd looked down at her plate for only a second, and when she'd looked up, Claire stood smiling at her.

It wasn't the same smiley smile she'd previously seen.

It was one of those little, nasty smiles with an edge and the potential for violence behind it.

"You look out of place," Claire said, looking stylish in black pin-striped slacks, a white blouse, and a fortune in bulky gold jewelry. "Feel free to leave. I'll take care of Bobby."

For a moment Cassie was speechless. Claire's rudeness was as unsubtle as a hammer blow.

"I'm sure Bobby appreciates your taking notes for him or whatever you do," Claire snidely added. "But now that I'm in town, I'll take over."

Take over? As in the new drug dealer in the neighborhood? Or as in second-string quarterback? "I'm not sure there's anything to take over," Cassie said, offering Claire a bland look. "If he has any questions about the museum or the collection, I'm there to help. You wouldn't be very useful in that capacity."

Claire quickly glanced around and then sat down beside Cassie and murmured, "Listen, darling—" the designation so chill it could have cooled the Sahara for a year. "I know

Bobby better than anyone, and he's not asking you any questions about the museum. We both know what's going on, so spare me the fabrications. I suggest you leave—now."

"You're kidding."

"Not in the least."

"You don't seriously think I'm going to go because you tell me to."

"If you don't, I assure you, you'll regret it."

"Are you demented?" Cassie asked. Those cold blue eyes did look a little strange. Maybe Claire and Jay should meet and they could stir their bubbling caldrons together.

"Perhaps you are if you think Bobby cares. Here's a news flash for you. Bobby fucks everyone," Claire calmly said. "He won't remember your name a week from now."

"I don't know what you're talking about."

"Of course you do. I saw the way he touched you as you walked in. He does that, you know, makes women think he's sweet and kind and normal. He's not. He doesn't live like you and"—she waved her hand in a dismissive gesture that took in the milling guests—"these Midwestern types."

"He lives like you, I suppose."

"Maybe he does," she said, her wasp nose lifted faintly in disdain. "He lives a privileged life. Did you know he's a French count? The Serres have been Comtes de Chastellux since the crusades; it's one of his father's lesser titles. Bobby has an estate in France along with his Montana land because some great, great something grandfather lived there at one time."

"And you fit into this privileged life."

"He married me, didn't he?"

"And divorced you." She couldn't help it, but then again, good manners weren't Claire's strong point, either.

"A mistake I think he regrets."

She'd seen Bobby in the car, his indecision and reluctance.

Was it because he didn't want to see Claire or because he wanted to see her too much? Did this woman understand him better than he understood himself?

"Look, whatever your motivation with Bobby, leave me out of the picture. I'm working with him on the Rubens theft. It has nothing to do with your plans. Feel free to re-enter his life in any way you wish." My God, she sounded mature and wise when she really felt like smacking the woman. "This isn't a contest or competition. I have a job to do for Arthur and the museum—that's all." Her lies were getting world-class. She should go on the stage.

"I don't believe you."

"It doesn't matter. If you'll excuse me." And rising to her feet, she walked away, holding her head high like Julia Roberts in that scene in *Pretty Woman* when she leaves Richard Gere at the hotel. Then she walked directly into the kitchen because she seriously needed a drink and if the waiters wouldn't come to her, she'd go to them.

Bobby found her a half-hour later sitting on a bar stool at the kitchen counter, commiserating with one of the waitresses on the dearth of honesty in relationships. Maybe she'd had a glass too many of champagne or she wouldn't have said with a faint sneer, "I suppose French counts have tons of women chasing them who want to be countesses."

"I wouldn't know. I don't use the title."

"I understand you're slumming here in town."

"Claire?" he gently asked.

"She's a real delight. I can see why you married her."

"Do you mind," he said to the waitress who was watching and listening with great curiosity.

"You don't have to go," Cassie said, feeling put upon and lied to, men in general back on her shit list.

"Please?" Bobby murmured, handing the waitress a hundred dollar bill.

A moment later they were alone, the sounds of the party faint, the festivities having moved out into the backyard where a pony ride was in progress.

"Counts certainly know how to throw around their money," Cassie grumbled, the thought of wealthy counts even more galling when she was poor as a church mouse with no tiara in sight.

"Have you passed your two-drink limit?"

"What's it to you?" she said like someone who'd passed their two-drink limit.

"I'd better drive."

"Don't bother. Claire tells me she'll be taking over. I don't know if that includes driving me home, but I doubt it. I'll call a cab, and you two can plan to watch the sunset of life together."

"No one's planning anything."

"That's what you think. Claire has plans, believe me. I was told to get out of town or there'd be a shoot-out at the O.K. Corral."

"Forget whatever she said. Okay? It has nothing to do with you and me."

"There's no you and me." But even as she spoke—her resentment fueled by alcohol and Claire's smug assurance—she felt like screaming DID YOU SAY YOU AND ME?

"You'll feel better when you come down a little," he calmly said, like he soothed distraught inebriated women who were angry with him every day. "Come on, let's go. I'll drive."

"You can't fit behind the wheel."

"I'll manage."

"I don't know where I left my purse."

"It's by the couch."

"Claire practically threatened me. I'm not sure I dare be seen with you."

"Give me a break," he muttered.

"Easy for you to say. You didn't look into her eyes."

"I'll protect you. Okay? Now are you going to come with me, or do you want me to carry you out of here?"

She almost said, "Carry me," because it would have pissed the hell out of his bitchy ex-wife, but she was still sober enough not to make a complete spectacle of herself when there was a possibility she might have to see some of these people again. "I can walk."

But he caught her as she slipped coming off the bar stool. "At least hold my hand. That way you won't fall into anything expensive."

"Except you."

"I'm free, babe."

The seductive warmth of his voice sent a megawatt glow clear down to her toes, and whatever resentment she might have harbored evaporated like water in the desert. "That remains to be seen," she said, trying to walk like a sober person, not willing to let him off the hook completely after having to endure Claire's unpleasantness. A drop or two of resentment may have resisted the sun's rays.

"I'll have to think of some suitable penance," he said, smiling.

"You already owe me for coming here."

"We'll work something out."

His voice was velvety and low, his strong hand engulfing hers, and even if she didn't know how they were going to work things out, it sounded as though he did.

They'd almost made it to the front door when a familiar female voice said with cloying guile, "Don't leave yet, darling. I wanted to give you your journal from the Thessalonika dig."

Turning around, Bobby deliberately placed himself between Claire and Cassie. "Why don't you send it to me? You have my address."

"Why don't we have lunch tomorrow instead, and I'll give it to you then."

I'll bet she'll give it to him, Cassie petulantly thought, various scenarios pertaining to Claire's immediate removal racing through her mind in cartoonish film-clip fashion.

"Sorry," Bobby said. "Arthur's pressing us on this recovery."

"But darling, I haven't talked to you for so long." Claire moved closer, her expensive perfume filling the air. "I was hoping we could have a chance to catch up while I was in town."

"I wish I could, Claire, but my schedule's tight. Jorge has that project waiting in the wings the minute I finish up here. It was nice seeing you again."

His grip tightened on Cassie's hand, and he turned to push the screen door open. "All the best on the Met job. Watch your step," he said in a different tone, guiding Cassie out the door.

And that soft indulgence in his voice triggered a small personal jihad in Claire Dumont, who wasn't familiar with losing. Particularly to a woman who probably didn't even own a good string of pearls.

TWENTY-FIVE

"SHE WANTS YOU BACK." THE TREES WERE rushing by slightly too fast for the suburban neighborhood. Cassie braced her feet on the floor.

"Too bad."

"I know she said something to you."

"Not really." No way was he going to say what Claire had said to him. He didn't want to be kicked out of her car while it was moving. Claire hadn't beaten around the bush, but then she never had. Maybe she was at loose ends after her polo player or maybe she'd really meant it, but it hadn't taken more than five minutes of conversation before he realized why he'd left her and never looked back. She still didn't know the difference between asking and telling. She still thought the world revolved around her. And turning on a man was still simply a means to an end for her.

"I'm mad anyway."

"That's because you're drunk."

"Am not."

"Whatever."

"Don't be condescending."

"I'm not. I'm just sober and you're not."

"Didn't you drink?"

"Pink champagne with cherries in it. I don't think so."

"I suppose counts only drink rare vintage champagne."

"Don't give me any grief. Claire never should have told you."

"That's not all she told me. She said you wouldn't remember my name next week. She said you live like an aristocrat."

"She's full of it. And I haven't seen her for five years. What the hell does she know about my life?"

"I think she's hoping to catch up. Does that mean fuck standing up?"

His hands tightened on the wheel. "Could we talk about this when you're sober?"

"I want to talk about it now."

He really should have had some champagne, he thought, cherries or not, and he wouldn't remember any of this tomorrow. As it was, the entire conversation was going to be a bloody waste of time, but she was making him hot just looking at her in that cropped jacket and tight jeans that showed off her big boobs and shapely ass. All he wanted to do was get her home and fuck the hell out of her. He didn't question the reason for his unusual obsession; he only looked forward to the hopefully swift consummation. "Ask me anything," he said, superpolite.

"Did she turn you on?"

"No."

"Why not?"

"Jesus, I don't know. She just didn't."

"She must have at one time."

"I suppose she did, but that was years ago."

"Try to remember."

"Why?"

"Just because." Even not exactly sober, Cassie understood how juvenile that sounded. "I mean—she must have *some* appealing qualities."

He almost laughed at her sweet bitchiness, but sensible and sober as he was, he stayed with good manners and vagueness. "Claire liked to travel. I did, too. She can pack one small bag and go around the world. I found that appealing."

Cassie had to turn and look at him, not sure his lack of sarcasm was for real. "So you married her?" she queried, suppressing her urge to snort. "Liar." *On both counts,* she thought. It was impossible to pack one small bag and travel around the world.

"Look, it just happened. We'd been seeing each other for—I don't know—quite a few years. She brought up the idea of marriage."

"And you rolled over?"

"Hey." He shot her a look. "No one rolled over."

Now we're getting somewhere, the little voice inside her head that hid below the alcohol line said. When his manly authority was at stake, the platitudes flew out the window. "Where were you married?"

"Florence."

Damn. There went her fantasy. "Are you sure?"

"Yes. Unlike you now, I was sober at the time."

"I was sober at my wedding."

Understanding there was a possibility of getting himself out of the mire of an inquisition about Claire, he quickly asked, "Where did you get married?"

"Hawaii."

"Why?"

"It was warm in January."

"Why did you get married in January?"

"My mother and Jay's mother wanted to go to Hawaii in January."

"I see," he politely said, when he was dying to say instead, "So you just rolled over?" But there was no reward for pissing her off. And it was still only three o'clock, which left plenty of time for fucking on this sunny afternoon. "I bet it was a nice wedding."

"Don't be so damned amenable. Is Claire staying here long?"

Shit. He'd overplayed his hand. "I doubt it. She hyperventilates when she's away from major cities of the world."

"Are you saying we're not a major city?"

There was no way he was going to tell her the truth. "I didn't mean it that way. I just meant more than ten million population." *The things I do for a piece of ass,* he thought. On the other hand, she wasn't exactly what you'd call a forgettable woman, and someday, when he had more time and she wasn't jumping down his throat, he might think about what the hell she was. Because this wasn't business as usual—that he knew. Particularly after the game of hide-and-seek with the birthday kids he and several parents had participated in to please Sarah and Paige. Particularly after stuffing himself into a small compartment under the back stairs and finding himself cheek-to-jowl with an unusual shopping bag hanging from a hook on the wall. His heart had damned near stopped. He'd unfolded himself out of the small cubby, carefully shut the door, and allowed his pulse rate to come back to normal before checking out the closets in the house, where he found what he thought he'd find. Only the pink beads were on the toes of tennis shoes. He wouldn't have figured that. Little pink beaded hearts.

The truckload of information currently overloading his brain would have to be weighed against his obsession with the hot, sexy redhead currently grilling him about his ex-wife. Did he leave or did he stay? Did he end his investigation or let it drift along? How much did he want Miss

Cassandra Hill? How consumed was he with the extraordinary sex they shared?

He slid a sideways glance at Cassie, and his libido made one of those instant decisions completely bereft of reason and logic. He'd better assuage Cassie's temper and misgivings about Claire if he wanted to enjoy what he intended to enjoy—he glanced at the dash clock—in about twenty minutes. "To tell you the truth," he said, perjuring himself for the sake of carnal harmony, "Claire made friends with my mother, and between the two of them, they decided I should be married. It seemed the right thing to do at the time. That's it, and that's why it didn't last long."

"How long?"

The real truth wouldn't be useful here, either. Five years might freak her, and he didn't want to go into a lengthy explanation about them being in different parts of the world for much of that time. He opted for a partial truth. "We were together maybe six months."

"Six months," she said, like he'd given her a really nice present—one you could pet and it purred back and made you feel all warm inside.

"That's about it." He was really hoping this conversation was over.

"What happened?"

He silently groaned. "She asked for a divorce." Lies, lies, lies. They were piling up like cordwood.

"Why?"

"Jesus, I don't know. Ask her."

Cassie did snort that time. "Not likely."

"Well, she did and I said, fine. End of story." *Please, God, have pity.*

"And you haven't seen her since?" Why did she feel she had the right to harangue him when she'd only just met him, when they were more or less strangers, when his past relationship with his wife didn't have anything to do with the sexual pleasure he could give her? Those very practical assessments swam upstream through the alcohol and punched her between the eyes.

"Nope."

Ohmygod, what was she doing? A small panic began to implode in all her brain cells. Was she trying to drive away the only real architect of mind-blowing sex she'd ever met? Was she *Insane???* "I'm really sorry for being such a bitch about Claire," she softly said, trying to look contrite enough to erase all the stupid questions she'd just harassed him with. "It's none of my business." God, she wished she could cry on cue. "I so apologize."

He almost ran off the road at her abrupt about-face but got a grip on his astonishment and said in the same gentle tone she'd used, "Don't worry about it. Claire can be difficult."

"Still, I shouldn't have behaved so badly. Something came over me. I have no explanation."

Other than the champagne, they both thought.

But then this wasn't one of those occasions when honesty was likely, what with this pleasant new rapport in the air.

"Except for Claire," he pleasantly observed, "I'm glad you came with me."

"Me, too." *Now,* she thought, that she'd regained her senses and could look at the situation from the perspective of gaining suitable compensation for her hideous encounter with his really nasty ex-wife. And honestly, wasn't life about compromise and concession? Wasn't a truly mature individual willing to navigate a compassionate midcourse through the shoals of life? She could overlook Claire, perhaps even forgive her if she lived long enough, and in that maturity be assured of reaping the reward of hours and hours and *hours* of unbridled sex with the very indulgent and talented Bobby Serre.

Less introspective, Bobby only knew it was going to be smooth sailing into her bed once again.

For perhaps the same reason, nuanced only by gender-defined sensibilities apropos speed and action, they were both smiling as he pulled into Cassie's driveway.

TWENTY-SIX

THEY'D NO MORE THAN STEPPED OUT OF THE car when Liv drove up behind them in her black Navigator and hopped out, her blonde curls bobbing, her tennis sneakers sparkling white to go with her tennis outfit that obviously hadn't been used yet because it was absolutely pristine.

"You weren't answering your phone or returning my messages so I came over before my game to see what was keeping you so busy. Now that I'm here, I understand completely." She smiled. "I'll come back later."

"Liv, meet Bobby Serre. Bobby, Lavinia Duncan. He's in town looking for the stolen Rubens. Liv is my high-priced lawyer friend. And come in," Cassie said, feeling guilty about sending Liv on her way when she hadn't seen her or returned her calls for days.

"Nah. I'll call you later. Nice to meet you." Liv turned back to her car.

"Come in and have a drink," Bobby offered, responding

to Cassie's invitation with politesse. "There are lawn chairs on the back deck at least. We can sit there."

Is he sweet or what? Cassie thought. "We might even have some leftover pudding." She nodded at Bobby. "He cooks. Can you believe it?"

Liv was having trouble believing movie-star types actually came to Minneapolis and, more pertinently, were standing in Cassie's driveway. Minnehaha Parkway would never be the same. "That's great," she said, keeping her voice even with effort. The man was gorgeous, and in those shorts and T-shirt, you could see just about everything he had to offer. "What kind of pudding?" she asked, because even in the presence of glamorous celebrity-type men, pudding held a strong attraction.

"Butterscotch with whipped cream. Made from scratch."

"Wow," Liv softly pronounced. "From scratch. Did she order you from some wish book?"

"My grandma was a great cook. I learned from her."

"Modest, too. Pinch me. I must be dreaming."

Bobby laughed and Cassie said, "Come in and try some," and moved toward the door. "We just came from an unpleasant duty visit for Arthur's sake. I'm feeling the need for some pudding myself."

Bobby felt some other needs, but restrained himself. It was still early.

"What are you doing for Arthur on Sunday?" Liv said to the back of Cassie's head.

"Attending his daughter's birthday."

"Since when are you invited to Arthur's parties?"

"Since Bobby came into town." Cassie led them into the kitchen. "He was invited, and I was persuaded to tag along."

"Ah," Liv said, her mind-reading abilities top notch. She was pretty sure what Bobby Serre's powers of persuasion might be and why he was employing them. Cassie was one of those astonishing beauties unaware of her looks. But Bobby Serre wasn't blind. And if Liv's nose for gossip was still fully functioning, these two were an item. She almost said, "You two are perfect together," but didn't, of course, because she wasn't thirteen and fervently romantic. She was, in fact, as cynical as a divorced female attorney who had scaled the slippery heights to partner could be. "So tell me what you two have been doing."

Two deer in the headlights was maybe a stretch, but their sudden constraint was palpable.

"With the theft, I meant," she diplomatically added, sitting on one of the counter stools. "Any progress?"

Cassie quickly replied, "Not a whole lot. Bobby's interviewing staff etcetera, and I'm making some calls around the country for him. But there's no certainties yet."

"It's early in the investigation," Bobby noted, moving to the refrigerator and opening the door. "Something like this could take time."

"How long—ballpark guess?" Liv kept her voice bland, her curiosity piqued on several levels.

Bobby turned with two bowls of pudding in his hands and the door swung shut. "Hard to tell. I doubt it's professionals. We haven't had any movement on the illicit market. But you never know."

Liv had been a trial lawyer long enough to read people with a certain degree of expertise. Or maybe her cynicism made her look at people harder. Bobby Serre didn't seem to be saying what he was saying. Or if he was, he was leaving something out. "Have you been doing this long?" she asked.

"Quite a while." Setting the bowls down, he pulled open a drawer, took out three spoons, handed them around, and sat down next to Cassie.

"You're company. You get your own bowl," Cassie said

with a smile, pointing her spoon at Liv. "Besides, I've already eaten two servings."

For the next few moments, a small silence descended as spoons moved from bowl to mouth, the quiet punctuated only by small sighs of satisfaction—female variety.

"I hope you don't have to leave too soon," Liv said, scooping up the last remains of her pudding, lifting her gaze to Bobby. "This is world-class cooking."

"We still have tons of people to interview, don't we?" Cassie said, glancing over at Bobby.

He smiled. "Unless we can narrow down the search some other way."

Liv got one of her little intuitive flutters again.

Cassie grinned. "He knows what he's doing, and I'm just taking orders."

"And doing it very well." The look Bobby gave her would have melted all the ice cream in the city. His gaze swivelled to Liv. "Cassie's been a great help manning the phones."

And as if on cue, his cell phone rang.

Pulling the phone out of his shorts pocket, he glanced at the screen. "If you'll excuse me," he said with a polite smile. "One of my contacts." And he walked from the room out onto the adjoining deck.

Following him with her gaze, Liv gave an appreciative whistle once the deck door closed and the women were alone. "I'm not kidding. He must have come from some fantasy catalogue. The man is flawless."

Cassie smiled. "He is."

"And? Fill me in. And don't tell me you're just friends because I can see very clearly that you're a whole lot more than friends."

"I don't want anyone at work to know, though. So don't tell anyone."

"How about him? How does he feel about keeping it

quiet?" Maybe that was the oddity she was picking up on. Maybe Bobby Serre wanted to keep this little liaison secret for reasons of his own.

"He agrees."

"Why?" Realizing her tone was whip sharp, Liv said with a smile. "Sorry. Bad memories of Don."

"I know. Don't worry about it. And the only reason Bobby and I are being cautious is because of Arthur. He's so incredibly gross about anything that smacks of sex. I swear he's an arrested adolescent—not a day over fifteen."

"That must be real charming for his various wives. Now give me a blow-by-blow because my sex life of late leaves a lot to be desired, and if I can't get any myself, I'll settle for a secondhand turn-on."

"Well, to begin with," Cassie said with a small sigh, "he's spectacular in every conceivable way. He's gentle and inventive, and he knows just exactly where and when to touch you, if you know what I mean."

"I'm not sure I do, but I'm listening," Liv said with a grin. "Tell me."

And while the ladies were discussing the finer points of hot sex, Bobby was telling Jorge in the vaguest possible terms that he might have a lead.

"Cut the bull," Jorge muttered. "If you know something you know something. Do you trust me or not?"

"Of course I do. The thing is, there's a woman involved."

"Shit. Why didn't you say so? Fine. You tell me whatever you want when you want to. And I hope you fuck your brains out."

"I'm trying to, believe me."

"So screw the Rubens. Wherever it is, it's not for sale, it's not even a whiff in the air. It can sit wherever it is until the cows come home."

"Seriously, I'll get back to the theft in a few days."

"It doesn't sound as though she's going to last long, but then they never do with you, do they, Bobby?"

"She's really beautiful and different—not slick."

"So? You thinking about babies, compadre?"

Bobby laughed. "No. She's just hot, that's all."

"And that's different for you, how?"

"Okay, okay, I get the point."

"Enjoy yourself, man. There's nothing wrong with twenty-four-hour sex, but you don't really want to meet the folks. That screws up all the fun."

"And you should know." Jorge had been married three times.

"Don't forget, I was at your wedding and saw Claire's parents."

"Don't remind me."

"I'm reminding you for a reason. I'm hearing something in your voice when you talk about this lady that's making the hair on the back of my neck rise. Just a warning, my friend. They still want to talk in the morning, they still want to give you advice, and the price of divorces is rising every year. Enough said?"

Bobby chuckled. "Maybe I'd better leave her house right now while my bank account is still intact."

"Don't laugh. It could be a real pricey piece of ass."

"Thanks for the warning. And with your track record, I'm taking it to heart, believe me."

"You're not leaving her house, are you?" Jorge grumbled.

"I think the saying is—not while I still have breath in my body. Wish me luck."

"Shi-it. As if you need luck with the size of your dick." The men had shared a small orgy a few years back in Miami.

"Thanks, Jorge, but I'm not your type."

"With enough Jack Daniels, who knows?" Jorge drawled.

"Me for one," Bobby muttered. "Keep your distance."

"Yeah, yeah, yeah, and you let me know what's going on up there with the Rubens. I have customers who are willing to buy it if it shows up."

"Sorry, Jorge. I promised Arthur I'd find it."

"Has he beat my record yet?"

"Nah. You two are tied—both on wife number three. He can afford it, but you could spend your money more wisely."

"Business is good, Bobby. You don't know how many drug lords and arms dealers want to upgrade their status. Everyone wants a museum-quality painting or two to add to the collection of shit stuff in their mansion. Who am I to refuse a man's aspirations for upward mobility?"

"You're lucky you're still alive."

"I'm not sure you should be cautioning me. I hope you carry."

"Sometimes. Not here."

"Would your new lady throw you out if she knew you were proficient with your custom 9mm Beretta?"

"It might be wiser not to mention it."

"So next time I talk to her, I'll be real polite."

"Damn right you will."

"Do I detect some soul-stirring emotion here?"

"No. You detect the best sex I've had for a long time. And now I'm done with this conversation. Good-bye, Jorge."

But Bobby stood out on the deck for a moment after he'd snapped shut the cell phone, struck by an uncomfortable sensation that the world was closing in on him. Or perhaps more that the freedom he relished and required might conceivably be at risk. It was a transient, hypersensitive feeling he almost immediately brushed off—blaming Jorge for riding him about women and marriage.

Luckily he was expert at disconnecting from serious emotion.

Five years of marriage to Claire had taught him well.

But he definitely felt some kind of feeling as he reentered the kitchen and saw Cassie's smile. Although this was more familiar and below the belt.

"I told Liv she could stay for supper if she wanted," Cassie noted. "We actually have groceries in the house."

"But I said no because I'd be in the way," Liv said with a grin.

"No you wouldn't. Tell her, Bobby. Tell her she's welcome."

Under any other circumstances, he would have taken issue with his plans for sex having been disrupted, but when Cassie looked at him like that, he felt a singular wish to please her. There was no explanation, or at least not one he cared to pursue. "Of course you're welcome to stay. We bought some tuna that's damned fresh this far from the ocean. I could grill it."

"If I had a grill," Cassie pointed out.

"Okay. I'll poach it with some dill."

"See? See how clever he is?" Cassie exclaimed. "I'm absolutely in awe of his cooking skills."

"It sounds great, but I promised Kelly I'd play a couple sets, and she's waiting as we speak. So thanks." Liv's gaze swung to Bobby. "I appreciate the invitation."

"Anytime," he said.

Like he might be here for a while, Liv thought, feeling better for Cassie, who deserved some happiness after her problems with Jay. And maybe there really were nice, kind, caring men in the world who looked like movie stars. Maybe she'd have to reassess her thinking. Maybe it was a glass-half-full kind of world after all. "Call me," she said to Cassie. "When you get time."

"Come for dinner tomorrow," Bobby offered.

Jeez, that half-full glass was filling right up to the freaking top. "Thanks. Maybe I will."

"Six-thirty," Cassie said.

Bobby nodded toward the empty dining room. "We'll buy a table and chairs."

"No we won't." Cassie scowled at him. Her bank balance was three hundred twenty-two dollars.

"We'll figure out something," Bobby smoothly said. He hadn't actually checked his bank balance for years, but he was guessing he could afford a table and chairs. "Drinks at six-thirty."

"Thanks." And Liv really meant it. She almost rushed up to him and gave him a hug but didn't want to give anyone the wrong impression. Especially Cassie. She hadn't seen her so happy in a long time.

As the sound of Liv's Navigator firing up reached the kitchen, Cassie said, "I hope you don't mind I asked her in?"

"Not at all." Bobby smiled. "It's early."

She smiled back. "Isn't that nice?"

"Yeah," he whispered, closing the distance between them and pulling her into his arms. "Nicer than hell. So what do you want to do?"

"Oh, I don't know," she murmured, reaching up on tiptoe and giving him a kiss. "Something sexual I thought. As my reward you know . . . for being a body shield."

"Speaking of bodies, I've been wanting to take this off ever since you put it on." He began unbuttoning the metal buttons on her jacket. "Your big boobs are being crushed."

"It's supposed to be tight."

"Like your jeans. Those will have to come off, too." He eased her jacket down her arms and tossed it on the counter. "Then you can breathe again."

"How considerate. That must be why I like you."

"Yeah, I figured you were into considerate men." He grinned. "From your screams."

She smiled. "I'm just expressive." He had her jeans and

panties half way down her hips. She kicked off her shoes, and he suddenly got taller.

"And a whole lot more accessible now," he murmured, stripping her clothes away. "As soon as I get this off." Unsnapping her black lace bra with finesse, he lifted it away.

"You're good at this."

He turned back from tossing her clothes on the counter, his brows raised.

"Taking women's clothes off."

He gave her a guarded look. "What do you want me to say?"

"Tell me you happen to be nimble fingered and I'm the first."

Was she serious? "You're the first," he said, going with his gut. She looked serious.

Maybe it was Claire, the bitch, and what she'd said. Maybe she needed lies right now. Maybe after that far-away look in his eyes on the boat and the afternoon from hell at Sarah's she wasn't in the mood for stark reality. "Am I really?" she said with a smile. "How perfect."

He laughed. "It's perfect for me, too." His gaze traveled down her lush nudity and back again to met her eyes. "Especially now . . ."

"And you owe me."

"I know."

"So I can ask for things."

He grinned. "Things?"

"You know."

"Give me a hint," he said with a sexy smile.

"For instance," Cassie said, surveying the kitchen. "Let's try the counter."

"Try?"

"Have sex on the counter."

"It won't hold me." He didn't want to crack her granite counters.

"Are you saying no?"

"Not at all," he said, picking her up and depositing her on the center island counter.

"It's cold!"

"You'll warm up."

He was stripping off his clothes, and he was right. She was really warming up. She squirmed faintly, the cool stone slick against her bottom.

In about ten seconds flat, he was lowering her down on her back. And from the looks of it she wasn't the only one who had been waiting for Liv to leave.

Pulling her bottom to the edge of the counter, he placed her feet on his shoulders and smiled. "Anything you want to ask for?"

"That." She pointed.

"Where do you want it?"

"Here." She pointed.

"Let me get this straight. You want my big cock in your tight little pussy. Is that right?"

She nodded. How did he do it? Those words, the image, his low, husky voice; she was practically coming already.

"Come on, babe. Someone who likes cock as much as you. You can say it."

"Please."

"Please what?"

"That's not fair."

"You don't strike me as the inhibited type."

"Maybe I am." But parts of her apparently weren't inhibited. Her vagina was hot, hot, and throbbing.

"Not this." He ran his finger up her dewy cleft as if he knew. "Say it and you'll get it," he murmured.

She said it like the words were racing for their lives, but

he gave her credit for trying and, putting action to words, gave her what she wanted. And what he wanted. And showed her that it was possible for her to come five times in a row without passing out.

She looked around her kitchen afterward, wanting to etch the memory—time, place, day, and incredible feelings. Who knew there were those degrees of pleasure? Well, maybe he knew, but she had been outside that particular loop until now. "That was . . . really fine—I'm practically speechless," she murmured. "It was so perfect. I may not ask you for another thing all day."

"Maybe you'll reconsider," he whispered, brushing her nipples with the most delicate touch. "It's still early . . ."

How did he know she'd reconsider?

No, don't answer that. She didn't want to know.

But in short order, she was more than willing to follow him out on the porch and get a breath of fresh air, as he put it.

She'd never fucked anyone in daylight on her back porch.

Or any time of day, for that matter.

She'd recommend it. Something about the impropriety and possible observation by the neighbors made her feel outrageously sexy.

Or maybe it was the warm sun.

Or maybe Bobby Serre was just that fantastic.

And afterward, he did one of those shockingly sweet things that only happened in movies. He walked down her porch steps as if he weren't nude, picked some lily of the valley, brought them back, and tucked them in her hair. "My own *Primavera*," he whispered, kissing her on the cheek. "More beautiful than Botticelli's by a country mile."

She was lying on the quilt he'd brought out, the sun warm on her skin, his smile more glorious than any sun in the sky, the heady fragrance of lily of the valley scenting the air. Life couldn't have been more perfect.

"Feel like some ice cream? I'm hungry," he said.

Life just zoomed into the more purified realms of perfection.

And when he went inside and returned with two pints of Edna Mae's—Rocky Road, her favorite, and Cherry Almond Swirl, his favorite—well, it really made her think.

Their sex was greater than great.

They both liked Romano instead of Picasso.

He cooked when she didn't—one of those yin-yang dovetail harmonies.

And a man who liked ice cream as much as she did?

Really. Some seriously astronomical odds were working here.

"I was thinking," he murmured, spooning Rocky Road into her mouth. "Maybe you'd like to come to Bulgaria with me after this. You could wait for me in Sofia while I give Jorge a quick assist with the *Isabella d'Este*. I could rent a villa for you."

Pinch me, I'm dreaming, she thought. "I've never been to Sofia," she said, playing it cool, like men asked her to a villa in Europe every day.

"You'll like it. It's off the beaten track. Some of the old churches date from the eighth century. We could explore afterward."

"If I can get away."

"I'll talk to Arthur. Clear the way."

And then she couldn't leave well enough alone. She had to say, "Why?"

"So you don't have to deal with Arthur."

"No, I mean, why do you want me to come along?"

He put a spoon of Cherry Almond in his mouth and took his time letting it melt before replying. "I don't know. I suppose I don't want this to end once the Rubens is found."

"Oh," she said, not daring to ask the next question: When will it end?

"We could go to Budapest after if you like. Have you been there?"

"Once, passing through to Constantinople. I saw the train station."

He smiled. "I'll give you the grand tour."

He already had, she thought, the one with prizes at every turn. "Maybe I will," she said.

"No maybe. Come. You'll love it. It shouldn't take long in Bulgaria. The Turks Jorge does business with don't screw around. If the painting's authentic, they'll name their price and they'll get it. A couple days, tops. Say yes."

"Okay. Yes."

He kissed her then, leaning over and brushing her lips with his. "To seal the bargain," he said.

The sweet taste of cherries lingered on her lips, the sweeter joy of his wanting her warmed her heart, although she was quick to remind herself that Bobby Serre probably wasn't in the market for hearts. But she didn't care. He made her happy. And that was enough.

Had she known Bobby had never invited a woman to his home in Budapest or to any of his homes, she might have fainted. Or thought about it. Even if women only fainted in Victorian novels.

But he was careful not to mention it. Not that he wasn't damned happy she'd said yes. More. He was relieved. He didn't want to let her go.

"Then, if you want to, we could go on to Avignon. Our vineyard is outside the city near a village almost untouched by time. Once the Rubens is found, we deserve a vacation," he added with a smile.

"I just want you to know, invitations like this could turn a woman's head," she murmured.

"And I want you to know, legs like this"—he ran the knuckles of the hand holding the spoon down her thigh, his dark gaze holding hers—"could turn a man's head."

"Then we're on the same page." Her voice was breathy, his touch doing predictable things to her addicted-to-love psyche.

"And I know a way to keep it that way," he said, setting down the spoon. "Open up, Hot Legs, I'm comin' in . . ."

TWENTY-SEVEN

CLAIRE WAS WAITING IN ARTHUR'S OFFICE when he arrived Monday morning.

"You're an early riser," Arthur said, his brows faintly raised, innuendo softly underlying his words. "I like your suit. Armani?"

"Jil Sander, but close." She looked him up and down. "You're staying fit, Arthur. I imagine your new wife appreciates it. Lovely party yesterday. Flora is enchanting. You must be proud."

"I'm fortunate," he said, moving behind his desk. "Are you enjoying your visit with Sarah?"

"Of course. We go way back." Claire watched him sit down in his leather chair and unbutton his suit coat. "She seems quite content," she lied. "I give you credit for maintaining friendly relations." Men like Arthur loved flattery.

"We try, Claire," he murmured, self-satisfaction in his gaze. "It seems more civilized to maintain a cordial relationship after a divorce—particularly where children are involved." It was a platitude he used often, the well-oiled phrases rolling off his tongue effortlessly.

"I'm glad you said that, Arthur, because I came to see you this morning for precisely that reason."

"Bobby," he said with a wicked smile. She wouldn't be here otherwise.

"Yes." She didn't respond to his smile.

"What can I do for you?" He preferred to cut to the chase.

"So blunt, Arthur," she blandly said.

She wasn't easily rattled, but then she'd never been, even as a young graduate student he'd met in Paris at a conference one summer. She'd tantalized him then as now. Was it her coolness? The fact that she looked as though she wouldn't warm up in bed? Or perhaps it was the opposite—that he knew she had to warm up in bed or Bobby Serre wouldn't have given her the time of day.

"There's no point in exchanging comments on the weather," he said with a small smile. What did she want, and what would he get in return? That was the exchange of interest to him.

"Very well." She leaned back slightly in her chair, glanced down briefly at the large ruby ring on her ring finger and once again met his gaze with a blue-eyed innocence she found especially effective on older men. "I need a favor, Arthur."

"Anything within my power, of course." He relaxed against the black leather, enjoying a piquant sense of anticipation.

"I want that redhead sent out of town on some assignment."

She didn't say *would you* or *I would like*—not Claire. But then that Maine lumber money—the old kind—gave one a certain peremptory authority. Damn, he wished he could help; he'd been counting on a friendly quid pro quo. "I'm afraid you're way off base, Claire. Cassandra's not Bobby's type. I had to beg him to take her on because she needed the consultant fees. Bobby finally agreed—very reluctantly, I might add."

Claire smiled tightly. "No offense, Arthur, but you must be blind. Bobby could hardly keep his hands off her at your party."

Arthur looked perplexed for a moment and then he softly swore. "So that's why Bobby asked if she could come along?"

Duh, Claire thought. Arthur's reputation for intellectual acuity was somewhere between Mickey Mouse and Britney Spears. Everyone knew he'd gotten through Princeton because his father had paid for a new library. "That would be my guess," she said mildly. "So if you could spare her for a few days or, more pertinently, if Bobby could be persuaded that she was needed out of town on some sensitive assignment, I would be most appreciative."

While Arthur might not solve *The New York Times* crossword, he knew how to negotiate. And when personal gain was at stake, he was capable of out-bargaining a genius like Einstein. He smiled. "I would have to have something in return—naturally."

"Of course. What would you like?"

You couldn't fault her for directness, Arthur thought, running through various options he might suggest, discarding a three-way with Bobby as being a probable deal-breaker.

Maybe she saw the look in his eyes. Maybe he was transparent as hell. Maybe she suddenly got cold feet when actually faced with Arthur in person. Although he was fit and trim thanks to his trainer, he was still fifty-five if he was a day and, honestly—compared to Bobby . . . "It would have to be something business related," she added.

Arthur frowned. "I can't imagine what you could offer that I need."

"Have you heard the Hermitage might be persuaded to

send some of their Impressionist collection to us?" She adjusted her options—this proposition more expensive in terms of calling in markers, but infinitely more palatable.

Us was the Met. Arthur began salivating. "How would that affect me?"

"The talks are just beginning." She smiled, cognizant of his avid interest despite his apparent nonchalance. "I'm involved, of course, because I did my internship with Serge Ravinsky."

Everyone, including Serge's wife, knew she'd been fucking Ravinsky, but she was beautiful and young and his wife wasn't. "I'm listening," Arthur said, keeping the excitement from his voice with difficulty.

"If you could accommodate me, I could see if Serge wouldn't mind sending a portion of the collection to you. I couldn't promise the entire show, of course. Your facilities aren't large enough."

"I understand. How many could we have?"

"What can you suitably hang? The Russians insist on superior conditions for their paintings—perfect humidity, lighting, surveillance . . . not to mention the necessary insurance."

"I could take thirty in our Ensted Gallery. It was completely renovated last year. Top-of-the-line everything, thanks to Ensted's widow."

"Very well. I'll speak to Serge."

His gaze narrowed. "I'll need more than a promise."

"I can't guarantee anything until I speak to Serge."

"Well, you let me know when you've talked to him," Arthur silkily murmured.

"I'm offering you a real plum, Arthur. You understand that, don't you?"

"Of course. But if you want Bobby all to yourself while you're in town—how hard is it to make a phone call?" His smile was oily. "I'm sure Serge will be understanding. You two are great friends, I understand." She was the one here at seven in the morning. And if she wanted what she wanted, she had to pay the price. Furthermore, if he wasn't going to join Serge in her bed, he was damned well going to get full payment some other way.

Claire knew it wasn't a question of Serge cooperating. He'd be more than willing, especially since his recent visit to New York. But Arthur was annoying—not taking her word on their bargain. As if she wasn't to be trusted. As if she wasn't handing him his biggest coup in a decade. If this wasn't so important to her, she would have told him to go to hell and also told him he was too old to be wearing his hair that long. "Why don't I get back to you?" she said cooly, preferring that he squirm for a time. Coming to her feet, she nodded a businesslike adieu.

But Arthur already knew he had the deal. Or maybe he just knew Bobby's effect on women. "I'll wait to hear from you," he said mildly, already planning the press release to the media as she walked from his office. It was going to be a spectacular occasion for the museum. Vodka would be appropriate at the reception—with caviar if he could find some member willing to allay the cost—and a string quartet playing evocative Russian music. He'd have to talk to some cultural activists in the Russian émigré community. Gypsy musicians would be superb.

Now all he had to do was come up with some reasonable explanation for Cassandra. Or, more aptly, for Bobby. Her trip out of town had to look, feel, and smell authentic as North Shore blueberry pancakes and maple syrup.

Which reminded him. Had Jessica made their reservations for the Madeline Island regatta?

TWENTY-EIGHT

"YOU GOTTA BE KIDDING," BOBBY SAID, scowling at Arthur.

"Not at all. William Spencer called me this morning. He's insisting Cassandra come down to Houston and authenticate his newest acquisitions. He bought Lord Boswick's entire collection, and you know that's Cassandra's field of expertise." As soon as Claire had called him with the expected approval from Serge, Arthur had called in a favor of his own. "She'll only be gone four or five days—a week at the most. I could find you another assistant if you wish."

"I don't wish." Bobby's voice was a low rumble. "She knows all the players now. Send someone else down to Spencer."

"Do I detect some personal attachment to Cassandra?" Arthur softly inquired, insinuation as high as Mount Everest.

"No, Arthur. It's nothing personal." Bobby slid up from his sprawl, planted his hands on the chair arms, and gave Arthur a black look.

"Then I don't see any problem," Arthur blandly remarked.

"If you need help, I'll find you someone else. If you don't, that's your call. And I apologize if Bill's request is inopportune, but that Boswick collection is first rate. I think Cassandra will be thrilled to go. Now, tell me, how's the search going?"

"Nothing so far, Arthur," Bobby brusquely said. And at the moment, he was so pissed he felt like throwing in the towel. Screw everything. Screw the Rubens, and for sure screw Arthur. And double-screw Lord fucking Boswick for assembling his collection. Damn. Sex yesterday had been so fantastic his nerves were still on edge. He was going into withdrawal just thinking of it. Fucking Spencer. Wasn't there someone else in the country who knew English narrative painting, for Christ's sake?

"As long as you're making progress," Arthur said, smiling, knowing he'd just brought Bobby's progress in the bedroom to an abrupt halt. "What more can I ask?"

"When does she leave?" Curt words, a matching scowl.

"This afternoon. Emma has her flight booked."

Bobby grimaced, came to his feet, and, with a nod of his head, turned and left a smiling Arthur lounging in his chair, visualizing thirty rarely seen Impressionist paintings under the soft lighting in the Ensted Gallery. That string quartet in the background was going to be perfect . . . maybe he should personally vet the musicians. Some young pretty faces would set an appropriate mood . . .

"HE TALKED TO you already?" Bobby stood just inside Cassie's office.

Cassie nodded. "Shut the door."

He did, but he didn't move from the door, feeling too much like hitting something to get too close. She'd be pissed if he busted up her furniture. "What did Arthur say?"

"Just that William Spencer needs me in Houston."

"And apparently he can't wait."

"I didn't dare ask."

"I did. Four or five days he said, maybe a week. I'm not real happy."

"I would have preferred going at some later date as well." She was still drifting on pink clouds after last night, but she wasn't stupid enough to make this personal. But she was glad he was unhappy, even if it was temporary and selfishly motivated.

"I don't suppose I could go with you?"

"It might raise a few eyebrows. Wasn't Le Corbusier your dissertation subject?"

"Jesus, it's annoying," he grumbled.

"I agree."

He gave her a look from under his lashes. "But you still want to see the collection, don't you?"

"It's a one of a kind, Bobby. I can't honestly say I *don't* want to see it. But would I rather go afterward? Yes, of course."

"What do you mean, afterward?" He was surprised he asked, but not enough not to want to hear her answer.

"I mean after you find the painting. After Bulgaria, say, and Budapest. After you're gone." She placed her palms on her desktop and examined her nails for a moment before looking up and meeting his gaze. "You're going to leave eventually. We both know it."

There was no polite response.

"I'm not asking for anything," she softly said. "When you go, you go."

"I just hate to see you go *now*," he murmured.

"Maybe I won't be in Houston long. The Boswick collection has been in one family for generations. There won't be many authentication issues." She smiled. "For sex like last night, I might be willing to work day and night and catch the red-eye home. I could be back in three days."

He grinned. "You pretty much say what you feel, don't you?"

"Pretty much." Except for the fantasy wedding stuff that would freak him out.

He blew out a breath, pushed away from the door, and, moving closer, sat down on her Mies chair. "Okay. Tell me again that you'll be back in three days."

"Three days tops. What do you know about English narrative painting? I might call you to expedite things."

"By all means call." Leaning toward her desk, he wrote two numbers on her note pad, ripped off the sheet, and handed it to her. "My cell and the houseboat. Call me anytime. And if you need help to speed things along, I'll get in touch with Ned Ashborough at the Tate. He owes me."

"Thanks, although maybe a break will do us good," she said. "Like—"

"Bull."

She half smiled. "I was trying to be polite."

"As if that helps," he groused. "What time do you have to leave?"

Moving some papers on her desk, she glanced at her e-ticket. "Jeez." She looked at the clock. "Three fifty. I thought it was five fifty. That barely gives me time to go home and pack. And I have to call Liv and cancel."

"I'll take you." They'd driven Cassie's car in this morning.

"If you want to use my car while I'm gone," she said, folding the e-ticket and reaching for her purse. "Feel free."

"Thanks, but Joe can keep me company."

She grinned. "I'll be jealous."

"And I'll be jealous of Bill Spencer."

"Don't be. I'm yours."

He was caught unaware, not sure whether it was her words or her smile that felt like a punch in the gut. But he recovered quickly because he was glad she was his. "Then I'll keep the home fires burning," he said with a grin. "Let me know when to pick you up at the airport."

TWENTY-NINE

AS CASSIE'S PLANE WAS FLYING HIGH ABOVE
Nebraska, Bobby was enjoying the sun on the St.
Croix. He'd made it an early day, not in the mood to
do Arthur any favors, and with a cold beer in hand, he was
lounging on the deck watching the boats go by. Another
beer and he'd walk over to the dock-side restaurant, eat supper, then come back and wait for Cassie's call. She said she'd
phone him once she was settled in her hotel room.

The sun was warm, the day balmy, and his mood less
sullen now that he knew she'd be back soon. He couldn't remember when he'd waited for a woman with such anticipation. Never, actually. Which might have been real unnerving
had he not been mellow after three beers. Which might
have been more than a little disconcerting as well had he
known of the phone call Arthur had made to Bill Spencer
not more than an hour ago, reminding Bill to keep Cassie
busy in Houston for at least a week.

And he would be way the hell more than disconcerted if

he'd been aware of the machinations leading to Cassie's trip to Houston.

But he didn't.

And for the moment, ignorance was bliss.

He ate Minnesota walleye for supper, the martini menu was extensive, the restaurant overlooking the St. Croix river busy on a spring evening, and he enjoyed the view and his martinis and the buzz of conversation around him.

The sun was low in the sky as he strolled down the marina dock, mentally checking off the hours from the three-day clock in his head. He'd survive, and someday he'd pay Arthur back. After several martinis, that thought brought a smile to his face. As Cassie had pointed out at their initial meeting, Arthur had his share of enemies—himself now included. But he wasn't in a rush for retribution. In a way, Arthur's whole life was a form of retribution. He was juggling a helluva lot of balls in the air, working up a sweat and not making much progress.

The two crewmen were gone for the night. Bobby had assured them as he'd left for supper that he didn't want the boat taken out that evening. He'd encouraged them to go, finding the idea of being alone when Cassie called appealing. Jesus, what the hell was that all about? Next thing you know, he'd be buying Hallmark cards.

He was on the gangway when he heard the phone ring and softly swore, cursing himself for not watching the time more closely. Sprinting, he leaped up the stairs to the second deck and, just as he reached the balcony off the bedroom, he heard a familiar voice purr, "I'm so sorry, but Bobby's busy right now. Would you like to leave a message?"

It was as if Wellington's battle plan for Waterloo had been laid out before him—after the fact.

Or the blueprints for the first nuclear bomb were suddenly

a brilliant visual in his brain—disaster blinking like a deto-
nator counting down.

And there was Arthur's voice coming through bright and
clear from some recording library in his brain saying,
"William Spencer called me this morning. He's insisting
Cassandra come down." *Like hell! Like bloody fucking hell!*

He'd strangle Arthur. He'd sell the fucking Rubens and
give the money to charity. He'd take Arthur's world apart
with his hands, piece by piece.

"Darling, how nice to see you." Claire stood in the open
glass-fronted bedroom doorway.

But first, he'd strangle Claire.

"What the hell do you think you're doing?" he growled.

"I just love when you sound all ferocious and male. And
I'm not doing anything," she said with wide-eyed innocence. "I just stopped by for a drink."

"You answered my phone," he said with a dangerous
softness.

"Is that a problem?"

"It sure as hell is."

"I'm sure whoever it was will call back," she said, over
sweet and smiling.

He doubted very much whoever it was would call back.
Not after the grilling he'd undergone in the car after Flora's
party. Not after all of Cassie's questions about his relationship with Claire. He could almost guarantee whoever it was
wouldn't call back until hell froze over, and maybe not even
then. "Why don't you get the fuck out, Claire," he snarled.
"Get on your broomstick and fly away."

"My goodness, that's not very friendly. I brought you a
very nice bottle of wine. A '56 Margaux."

"Listen," he said, ultra softly. "Just go. Stay out of my
life. And whatever you gave Arthur for this, I hope like hell
he chokes on it."

"Really, darling, you're overreacting," she said, her model's smile in place. "There's no Machiavellian motive behind my visit. We haven't seen each other for a long time. I thought we could have a glass of wine and chat."

"*Chat?*" His voice sounded explosive in his ears, and he forced himself to inhale and exhale, told himself Claire wasn't worth the aggravation, and said, "I don't chat, and if I did, I wouldn't with you. You and Arthur are playing some game, and I don't want to be a part of it."

"No one's playing any game. It's a beautiful evening. You're alone. I'm alone. Why can't we have a drink and talk?"

"Look, Claire, I don't know how to put this politely, but we're divorced for a reason—for a whole lot of reasons—and I'm not interested in picking up where we left off."

"You looked interested that first day at Sarah's."

"I was surprised to see you."

"Are you sure that was all?"

"Yeah, I'm sure." He'd had time since then to see her in action again, to sort out his feelings, their conversation at Flora's party reminding him of her blatant selfishness and her ungenerous nature. And now this flagrant manipulation. Jesus, did she think he was a complete moron? "I'd like you to go."

"It's because of her, isn't it—that Cassandra."

"No. It's because you and I don't have anything left to say."

"We could talk about the weather," she playfully murmured. "And drink this great Bordeaux while the sun sets."

It was amazing how his reaction to her had changed since he'd first seen her getting out of that cab. She wasn't any less beautiful. In fact, she was dressed for seduction in a low-necked, short-skirted dress and high heels. He was sure she could turn on most of the men on the planet. But just not him. "I've had enough to drink tonight. Please go."

"Good Lord, Bobby. Lighten up. It's just a drink." She moved from her languid pose in the bedroom doorway and began walking toward his bed.

"I'm serious, Claire. Go or I'll call the cops."

She turned and gave him a pouty look. "You needn't be melodramatic. I'm just going to check out your bed."

"I don't know how fast the cops show up here, but if you don't want to do a lot of explaining, I suggest you get your ass in gear."

"You wouldn't."

"In a fucking second. Breaking and entering. I think my Piaget watch is missing."

For a taut moment they did the equivalent of a Mexican standoff north of the border.

Her cool blue eyes had turned icy. "I think you're losing your mind."

"Just go."

She lifted her chin faintly. "I don't have to."

He took a step forward, and something in his face changed her mind. Brushing past him, she stalked away, moving down the narrow staircase with remarkable speed considering her spiky heels. He watched her stalk down the marina dock, quickly ascend the stairs to the river bank, and disappear behind one of the repair sheds.

And then he sat down on a deck chair and stared out at the river, racking his brain for an explanation Cassie was likely to listen to. Hoping like hell the bedroom phone had caller ID. Thinking maybe he should just fly down to Houston and talk to her in person. Shocking the hell out of himself that he would consider such a dramatic gesture. Which resulting tumult caused him to stare at the busy river for several minutes more while his brain stopped short-circuiting. Jesus, how deep was he in this—he hesitated on the word *relationship* and finally gave up—what the hell . . . relationship?

Deep enough to ruin his very comfortable life? Deep enough to make him forget the disaster of his marriage? It was frightening in a way that he was even thinking about such bizarre possibilities after having been unlucky enough to experience his ex-wife in all her deluded glory.

Maybe he'd have another beer to relax.

You know, put everything into perspective.

Then he'd check out the caller ID. If there was one.

Otherwise, he'd have to call Emma. She'd made the reservations. She'd know the name of the hotel.

There.

He had time.

He didn't have to rush into anything. It was always better not to rush into any serious decisions.

Although in hindsight, delay might not have been a good idea.

It might be construed as indifference.

But consider, his world was being rocked.

Seriously.

THIRTY

WHEN HE CHECKED THE PHONE, IT DID HAVE caller ID. Punching in the number, he counted the rings, hanging up on ten with a sigh. What did he expect?

But intent, he called back, then called again and again until Cassie finally picked up.

"Let me explain."

Click.

At least she'd answered. He was encouraged.

But she didn't answer for—he lost count—but redial was easy, and he wasn't about to give up. Sort of like when his team was behind by two touchdowns and he'd keep throwing those passes. Besides, he had plenty of cold beer, and getting to work early tomorrow wasn't on his radar. After his talk with Arthur, he'd temporarily shut down the radar. So—redial. He watched the numbers dance across the screen, listened to the first ring, the second, the third— lifted his beer to his mouth and almost choked when Cassie picked up.

"Whatever you have to say I don't want to hear," she said, clipped and curt.

Thank you, God. He felt like a hostage negotiator who finally got through to the kidnapper. "Listen for ten seconds before you hang up."

"One one thousand, two—"

"This is all a setup, your trip to Houston included, and Arthur's getting something for it."

"Good-bye."

"Claire's gone," he quickly said.

"You must be tired." Sarcasm dripped from every word.

This was one of those times when "Screw you" wasn't going to work. "I came back from supper and she was here. Thanks to Arthur. Like your trip was thanks to Arthur. He planned this."

"Why?"

Bobby took a small breath, knowing the dicey part was coming up, the part about Claire. "He and Claire made some deal, I'm guessing."

"You're guessing?"

"I didn't talk to her. I just told her to go when I found her here."

"She answered your phone."

He exhaled. "Yeah. I know. I was a second too slow."

"Or you would have stopped her and pretended she wasn't there?"

The truth wasn't going to be helpful here. "I'm not sure." Would ambiguity move them on to something less fraught with disaster?

"Not sure you would have stopped her, or not sure you would have pretended she wasn't there?"

Shit. He wasn't going to get out of this one. "To be honest," he said, making one of those figurative Hail Mary passes of candor and frankness, "I wish I'd come back from supper earlier and sent her home before you called. Then you wouldn't be mad, and I wouldn't be trying to figure out how to make it up to you. I don't want to say she's nuts because she isn't, but she's—"

"A malicious bitch?"

At least Cassie was talking, although the heat in her voice still gave him pause. But he knew how she felt because he'd been ready to strangle both Claire and Arthur not more than three beers ago. "Yeah," he said. "She is."

"And now what, Bobby?" She was so pissed she dared put him on the spot.

There was a scary question, especially when it was uttered in that clipped, crisp tone. But he'd always more or less faced the various crises in his life so he said, "Why don't you come back? Tell me what you want."

"I can't come back and possibly irritate Arthur. I need my job."

"I'll run interference for you."

"Maybe you've done too much of that already."

"What the hell does that mean?"

"It means I'm going to stay down here and authenticate Spencer's collection as instructed, and when I'm finished I'll return. Whether Claire and Arthur have some deal going has nothing to do with me. Claire's your problem. When you return to your life, I'll still have bills to pay and Arthur to placate if I want a relatively peaceful work environment. We can't all be independently wealthy."

"So when will you be back?" This time *his* voice was clipped and crisp.

"Four or five days. The collection is huge."

"And Spencer's nice, I suppose."

"Hello. He's married with children and grandchildren."

"So that means he can't be nice to you?"

"I don't like your tone. For your information, he's pleasant, I'm pleasant. Everyone's pleasant."

"And I know how pleasant you can be," he silkily murmured.

"Unlike you, we don't all jump into bed with anyone at all," she snapped.

"You could have fooled me."

The line went dead, but he didn't care because he felt like ripping the phone from the wall anyway. *Pleasant, my ass.* He'd met Bill Spencer. And he'd met Bill Spencer's girlfriend, or at least current girlfriend, one night at an intimate little bar on the Upper East Side. God almighty, Cassie was naive.

Or maybe she wasn't.

Maybe she was in the running for Bill Spencer's newest girlfriend.

Shit. Lifting his beer to his mouth, he walked outside and stared at the darkening sky, too resentful to notice the evening star and the beauty of twilight.

Claire was to blame, of course. But regardless of the dynamic behind this travesty, Cassie could have been more understanding. It wasn't as though *he'd* done anything wrong. Hell, he'd been an innocent bystander. And if Cassie had really wanted to, she could have told Bill Spencer to stuff it and taken the next flight out. Spencer couldn't have argued; he knew the whole setup was a sham. But no, she was going to stay down in Houston and finish her bogus assignment.

What the hell was going on with that?

As if he didn't know when the hottest piece of ass he'd ever seen decides she needs to placate Arthur.

As if Arthur needed placating when he'd been exposed for a fraud.

What the hell could he do to her?

Obviously she had other things on her mind besides bills that needed paying.

She had another Bill to pay, although he guessed that payment would be one of those mutually satisfying expenditures. It looked as though she was moving on; he might as well.

Hell, he'd just gotten rid of one bitchy wife, he sure as shit didn't need another woman complicating his life.

He'd meet with Arthur in the morning and settle up.

THIRTY-ONE

AT THE FOUR SEASONS IN HOUSTON, HER current posting thanks to Bill Spencer's largesse, Cassie was waiting for room service with a kind of suppressed panic. She really, really, *really* needed the chocolate torte and chocolate malt and chocolate mousse if she was going to retain her sanity, because she was *this* close to losing it. She hadn't actually cried yet, steeling herself against giving way to her tears until the room service guy left so she wouldn't have to answer the door all red-eyed and puffy faced.

That first sound of Claire's cool voice answering Bobby's phone had precipitated anger rather than tears anyway. She'd contemplated more physical responses to his ex-wife—all of which were forbidden by the justice system, of course. And realistically, for someone who stepped over ants on the sidewalk and fed the racoons when her neighbors shot them with BB guns, her revenge fantasies were not too likely.

Then her anger had shifted to the real culprit—the man who made women swoon all over the world—and she'd been able to sustain that anger for maybe a whole five minutes because he made her feel *soooo* good. Okay, she admitted it; she wasn't rational about Bobby Serre. Her actions of late a case in point.

That's why she'd finally picked up the phone, half hoping he'd have a perfectly reasonable explanation for why the black-haired bitch had answered his phone on the houseboat. But no, he'd blamed Arthur and Bill Spencer, and in the end, she was getting the idea she was at fault. Figure that. It would be a cold day in hell when she slept with Bill Spencer. Not that she hadn't been propositioned about ten minutes after meeting him, but she knew how to deal with men like him. She'd had lots of practice with Arthur.

But old guys and their egos aside—seriously—was life unfair or what? Just when you think you've found someone really nice and really, really fantastic in bed, they turn out to be a grade-A jerk. On the other hand, she might just have been super-gullible like a teenage rock-star fan with starry eyes and no sense who can't separate the stage presence from the man. But either way, she was sad and blue and half in the mood to belt out a Patsy Cline song if she'd actually ever listened to a Patsy Cline song. But she knew the singer was all about heartache and despair and losing your man, and she was feeling it big time. In fact, if she wasn't so depressed, she might have had the energy to find the country music channel on cable, scroll through it, and find Patsy to sing her to sleep.

Her one small—very small—consolation was the collection she was working on. The paintings were gorgeous, absolute gems, and if she didn't have to sidestep Mr. Bill all day long, she would have finished sooner. Not that she was about to admit that to Bobby. He'd been way too fucking male, assuming just because she slept with him she slept with everyone. He should talk. And bottom line, after Jay, she wasn't likely to roll over and apologize. The way she saw it, he could apologize to her.

Which he hadn't.

Not even slightly.

When he was the one with Claire answering his phone.

Damn, it was really too much like a replay of her life with Jay, the lousy excuses and nonapologies and I'm-right-and-you're-wrong conversations.

One thing she'd learned since her divorce was that she was through apologizing for no reason. As for her staying on in Houston, she *did* need the job, and because of that, Arthur's tacit approval at least. She really liked her work. If Bobby Serre couldn't understand the needs of the plebeian laboring class, that was his loss. A little spurt of that female power thingy marginally raised her spirits.

Once she was back home, she and Liv would go out, have a few drinks, and compare notes on the deplorable lack of nice men in their world.

A shame some of them were so well hung and knew how to use it.

With that disquieting thought, she quickly flicked on the TV.

Alone in bed, she didn't *dare* think of Bobby Serre.

THIRTY-TWO

"YOU LOOK TIRED," ARTHUR SAID, SURVEYING Bobby from across his desk.

"No sleep does that to you. By the way, thanks for all the heavy-handed manipulating. I hope like hell you got something of value from Claire."

"You didn't?" Arthur roguishly inquired.

"In my case, it's not possible. But you ruined my night. I hope it gets you off."

"It was a business arrangement."

"I figured. Isn't it always? Now then, I have some information for you. Do you want the good news first or the bad?"

"Either." Arthur was in fine spirits. He didn't know yet that Claire had canceled on him.

"I found the Rubens."

Arthur's face lit up. "My God, that's unbelievable news!"

"Brace yourself, Arthur. I found it at Sarah's. Under the back stairs when I was playing hide-and-seek with the kids on Sunday."

"I don't believe it. Are you sure?"

"Unless Sarah has become a world-class artist overnight and by coincidence painted Isabella in the nude, I am. By the way, it was casually slipped inside a shopping bag. All twenty-two million dollars worth."

"Jesus." Arthur slumped in his chair.

For a fraction of a second, Bobby almost felt sorry for him. Until he remembered his conversation with Cassie last night. "The insurance people are going to want to prosecute. That's a given. They like the headlines; it's good for their bottom line. I don't know how you want to handle this, but my part is over." He stood up. "You know where to send my check."

"Christ, Bobby, you can't just leave. Sarah didn't mean it, you know she didn't. Sarah, Paige, and I have been arguing about money lately. She must have gotten it into her head to take drastic action. Jesus, what the hell am I going to do?"

"The justice system is outside my bailiwick. I suggest you call a lawyer."

"Wait, wait!" Arthur jumped up. "Don't go! I need help! You know how these insurance companies work. You do this every day. There has to be a way out short of prosecution. This can't go to court! She's the mother of my child! It was some damned prank or misunderstanding! You know she wasn't serious. Help me, please. Name your price!"

Take back last night, Bobby wanted to say, but it was a little too late. Actually, Arthur's machinations aside, it might have been too late the moment Bill Spencer laid eyes on Cassie.

"Jesus, Bobby, give me some help here!" Arthur had come around from behind his desk and grabbed Bobby's arm. "I mean it. Money's no object. You know all the angles. Christ, there must be some way to bend the rules. If the police are brought into this . . . it's over." He suddenly looked old, his face ashen. "The museum can't afford the scandal. I can't afford the scandal. And poor Flora. God. Why did Sarah do it?"

Bobby was surprised he could feel sympathy for Arthur. He wasn't a man who inspired those feelings—his entire life a paradigm for selfishness. Maybe it was the shocking change he saw, Arthur's sudden aging as though some time machine had passed over him. Or maybe it was the fear he felt emanating from the taut grip on his arm. Or perhaps the thought of Sarah and Flora having their life taken away was the most powerful motive. "If I help you with this," Bobby abruptly said, "I'll need a couple things."

"Anything. I swear. Anything." A spark of life revived in Arthur's eyes. "Tell me what you want and I'll see that you have it."

"Give Cassandra Hill a raise."

"Of course. How much?"

That threw him for a moment, his familiarity with salaries nonexistent. "Triple it," Bobby said, thinking of Cassie's empty house. "And I want a contract drawn up for her that gives her a permanent position here if she wants it."

"She's already guaranteed a job with the Palmer trust, but, yes, yes, I'll have our lawyer draw up something imme-diately," he quickly asserted at Bobby's frown.

"That's it, then."

Arthur opened his mouth to speak, thought better of it, and shut it again.

Bobby smiled faintly. "I don't need your money, Arthur. Count your blessings."

"I will, believe me. Just tell me how to deal with this fiasco, and I'll be eternally in your debt."

Bobby knew Arthur's eternal was about as long as Claire's, but he wasn't looking for gratitude. He just thought Cassie should have some furniture. It was the least he could do for all—shit—he forced his mind back to the present because the sudden images flooding his mind were sexy as hell and not at all helpful. "Sit down, Arthur. Tell Emma you don't want to be disturbed, and we'll walk through some feasible scenarios for returning the painting. Then we'll go see Sarah. Call her and tell her you're coming over with some belated presents for Flora."

He waited while Arthur made the calls and then said, "Here's what you have to do. We'll need some storage area that's rarely used and an excuse for you to come back here tonight. Nothing weird. You must work in the evenings occasionally. Christ—okay you don't . . . tonight, however, you'll have some emergency. A donor you have to call overseas—six times zones away—and you don't want to call from home. Get some name from Emma; we want to make this look real."

Bobby kept talking, and Arthur kept nodding his head. When Bobby finally stopped laying out the drill, he said, "We'll stop at a toy store. The visit to Sarah's has to be as authentic as possible, too. While Flora's opening her present, I'll make a bathroom run, remove the painting out of the space under the stairs in the back hallway, and bring it to the car. When I return, we'll thank Sarah for the visit and leave. You don't want to tell her you know. You don't want to be involved in any way. I doubt she'll call the police and report the painting missing. And when the police question you, you know what to say."

"The painting was found in a storage unit. How it got there is a mystery."

"Why wasn't that storage unit searched?" Bobby tipped his head.

"It was considered much too small for the Rubens."

"That's good, Arthur. No excuses. A simple answer. Don't elaborate. Let's go toy shopping."

"I'll owe you, Bobby. I mean it sincerely."

Bobby had never heard that humble tone from Arthur. He

wished he had a recorder so he could play it over when he needed solace for losing someone he would have preferred not losing.

But hey, how long could their relationship have lasted, anyway? Jorge wanted him in Bulgaria ASAP. Which reminded him—once the Rubens was back at the museum, he'd give Jorge a call. "We'll take your car," Bobby said to Arthur. "I don't want Joe involved. I'll go down, send him home, and meet you in the parking lot."

THIRTY-THREE

SARAH LOOKED WARY WHEN SHE OPENED the door and saw Bobby with Arthur, but once she saw the presents in Arthur's arms, her expression changed. "Come in. Flora's in the playroom. She'll be thrilled with more presents."

"I hope you don't mind that I tagged along," Bobby said. "Arthur and I have an appointment afterward—one of the trustees wants to meet me. Did he say he knew my father or mother?" Bobby glanced at Arthur.

"Your mother," Arthur quickly replied, familiar with prevarication. "He met her in London a couple years ago apparently and was charmed."

Bobby smiled. "Mother can do that." He turned to Sarah. "She had her own PR firm in Washington for years. Where better to learn the usefulness of charm?"

"Claire mentioned that once," Sarah said. "By the way, she left early this morning. Some emergency in New York." At the sudden silence, she quickly added, "Would anyone like coffee before we see Flora?"

Bobby shook his head.

"Nor I," Arthur seconded, wanting nothing more than to expedite the return of the painting. "Because these presents were overlooked on Sunday, I thought Flora would rather not wait for them."

"She adores presents, but then what child doesn't?" Sarah added, a note of caution still in her voice as she led them down the hallway to the playroom.

If not for Flora's squeals of delight as she opened the presents, the visit would have been uncomfortable. Sarah was patently tense. Every few moments she would glance apprehensively at Bobby, and now he knew why. Arthur, too, was unusually restrained. Normally one to dominate the conversation, he was practically mute.

Taking the first opportunity to excuse himself, Bobby went to the back hallway instead of the bathroom, opened the small doorway under the stairs, and lifted out the Rubens residing in a green-striped shopping bag from the museum bookstore.

With the sound of Flora's new playtime piano echoing through the house, Bobby quietly opened the back door. Having purposely parked in the drive, he covered the distance to the car quickly, placed the shopping bag on the backseat of Arthur's black Mercedes sedan, and relocked the car. Time elapsed, a minute ten. A swift trip to the bathroom to flush the toilet in the event someone was listening and moments later he returned to the playroom.

"We should leave, Arthur, if we want to make that appointment," Bobby suggested, standing just inside the door.

"Of course. We don't want to keep Chester waiting." Arthur jumped up. "Business, business," he murmured with a smile.

Flora was too intent on pounding the oversize keys on the piano to take notice of the adults.

Sarah seemed to relax the moment Bobby spoke of leaving. "Paige and I and the children are going up north tomorrow. I hope you don't need the cabin this weekend."

"No, no, not at all, you go up anytime! Anytime at all!" Realizing his voice held a note of hysteria, Arthur quickly added in a slightly more normal tone, backing out of the room as he spoke, "I know the children always enjoy the lake. Call Marv Gertz and have the children's swingset put together; I told him it would be going up as soon as the weather warmed up. Or if you'd rather wait, I mean—suit yourself, of course, but I did tell him—"

"It was nice to see you again, Sarah," Bobby interposed, cutting Arthur's rambling short, quickly stepping aside before Arthur backed into him. "And you, too, Flora," he politely added, although little Flora was doing the Shroeder thing with the piano and wouldn't have noticed if the sky fell.

With a wave and a smile, Bobby followed Arthur, who was practically running out of the house.

When they reached the car, Arthur whispered, "Did you get it?" His eyes were flicking from left to right like an amateur spy in a bad movie.

"Relax. It's in the backseat." Unlocking the car, Bobby tossed the keys to Arthur. "Don't look right now, and don't hit anything backing out of the drive. This is no time for an accident report to the police."

But several blocks away, Arthur pulled over to the curb and glanced over his shoulder. "Jesus. It's really in a paper bag?" he said on a suffocated breath.

"Yeah. I'm guessing your ex-wife has some serious issues with you."

"No shit."

"I'm also guessing you haven't changed the security codes at the museum for a long time. And just a wild guess, but dealing with the security code and taking the painting is a two-man job. Or I should say, a two-woman job."

"You're kidding!"

"Uh-uh. Maybe some therapy or perhaps some restructuring of the divorce settlements would be my suggestion. For sure, change the security codes. You must have given them the numbers at some point."

Arthur looked sheepish. "I might have." He exhaled. "And they've both been needling me about more money."

"And you've been blowing them off. A word to the wise. Call your lawyer and start a dialogue with them. Upping their support will be a lot cheaper than what I charge."

"As soon as I get back to the museum, I'll call Harvey," Arthur said, pulling away from the curb. "He can call Sarah's and Paige's lawyer and get the ball rolling. Next, I'll have the codes changed."

"Good. You wouldn't want a repeat of this little disaster. Although I'd be very careful about pissing off your ex-wives."

"They should be warned about the consequences," Arthur grimly muttered, pugnacious once again, having overcome the specter of personal and professional ruin.

"Rein it in, Arthur. You can't speak of the theft to either of them. Understand? You'd be an accomplice, and you don't want that. Let it ride."

"I suppose I don't have a choice," Arthur testily acknowledged.

"Not really. We're agreed then?" Bobby waited for the requisite nod so Arthur couldn't say he'd never heard the conversation. "Fine. Now the painting stays in your car until tonight, when we'll transfer it to the storage locker. The locker you'll have opened tomorrow—why?" Bobby prompted.

"To bring up the Chinese jade stored there," Arthur recited.

"And why do you want the Chinese jade?"

"To inventory what we have against the Walker accounts recently sent to me by the family."

"Those were sent to you directly?"

Arthur nodded, giving the agreed-upon answer. "Emma opened the envelope, but she didn't study the accounts. That was up to me."

"Okay, we're good to go then. Drop me off downtown. I'll meet you back at the museum at closing time. And keep an eye on your car. This wouldn't be a good time for a casual auto theft."

"I'll leave it in the valet zone. No one will touch it within sight of the front entrance."

Bobby checked his watch. "By evening your troubles will be over."

"Thanks, Bobby. I really mean it."

"You're welcome, Arthur." Bobby grinned. "And my bank account thanks you, too."

BUT THE NEXT day, after the Rubens was safely rediscovered and Arthur had dealt with the police, Bobby made a short detour on his way to the airport.

He left the cab waiting at the curb outside Sarah's house.

When Sarah came to the door in response to his knock, she cast a furtive look around to see that he was alone and then blurted out like every amateur thief he'd ever known, "You found it, didn't you?"

"Sarah!" a voice from behind her exclaimed. "Keep your mouth shut!"

Paige came up behind Sarah, a scowl on her face. "What do you want?"

"I'd just like to let you know the alarm codes have been changed at the museum in case Arthur forgets to mention it."

"Ohmygod," Sarah gasped.

"I don't know what you're talking about," Paige coolly remarked.

"Just a general FYI, nothing personal. You two have a great day." And turning away, Bobby walked back down the sidewalk to his waiting cab.

Knowing Arthur wasn't allowed to bring up the subject, he'd thought he'd give warning to Arthur's two exes—in his capacity as a professional bounty hunter, of course. Just some general information for the usual suspects on his list, he'd say, if anyone ever questioned his stopping by.

He had to admit, deep down, he even understood why the ladies copped the painting—acting out their frustration and anger with Arthur, finding a way to embarrass and humiliate him. Those motivations were probably more appropriate for a therapist's couch, though. But hell, he knew about anger and getting even. He could even sympathize with Sarah and Paige, to a point. Arthur could be impossible to deal with. It was his way or the highway. At least his exes had Arthur's attention now, and hopefully the lawyers could iron out all the money issues. But he sure hoped they weren't stupid enough to try it again. Next time, he might not be around.

As for *his* anger, he was going to get as far away as he could from the woman who engendered those unwanted feelings.

And with luck and enough distance, hopefully they'd fade away.

And if they didn't, he'd find some appropriate diversion. That had always worked in the past.

THIRTY-FOUR

CASSIE HAD HEARD THE BOMBSHELL NEWS OF the Ruben's recovery while in Houston. That meant Bobby Serre would no doubt be gone when she returned to Minneapolis. Bingo there, she discovered on arriving at the museum. Emma gave her all the details in the coffee room, where she'd stopped for a little extra caffeine fortification. Not that Bobby's leaving was a huge surprise after her last phone conversation with him. Still, there was a blunt finality to it now. He was really, truly gone.

She walked to her office, knowing her life was definitely back to normal. Not that she hadn't expected as much.

But she'd no more than walked into her office when Arthur called her in for a meeting.

And gave her the real bombshell news.

"I've decided to give you that raise you asked for, Cassandra," he said, moving around several items on his desk top as he spoke.

She'd never seen Arthur nervous before. That in itself

was scary. Nor had she expected him to discuss her raise so quickly after her return. Getting money out of Arthur was a little like breaking into Fort Knox—difficult if not impossible.

She quickly measured the distance to the door. Was he about to suggest some sordid sex act as quid pro quo for her raise? But she replied in what she hoped was a normal tone. "Thank you, Arthur. I certainly appreciate it."

"The new figure will be"—and he mentioned a sum that made her gasp—"beginning with the next pay period. And I was thinking, too, that you might like some additional guarantees in terms of your future, so I had our attorney draw up a simple contract that ensures your position beyond Isabelle Palmer's trust stipulations."

His smile was more a grimace than a smile, and everything suddenly became crystal clear. Bobby Serre had had a hand in this. For a moment she didn't know if she should be grateful or offended. Was this payment for sex? Was she his high-priced call girl in Minneapolis? Because the sum Arthur had mentioned was colossal.

And then the old Arthur resurfaced. "I will naturally expect a superior performance in the future for your new compensation package."

She felt herself relax. This was the Arthur she knew and disliked. This was a dysfunctional comfort level she understood. This was business as usual at the museum she loved. "I understand. Thank you, Arthur. Is there anything more?"

"You really should get a haircut."

"When I need grooming tips, I'll let you know, Arthur."

"I just meant he might have stayed if—"

"Don't go there, Arthur. Not if you value your life."

"It was meant as—"

"Send my contract to my office," she interrupted, rising

to her feet. He knew and she knew that he was obliged to give her that contract or Bobby would have his balls. And he knew and she knew that contract meant she didn't have to take any crap from him.

She walked out without a backward glance.

THIRTY-FIVE

LIV MET HER FOR DRINKS AFTER WORK BECAUSE Cassie couldn't bear walking into her house without an alcoholic buzz after dealing with the overwhelming rush of potent memories her first night back from Houston. Or actually *not* dealing with them, sort of half sitting up all night watching reruns of old John Hughes movies on cable.

The minute Liv saw Cassie's doleful look and tall glass of Long Island ice tea with six shots of everything, she said, "He really is gone, isn't he?"

"Yeah."

"Where?"

Cassie shrugged. "Wherever high-priced bounty hunters go. Actually, in this case, maybe Bulgaria. One of his contacts wanted him to go with him to check out a Titian that's been missing for a couple centuries."

"Are you sad, heart-broken, going to live, or not going to live?" Liv asked as she slid into the booth and motioned for the waitress.

Cassie raised her lashes marginally. "It wasn't as though I expected him to stay and set up housekeeping with me."

"That's the rational part. What about the rest?" Liv held up three fingers to the waitress. "Single malt scotch, three fingers over ice."

"I'm here because I don't want to go home. What do you think?"

"Oookay. Gotcha. So do you want to sleep over?" Liv asked with a grin. "We could have pizza delivered and watch six episodes of *MI-5* and paint our nails."

Cassie tried to smile and shook her head. "I have to go home eventually. A couple more of these, and I'll fall into bed without knowing where I am. And Bobby got me a raise anyway. A huge raise *and* a contract so my position is secure until the end of time."

Liv winked. "So he's not all bad."

Cassie snorted. "The only bad thing about him is he's gone."

"You know what they say. Get back on that horse."

She wrinkled her nose. "I don't even want to look at another man. How bad is that? I must be jinxed. Do you think I'm jinxed?"

"Because the movie star didn't stay? Reality check, sweetie. You knew from day one he wasn't going to stay."

"Don't confuse me with the facts." Cassie grimaced. "I'm doomed to spinsterhood, 'cuz no one looks good anymore."

"You haven't exactly been running a dating marathon since Jay. No one looked good before Bobby came, either."

"Well, if nothing else, I'm absolutely sure I have no judgment when it comes to men. First Jay and now, when I should have known better, of course, I didn't. I let myself fall into some sticky infatuation trap. You have to agree I don't have a clue when it comes to men. I can't recognize good from bad or liars from nonliars, stayers from goers, or, more pertinently, when the goers will go."

"But you can tell big dicks from small dicks, I'll bet."

Cassie groaned. "Don't remind me. He should be in the *Guinness Book of Records*."

"Look at it this way. You scored for a couple weeks. How bad is that?"

"I don't feel like being reasonable right now. Okay? I want to wallow in my misery and moan about love and loss until I'm sick of sniffling and hearing my own whiny voice." Cassie half smiled. "It's the normal way to deal with problems, isn't it?"

"Don't ask me. I usually scream at whoever's in range. But then, I come from a long line of screamers and you don't. I remember going to your house when we were kids and figuring someone must be sick 'cuz the house was so quiet. In my house, the din was deafening. But hey, did you say *love* a while back?"

"No."

"I think you did."

"Think again. That word and Bobby Serre aren't in the same galaxy, believe me."

"Maybe you forgot for a second and let the word slip out."

"You're hallucinating. I still have a few brain cells operating even though I'm way ahead of you with these ice teas. I'd never say anything so stupid."

"Fine. Whatever." But Liv had heard it, and she had perfect recall, which always came in handy during cross-examination. "So what do you think of that guy over there at the bar? The one who looks like that young Nordic stud Samantha is having her way with on *Sex and the City*."

Cassie gave a quick look and shook her head. "I'm not interested in blonds."

"Since when?"

"Since forever."

"What about Sonny White and Max Martell and your ex?"

"Okay—I've lost my taste for them. He's all yours."

"Later . . . maybe. If his girlfriend or wife doesn't show up. So tell me, what did you do in Houston?"

"I checked out eighty paintings—really great ones—and gave them my seal of approval. I cried myself to sleep at night and in general worked long days so I didn't have to stay there any longer than necessary and whined to you, as you well know. Sorry about calling so late at night."

"What are friends for if they're not available twenty-four seven? And you weren't whining so much as weeping on the phone. Which is why I bought you this." Pawing through her very large shoulder bag, Liv came up with an official-looking paper and handed it across the table to Cassie. "You might as well profit from your misery."

Unfolding the crisp sheet, Cassie smiled. Five shares of Edna Mae's Ice Cream Company Ltd. "Thanks, Liv, you're a sweetheart. I'll treasure this always." Her brows lifted. "And probably add considerably to Edna Mae's bottom line. Now that I'm a stock holder, I'll have to remember that ice cream isn't just for breakfast."

"It's good for hot sex, too, don't forget. Like in you eat it off me and I'll eat it off you and we'll get our calcium with a whole lot of lovin'." Liv grinned and signaled for another drink. "Speaking of eating things, that blond is looking better all the time . . ." Her gaze narrowed.

"Go and talk to him," Cassie offered. "My iced tea and I will be fine."

"Maybe later. You need company, and I could use another drink. It's a work day tomorrow, too." She shrugged. "And I have a seven o'clock meeting, so maybe I'll have to leave thoughts of ice cream and pleasure for another day."

The word *pleasure* ironically offered up a sharp contrast in Cassie's mind. "Meg called," she muttered.

"Oh, oh. She's going to be lining you up again. Right?"

"I swear, she'd no more asked if Bobby was still around— she'd heard the Rubens had been found—when she's telling me about a friend of Oz's who's divorced and would be just perfect now that I have time on my hands again."

"So when are you going for dinner?"

Cassie's eyes widened, her surprise perhaps the result of almost two Long Island iced teas rather than Liv's conjecture. "How did you know?"

"Hello. It's Meg. The girl who's been telling you who to go out with since the tenth grade. The same one, by the way, who doesn't take no for an answer and keeps calling and calling and—"

"Tomorrow, although I tried to refuse. I really did. But she caught me about a minute after I'd come into work and hadn't had enough caffeine yet. My brain wasn't fully functioning."

"She's sneaky. She knows."

"I'm going to cancel."

Liv laughed. "In your dreams."

"I suppose I could go and not talk, just drink and leave right after dessert."

"You're too nice. You won't."

Cassie groaned. "So you see why I'm drinking. It's not just Bobby. It's the potential blind date who's not going to be my type because no one ever is except well-hung bounty hunters, I suppose."

"But then Bobby Serre's everyone's type. I don't want to be too harsh, sweetie, but you know he is."

"I know. Give me another week or so, and I'll get over this infatuation with hotter-than-hot sex. It's probably not him I'm missing so much as the thirty orgasms a day . . . and night . . . and everything in between." She smiled. "He was definitely high octane."

"To good memories," Liv proposed, lifting her glass.

Cassie clinked glasses with Liv and smiled faintly. "Which are better than no memories."

"Amen to that."

THIRTY-SIX

BOBBY HAD BURNED THROUGH THE BULGARian venture like a man with a hit squad on his trail. He'd authenticated the Titian for Jorge, backed him up in a falling-down palace in Sofia where the money changed hands, then escorted him and the painting as far as Marseille. In that port city, Jorge found a captain and oceangoing craft for hire, lined up some bodyguards he trusted from friends in Europe, and made ready to sail to Miami with his rare find that would add nicely to his retirement fund.

"Are you gonna be okay?" Jorge asked as they took leave of each other.

"Sure. I'll be in Budapest tonight."

"You've got something on your mind. I'd say women troubles, but not with you. If there's some job you need help with, just say the word. My sailing schedule is flexible."

"I'm good. Tired, that's all. I've had a few too many sleepless nights." Bobby shouldn't have said that, his statements bringing disastrous memories to the fore—the ones with

Cassie during their all-nighters. The ones he couldn't shake, no matter how hard he tried.

"You're sure?"

"Absolutely. Have a good trip, Jorge. You have my numbers if you need anything."

Then Bobby caught the first flight out to Budapest, but he'd no more than landed in the city than he changed his mind. Booking a flight to London, he had a brief layover at Heathrow before boarding a nonstop to Denver. It was the closest major city to his home in Montana, and in the mood he was in, he wanted nothing more than to sit on his porch and watch the grass grow. He didn't want to think; he didn't want to feel—although that wasn't too likely, with misery clinging to him like a shroud. But at least he'd be home—his best home.

And if there was peace to be found, he would find it there.

THIRTY-SEVEN

AS IF A BLIND DATE DINNER AT HER SISTER'S wasn't about as gruesome an evening as she could imagine, Cassie almost had a heart attack when she arrived at Meg's and saw her parents' car parked in the drive. Weren't they supposed to still be in Florida? Didn't they always wait until Memorial Day to return to Minnesota?

If Meg hadn't been waving at her from the front porch, she would have turned the car around and called with some excuse like the heart attack that might actually be imminent. With a groan, she braked.

She was screwed.

Knowing Cassie's strong inclination to avoid family dinners, Meg stayed on the porch as a deterrent to that impulse until Cassie parked and walked up. "We've already started eating. You're late. I've been calling and calling. Why don't you answer your phone?"

Cassie hadn't answered her phone at home because she had caller ID and was still trying to think of some excuse to back out of Meg's dinner. She was late for the same reason—the backing out one. She'd been driving around aimlessly, trying to think of some excuse that would fly. And she hadn't answered her cell phone that had caller ID, too—thank you, God—because her excuse machine seemed to be out of commission. She decided she should have spent a lot more time lying in her life and she'd be a whole lot better at it. "I can't stay long," she said, desperately tossing out her last lifeline. "I have to get up early tomorrow to go shopping with Liv."

"I just talked to Liv when I was trying to find you. She's playing tennis tomorrow, not shopping. But you just wait and see," Meg said, rolling over Cassie's excuse like a bulldozer while pulling her into the house. "You're going to just love Drew."

If Meg hadn't said that to her about ten thousand times in her life—okay, maybe she was exaggerating . . . but a thousand for sure—Cassie would have been more apt to look forward to this meeting with the man she was going to love. But once burnt, etcetera, etcetera, and she was working on a thousand burns, so she wasn't likely to fall into that trap. "I'm not staying long, Meg. I mean it." She tried to sound really, really firm.

"You look great tonight, Cassie. Drew is going to adore you."

Why was she getting the idea her words were falling on deaf ears?

Why did she feel like running even though she was wearing strappy heels that would make her fall and break her ankle if she ran five yards?

Why was she getting that familiar sinking feeling in the pit of her stomach?

"Cassie, honey!" It was her mother's voice. "I hear you out there. Come and meet this sweet young man Oz knows!"

That's why, she thought, mortified.

She was going to have two take-no-prisoners marriage brokers working on her case tonight.

As she entered the dining room, she felt as though she'd walked on stage—everyone was staring at her. "Sorry I'm late," she murmured. "Traffic." That was lame, but she couldn't help it. She was coming up blank for excuses tonight.

"You know everyone except Drew," Meg said in her most charming voice. "Drew, this is my sister, Cassandra Hill. Cassie, meet Drew Nyberg. Sit there, Cassie, right next to Drew," she said in her totally unsubtle way.

My God, he could have been a twin to Samantha's stud, the blond guy from the bar.

He came to his feet as Cassie approached and smiled. "Hi. I think I have most of your grade school teachers memorized."

"Jeez, Mom, thanks." She shot her mother a look as she sat down. "When did you and Dad get back in town?"

"Just a few hours ago. Isn't it perfect? We can all have dinner together."

Cassie wouldn't have used the word *perfect*. A disaster waiting to happen, maybe; sure-fire embarrassment, for certain.

"Meg said you've just returned from Houston where you were helping with some collection there," her mother said. "Cassie's very well respected in her field," her mother added, smiling at Drew. "Everyone comes to her if they want to know about—what is it you study, dear? I always forget."

"Nineteenth-century English narrative painting." Her mother could remember the temperature on her birthday in 1980, but she couldn't remember Cassie's field of study. Was art history really that boring?

"Isn't she amazing?" her mother exclaimed. "I'm always amazed. Your father is, too, dear. Why, he just said to me the other day—'Isn't Cassie so clever about'—your narrative painting thing. Didn't you, dear?"

The look her father was getting required only one answer. "I certainly did. Hi, pumpkin," her father said with a grin. "Long time no see."

"The fishing was just terrible in Florida this year. Your father was distraught."

"It didn't matter," Jim Hill said. "I had more time for golf."

"But he likes his fishing more. Do you fish, Drew? Everyone in Minnesota fishes."

"I'm from southern Minnesota. There aren't too many lakes where I was raised. We hunted pheasants in the fall."

"Girls, your grandfather Peyton used to hunt pheasants." Her mother's voice implied that Drew had gained the Mothers of America's very largest seal of approval. "The girls just loved their grandfather Peyton, didn't you, girls?"

"Yes, Mom," they both replied, understanding there was no point in arguing with their mother or mentioning that they were three when their grandfather had died.

Mitzi Hill was the dynamo who drove the family. A diminutive redhead who had long since resorted to a chemical version of her original hair color, she kept her husband's social schedule busy and tried whenever she could to do the same for her daughters.

Although she was finding it more difficult to coordinate her daughters' lives since she and her husband had sold the family farm to developers. More wealthy now than they'd ever imagined, they spent six months of the year in Florida. It wasn't that she didn't try to give orders or suggestions or practical advice, as she called it, but her authority was considerably diminished by distance.

For which both of her daughters were supremely grateful.

But now that she was home for the summer, she was making up for lost time.

"You must tell us what do you do for a living," she cooed to Drew.

"I help run my father's bank."

You could practically see the calculator totaling the numbers in Mitzi's head. "Isn't that sweet? Helping your father. In our case," she said, affecting a small stricken look, "neither of the girls wanted to take over the farm. Not that I blame them, of course, with the price of corn lately, but I think Jim would have enjoyed it."

Jim had been watching the suburbs move north for ten years, waiting for the price of land to reach his set point, but he knew better than to disagree with his wife's fiction. "There were times, I suppose," he said, in lieu of an outright lie.

Cassie smiled, and he winked at her. She and her father came from the same mold. Tall, slender, fair-skinned, and with classic features, neither were motivated by a busy social schedule. The only quality Cassie had inherited from her mother was her hair color. She got along with her mother, but they were not personality soulmates. Mitzi liked to set things in motion and give them a good shove. Meg was a chip off the old block.

Cassie and her father were more apt to sit back and watch the action. They participated on occasion, but neither was interested in a full-out marathon every day.

"How long have you been—um . . . helping your father?" Mitzi sweetly inquired.

"Since I graduated from college."

"Where did you go to school, dear?" Mitzi's smile was all gracious charm.

"Harvard."

"My goodness. Isn't that nice? Those Ivy League schools

have a very good reputation. Our Cassie and Meg went to Stanford. They wanted more sun when they were young."

"I don't blame them. Minnesota winters can be long."

"But now both girls are back home, and we just love it, don't we, dear?"

"Couldn't ask for more," Jim Hill said on cue. He didn't fish and golf just for the exercise. Much as he loved his wife—and their thirty-seven-year marriage had been happy—there were times when he needed a break from Mitzi's management skills.

"Meg, pass your sister the beef roast," Mitzi ordered, switching smoothly to her nurturing mother mode. "You look like you could use a good meal, Cassie, dear," she added, her gaze benevolent yet competent in the feel-good style of a TV ad for Johnson and Johnson where a mother soothes and bandages her child's knee. "I don't suppose you've been doing any cooking."

"Not in Houston, Mom. But the Four Seasons had a good chef."

"Obviously, you didn't make use of him. You're thin, darling, maybe just a little too thin. Don't you think so, Meg?"

"I made blueberry pie for dessert," Meg said, as if pie were the answer to every nutritional deficiency.

"My favorite," Oz murmured.

Oz didn't talk much, but then their marriage dynamic was driven by the Mitzi Junior syndrome where his position didn't require much speech. But he didn't seem to mind as long as he could watch the football season on TV with a minimum of interruptions.

Cassie really liked him and his easygoing manner. He was a hands-on dad, too, and could take over and watch the kids without having to ask where their clothes were or when they went to bed or whether one disliked peas and the other carrots. He was involved enough to know. Meg was really lucky.

That thought brought up Cassie's own poignant lack of a significant other, and inexplicably her eyes began to fill with tears. Quickly reaching for her wine glass, she took a few swift gulps and tried to distract her mind with the immediate sensations of a very good, full-bodied, velvety Bordeaux swirling down her throat.

"Tell us about that fancy English collection you worked on," Meg said.

Could Meg tell she was near to embarrassing herself? Was she deliberately jogging her out of her sudden melancholy? Cassie didn't dare look up for a moment until she'd blinked away the wetness in her eyes. "The original Lord Boswick was Chancellor of the Exchequer for Lord Palmerston," she offered and went on to deliver a thumbnail sketch of the collection and the current owner, finishing with a description of the thirty-thousand-square-foot home Bill Spencer and his family occupied.

Then her mother began detailing the numerous six- and ten-million-dollar homes she'd seen in Florida, which pretty well got them through dinner and into the blueberry pie and vanilla ice cream that smoothed over Cassie's hopefully unnoticed awkward moment of near tears.

Fortunately, there was never any lack of conversation with Mitzi and Meg in the same room—a blessing in Cassie's current unstable condition, mood wise. She wasn't capable tonight of any light, vivacious, I'm-your-date-for-the-evening-what-are-your-favorite-books-or-movies kind of conversation. She was more interested in bolting just as soon as she could—no offense to the good-looking, nice, and polite Drew, who seemed to be very mellow about this whole stupid situation.

But it had really hit her somewhere between dessert and coffee, how she wasn't responding even slightly to handsome, pleasant Drew, who might just as well have been a wooden statue seated beside her.

She wasn't getting a single vibe.

She didn't have a scintilla of interest in seeing him again.

She didn't even care if he had ten million dollars of his own money in his daddy's bank. She was completely indifferent to his looks, charm, and status.

Not that she'd ever been concerned with status.

But certainly, she'd never been blind to looks and charm.

Don't go there, her voice of reason warned. *Not even for a second.*

Just stay the hell away.

Maybe she'd drunk too much wine. Maybe the three cups of coffee so late at night were making her shaky—her psyche included. Or maybe she'd been trying so hard not to think of Bobby that her circuits had tripped and all the power stations holding back those thoughts had shut down.

What was he doing now, she wondered? What time was it in his current time zone? Was he with a blonde or a brunette, or had he found another redhead? She never questioned the fact that he'd found company—unlike her. He was pursued big time, and she doubted he was running very fast.

"Cassie! You're daydreaming again!"

Meg's voice brought her back with a start.

"You must be tired, dear," her mother murmured. "She's been working too hard," she added, giving Drew a small, sad smile. "I know her supervisor—what's his name again, dear? Arthur, that's it. Well, he's not a very nice man, and I don't mind saying it. Don't look at me like that, Cassie. He's been married three times, and who knows if he'll be stopping at three. He doesn't seem to realize this isn't Hollywood. And he insists Cassie get to work early when there's really no need for anyone to be at their desk at seven o'clock. Can you imagine seven o'clock? With the terrible rush-hour traffic and all. Well, he's just a dreadful man, and that's a fact."

One of Cassie's greatest fears was that her mother and

Arthur would meet someday because, despite her trouble-some meddling, Mitzi had the heart of a lioness when it came to her daughters' welfare. "He gave me a nice raise, Mom, so he's not all bad," Cassie offered in an effort to soothe the wild beast.

"Well, you deserve one. I'm glad he finally realized it. What with Jay's well—unpleasantness—and you with that big, empty house and all. A little extra income won't hurt. Meg tells me you're divorced, too, Drew. I hope your divorce was more agreeable than poor Cassie's. Although Jay never did strike me as husband material, and I said it more than once."

When Drew didn't reply to such a loaded question, Mitzi prodded. "Are you still on speaking terms with your wife, Drew?"

"We get along." His voice was neutral.

Oz smiled because he knew Drew's wife, and no one got along with her. She gave orders like a drill sergeant, a fact unknown to Drew until after the marriage.

"Were you married long?"

"Six months."

Mitzi's eyes flared wide, and it was obvious to even the most obtuse that she was reconsidering the merits of a man, however rich, if he couldn't stay married more than six months. Her daughter didn't need any more heartache. "How interesting," she said in a tone of voice that was clearly probationary.

And when you said "How interesting" in Minnesota, it meant you didn't like it or you probably weren't going to like it or you thought the particular person, place, or thing was weirder than a three-dollar bill.

For her part, Cassie found the six months thing intriguing. Not enough to actively pursue, but at least Drew wasn't the complete perfect, bland image he projected—handsome, pleasant, heir to his daddy's bank. That six months thing gave him character.

Her smile projected her approval.

"She screamed," he murmured under his breath. "It was a shock."

"Good for you," she murmured back. And she meant it. If she'd had half a brain, she would have dumped Jay the first time he gave her some lame excuse for coming home late. But no, she was willing to forgive and forget. Wasn't that what a mature, reasonable adult was supposed to do? Was she stupid or what?

"I hate blind dates," he whispered.

"No kidding."

"Not tonight, though."

"If only."

"There's someone else Meg doesn't know about?" he said with a grin.

"Maybe when hell freezes over there might be."

His brows rose. "Unrequited love?"

"It wasn't love."

His smile projected a small heat. "Then let me say, if you ever change your mind, give me a call. Your sister has my number."

"I'll keep it in mind. On the other hand, I have a friend who was looking real hard at someone who could have been your twin last night."

"I really do hate blind dates."

"Think about it. She's nice. Her name's Liv, and her number's S-E-E-S-N-O-W. She likes to ski."

"Okay. I'll think about it." He suddenly looked up. "We seem to be alone."

Cassie had noticed her mother shooing everyone out of the dining room, but she wasn't about to say stay and embarrass

Items purchased at Walgreens may be
returned to any of our stores within
30 days of purchase.

Items with a receipt will be exchanged,
refunded in cash, credited to your account,
or refunded to a Walgreens cash value card.

Items without a receipt will be exchanged or
refunded to a Walgreens cash value card.

For any return you may be asked for
acceptable identification.

Items purchased at Walgreens may be
returned to any of our stores within
30 days of purchase.

Items with a receipt will be exchanged,
refunded in cash, credited to your account,
or refunded to a Walgreens cash value card.

Items without a receipt will be exchanged or
refunded to a Walgreens cash value card.

For any return you may be asked for
acceptable identification.

her some more. Apparently, Drew's money had trumped his brief marriage. "Wanna get out of here?"

"Definitely."

"I'll say we're going to a movie. You watch my mom and Meg smile widely like they just picked the winning bachelorette and then we'll make our escape."

"No movie?"

"Sorry."

He grinned. "It was worth a try."

"Has anyone ever told you that you look like the guy on *Sex and the City*?"

"Not more than twenty times a day."

"*Okaaay*. Then pretend I'm Samantha, and follow my lead."

Cassie was right.

They were practically pushed out the door by her sister and mother. She told Drew thanks as they walked to their cars and really meant it. Maybe she should feel guilty about skipping out, she thought, unlocking her car. But she didn't. She felt exhilarated. And the evening hadn't been all bad, she decided, pulling her car out onto the street. The blueberry pie had been prime.

THIRTY-EIGHT

IN THE FOLLOWING MONTH, CASSIE KEPT herself as busy as possible. She actually played tennis with Liv, and she hated tennis. She went into the museum on the weekends, when she rarely did. She worked in her gardens until there wasn't a weed in sight and the flowers were blooming their heads off thanks to her vigilance. Even her temperamental roses were at their peak, the scent and color and riotous growth a testament to her on-the-brink-of-melancholy pampering.

On occasion, Arthur would make some remark about Bobby just to jerk her chain, but she always ignored him and with their personal dynamic shifted, he didn't press the point.

But one day, over lunch in the coffee room, Emma said, "Bobby Serre is back in the States—in Montana. I heard Arthur talking to him—something about an insurance report."

It shouldn't have mattered. Whether Bobby was in Europe or Montana or down the block had no impact on her life. He lived in a different world—one with legions of women clamoring for his body. A world that had nothing to do with her. "I imagine he's living the good life as usual," she said, trying not to sound bitter or rejected or *dejected*. And failing miserably.

"You could call him, you know. What do you have to lose?"

"My self-respect. He's not waiting for a phone call from me."

"How do you know? You two seemed to get along pretty well while he was here."

"*While he was here* is the operative phrase. He's the poster child for that old Bob Dylan song, 'Like a Rolling Stone.'"

"Montana's not so far," Emma said, pressing the point because Cassie had been in the doldrums since Bobby left. "I could get his address. Arthur must have it."

"Perfect. So I show up on his doorstep, he opens the door and says, 'I didn't order any pizza,' or 'The cleaning ladies have already been here,' the possibility that he'd actually remember me totally erased by the ten thousand females that have passed through his life since May."

"And then you say, 'I'm not wearing any panties,'" Emma said with a grin, "and he'll let you in."

Cassie laughed. "The worst thing about that scenario is you're probably right."

"I know I'm right."

Cassie grinned. "Personal experience?"

"Try it. It works every time."

"I wish I had the audacity."

"Well, if you ever change your mind, let me know. I'll give you his phone number."

IN THE SAME general time frame, Bobby Serre was out of phone range, as he'd been for most of the last month. After sitting on his porch for approximately one and a half minutes, he'd called his cousin who lived on a ranch in the valley and asked him if he wanted to hang out in the mountains for a while.

"How long a while?" Charlie Wolf asked.

"A week or two."

"Or three or four—I know you. My wife will complain. But tell you what. I'll go with you for a week and see if Marlys sends up one of the kids to get me. If she doesn't, I'll stay longer."

"Great. How's tomorrow for you?"

"Afternoon will do. That'll give me time to settle things with my foreman . . . and Marlys."

"I'll ride over about four."

The men had ridden their ponies up into the Madison Range where they'd spent weeks and months as youths. And when Marlys hadn't complained, Charlie had stayed another week. But his oldest son came to get him after the second week, and when Charlie got home he told Marlys he hadn't seen Bobby so bummed out since Cathy Sue Gardener had turned him down for the tenth-grade homecoming dance.

The fact that Bobby Serre was thinking seriously about a woman was a hot topic of conversation at the Dugout Bar in town. Not that he'd actually mentioned her name, Charlie had said, but he and Bobby had been close since they could walk, and this was the Cathy Sue syndrome all over again. He'd bet his best palomino mustang on it.

Bobby came down from the mountains toward the end of the month, unshaven and noticeably thinner, his skin even darker from the sun, his hair pulled back in a ponytail, his palms calloused from weeks of riding. He was planning on meeting his folks and brother in Nantucket for the Fourth, he told Charlie. Then he'd probably go over to France for the rest of the summer. Something about a new manager at his place over there, Charlie told all the regulars at the Dugout Bar. Then conversation shifted to Cathy Sue, who had gone on to Hollywood and was one of those presenters on *The Price Is Right*. Everyone thought she still looked mighty sharp in a strapless gown.

THIRTY-NINE

CASSIE HAD BEEN AVOIDING THINKING about the Fourth. She'd always loved the holiday, ever since she was a kid and her whole family had packed up and gone into their small town—that had since become a suburb—and took part in the festivities. They'd sit on the lawn chairs her father had brought in the back of the pickup truck on a strategically located curb and watch the parade go by: the recycled floats sporting area princesses and queens; the Cub Scouts and Brownies in their uniforms; the Legion ladies and Color Guard, who got a little fatter every year; the clowns from the Shriners in the cities; the local school band in their wool uniforms that made them faint on the really hot Fourth of Julys; the implement dealer's son driving their hundred-thousand-dollar John Deere with air-conditioning and a TV; the retirees from Green Acres in the horse and buggy; and every pickup truck driver in town who wanted to get into the parade.

Then, when the parade was over, everyone would walk the few blocks to the town park, where the carnival had been set up, and ride all the rides and eat cotton candy, mini-donuts, grilled corn on the cob, and pork chops on a stick until they almost puked. And the street dance at night was fun for all ages, the adults tolerating the little kids getting in their way on the temporary Second Avenue asphalt dance floor between Maple and Main.

But Cassie couldn't get herself in the mood this Fourth. The small town was more or less swallowed up by the suburbs, and everyone was going up to the lake anyway, she told herself, as if that hadn't been true for the past ten years. But she was looking hard for reasons to stay home, particularly because her mother and sister had been pressing her to come up to the lake. So far, she'd been able to fend off their appeals.

So far, she thought, glancing at the cell phone beside her on the bed, the ring vibrating through her still more or less empty bedroom.

It was Meg's number on the screen.

Be a grown-up.

Answer it.

Reluctantly, her hand went to the phone and even more reluctantly, she hit the talk button and put the phone to her ear.

"We're going up to the lake tonight. We'll stop by and pick you up."

"I'll come up tomorrow. I have some reports to finish tonight."

"On the day before the Fourth? You've got the whole weekend. Bring them with you. I'll help you."

"It's an inventory of some drawings. I'm matching them with a catalogue raisonne. But thanks for the offer. Tell Mom I'll see you all tomorrow."

"I can't get you to change your mind?"

"I'll be up in the morning. The traffic won't be so bad."

"Promise?"

"Yeah, promise," Cassie lied, figuring she'd have all night to come up with a really good excuse. "Drive carefully."

Her mother must have been working her mental telepathy because Cassie had no more than clicked off the phone than it rang again.

"I'm not going to let you sit home and mope on the Fourth. And your father agrees with me. Don't you, Jim?" Mitzi shouted.

"Hi, Mom." Cassie pictured her mom in the kitchen at the lake and her dad out on the deck drinking a beer and reading his paper like he always did. Then he watched the evening news and ate supper. There was something comforting about the regularity of his schedule, undeterred by rain, snow, or dark of night. But not quite comforting enough to induce her to spend a weekend at the lake with her family when it was so much easier to remain immobile before her TV screen.

"Your dad says you have to come up," Mitzi commanded. "He'll take you fishing."

"Thanks, Mom. I already talked to Meg. I'll be up tomorrow. The traffic won't be so bad." Or in her case, nonexistent, but she wasn't suicidal. She continued the lie. "Do you want anything from Tobie's?"

"That's sweet, dear. A dozen of the raised donuts and some of those maple frosted long Johns your father likes. And drive carefully."

"Yes, Mom."

How easy it was to lie over the phone. No one could see your eyes or whether you were blinking like crazy. Or that your bed looked like a garbage dump after a day in bed— she hadn't dared tell her family she hadn't been to work. Just like she hadn't told anyone at work that she wasn't really going up north early for the Fourth.

Because getting in her car and driving up north would

require she first work up enough energy to pick up the sticky ice-cream sandwich wrappers on her bed and the two almost empty bags of salt and vinegar chips and the nearly empty carton of malted milk balls—okay *empty,* but you couldn't tell by looking so she was allowed her delusions. She'd thought about getting up and making herself a chocolate milkshake for a really long time, but that would have required mega-watts more initiative than she currently possessed.

In fact, she was seriously wondering if she'd contracted mono, she was soo lethargic. Although the only person she could have possibly contracted mono from was thousands of miles away, oblivious of her and, let's face it, so physically fit he couldn't possibly be unwell.

The reminder of Bobby's superb fitness almost made her sorry she hadn't been enough of a modern woman or pervert—depending on your view of sexual amusements—to have taped an evening or two of his splendid body and in-credible endurance. If she *had* been so inclined, she would have had the additional possibility of becoming fabulously wealthy like that man who taped spring break in Florida and Mexico using all the drunken, half-naked coeds on the beaches and was now residing in a multimillion-dollar home in Beverly Hills.

If it was possible to black out her face somehow, she would definitely be inclined to consider such a proposal be-cause Bobby Serre really should be available for the masses. Or at least as long as he didn't want her, he should.

She wasn't being vindictive—okay . . . maybe just a little. But really, if she had tons of money she might be completely happy again. Not that Bobby hadn't been more than generous with Arthur's money. All her bills were paid now, her bank account was smiling, and someday, when she felt more like shopping, she'd actually go buy some furniture for her house.

She'd get the chair paid for by Bobby Serre and the couch paid for by Bobby Serre and the dining room table he'd wanted, kind of like the house that Jack built, only hers would be the house that Bobby furnished.

Could she get on the Home and Garden Network with her makeover funded uniquely by hot sex? Was there a niche market for such a show?

Don't be bitter, she told herself. *Think of yourself as the recipient of pleasure formerly beyond imagination. Think of yourself as Bobby Serre's starlet in Minneapolis. Think of yourself as a thirty-two-year-old woman who will never again meet a man to compare. And I don't care what anyone says,* she thought. *That would make* anyone *bitter.*

She desperately needed a drink or a chocolate bar or both.

Sliding over her wrappers and crumpled bags, she rolled out of bed, walked into her kitchen, and rummaged through her cupboards. After a certain amount of cursing, she managed to ferret out a single bar of Valrhona hidden behind a tin of steel-cut oatmeal that had to be at least two years old, remnant of one of her temporary fits of good nutrition. It remained unopened.

The Valrhona, however, was not.

It was half-eaten. Damn.

Like a recent escapee from a fat farm, she scarfed down the bar in a few seconds, licking the wrapping afterward for any small scraps that yet remained.

She was becoming really pathetic.

Get a grip, she silently commanded. *No man is that good. No man is worth this amount of ennui and brooding. For God's sake, not more than two months ago you'd resolved to remain celibate indefinitely.*

So indefinitely has arrived.

Simply embrace it, she told herself, *like some enlightened guru might or a yogi who was completely centered.*

There. She felt better. The no-man-is-worth-it mantra would be her guiding light.

Having gently bitch-slapped her psyche, she took out a chilled bottle of champagne she'd been saving for an occasion, telling herself self-actualization and personal validation were certainly an occasion and man-handled the top off. Men always made twisting off a champagne cork look so easy. In her current easily irritated mood concerning men, that annoyed her, too—not as much as their seemingly innate need to be a rolling stone—but mildly.

She would find something self-indulgent on TV to watch.

She would soothe her bruised ego with this—mmm—very nice champagne while she watched. How opportune, she noted, checking out her cable guide—Exxon Mobil Masterpiece Theatre was showing *Warrior Queen*. That's just what she needed—a story about an upstart female warrior in first-century Britain who takes her revenge against the might and power of Rome.

Yay! Female power!

You go, girl!

The fact that Queen Boudica died a miserable death in the end, if she recalled her history, did not at the moment sabotage Cassie's reinvigorated female power sensitivities.

Had Queen Boudica not killed a great number of men who had done her wrong before her tragic demise?

Such a soothing thought.

FORTY

BOBBY HAD VISITED FOR TWO DAYS IN Nantucket. The weather was perfect, the town was mobbed with tourists, and he was playing uncle to his brother's kids and teaching them how to sail. Strange, though, despite a seemingly idyllic holiday, he couldn't shake his discontent. No matter where he was or who he was with or what he was doing. If he didn't know better, he would have ascribed his moodiness to overindulgence. But no monk could have lived a more austere life than he the last few weeks.

Even his mother had asked, "Are you coming down with something?"

His brother had said instead, "What you need is a night on the town."

That night consisted of several hours too many drinking in the local pubs and one helluva headache this morning.

With his sour mood undiminished.

But he took his nephews for their sailing lesson, and for a few brief hours, he forgot what was more or less constantly on his mind. Once back on dry land, however, his specters of gloom returned.

He talked with his father that evening about the new manager at their estate in Avignon, told him he was going over soon, and they compared notes on what had to be done. He played the piano for his mother because she always insisted and he didn't have the heart to tell her he only played when he was home. But he went through his repertoire of all her favorite songs, ignored his brother's jibes, played one or two of his sister-in-law's special requests, and excused himself for the night.

"Something's wrong," his mother said when he'd gone.

"He needs a haircut, for one thing," his brother said, his own surfer locks short for easy upkeep.

"I think he's in love," his sister-in-law said.

Everyone thought *what does she know,* because his family knew him so much better. Even when Bobby had married Claire, no one had been under the illusion it was for love.

"That'll be the day," his brother said.

"I think you're wrong."

"Maybe Alexis is right," his mother said politely, her PR background coming to the rescue.

"If he is, he'll let us know in his own good time," his father said. A man of a pragmatic bent, he rarely engaged in the art of possibility.

So as Bobby packed his carry-on upstairs, his family discussed him.

When he returned downstairs, he stood in the arched opening between the front hallway and the living room as though already poised for escape. "I hired a plane to take me to the mainland. There's a matter I have to look into. I'll call you in a few days."

"See," Alexis proudly said.

"Where are you going?" his brother asked.

"West," Bobby said.

"Anyplace special?" his mother asked.

"Leave the boy alone," his father said.

"I'll give you a call when I get there."

The front screen door slammed a second later.

"He won't call." Jake smirked at his wife.

"Wrong, wrong, wrong." Alexis had a feeling. "You just wait and see."

FORTY-ONE

SELF-INDULGENCE WAS ALL WELL AND GOOD, Cassie decided, as long as an entire bottle of champagne wasn't included in the scenario. She had a mother of a headache, and what little energy she possessed yesterday had entirely disappeared.

Could she get a delivery of waffles with blueberry sauce, whipping cream, and a side order of Canadian bacon and fresh squeezed orange juice?

She knew the answer, which further lowered her mood.

She would be obliged to actually shower, dress, and drive somewhere to get the sustenance she desperately required.

Just as she was debating whether her head would crack open if she moved, the phone rang—a particularly jarring sound in her current condition. She could neither move fast nor make the phone stop ringing by shouting at it, but eventually she was able to reach it and, hitting the talk button, grumpily said, "Hello."

"Good morning, sunshine," Liv said. "Am I interrupting something?"

"I wish, although not right now because my head is splitting open, which would no doubt deter any possible pleasure."

"Come with me to Drew's party. A couple quick Bloody Marys and you'll feel like new."

"Please . . . I'm going to barf. Do not mention alcohol ever again."

"Okay, fine, but get dressed and I'll pick you up in twenty minutes. Drew's taking his yacht down to Lake Pepin. You'll love it."

"You'll love it, I won't."

"Drew said he invited someone you have to meet. It's only fair, he says, as you gave him my phone number."

Liv and Drew had been seeing each other for three weeks, their instant rapport such that they were seriously thinking of buying into the soulmates theory.

"Come on," Liv cajoled. "You don't want to sit home alone on the Fourth. I won't take no for an answer."

"No, no, and no, but thank you for asking for the thousandth time. I appreciate your persistence."

"It's not good for you to be by yourself on the Fourth."

"Believe me, I'd ruin any party I attended. I've been in a foul mood for—"

"Six weeks?"

"Am I pathetic or what? Tell me to snap out of it."

"Snap out of it and come with me. You'll enjoy yourself."

"I can't . . . really. You have a good time *for* me."

Liv knew that tone, soft but final. Like all the other times she'd asked her to come along. "You're sure now?"

"I'm sure. Actually, I've been thinking of going to every movie at the Lagoon today. It's dark in there so I can hide from the Fourth, those foreign films are slow moving so I don't have to think too fast—which would be difficult today—and their popcorn has real butter on it. Not to mention they have

espresso and prime chocolate." Just thinking about the popcorn, espresso, and chocolate made her mouth water. Maybe
she'd try to make the first movie at twelve thirty. Then she
could eat her breakfast there.

"If you change your mind, call me."

"Will do."

Both of them knew she wouldn't.

But mildly energized by the prospect of junk food, after
she said her good-byes to Liv, Cassie gingerly rolled out of
bed, managed to remain standing in the shower long enough
to wash, and, after resting on the bed briefly, dressed. The
summer air revived her somewhat as she walked to her car,
and shortly after, she was on her way to the Lagoon.

Two of the five movies on the billboards actually looked
like something she'd like to see. The other three would tax
her intellect or credulity, but she could always sleep in the
slow spots. She looked like someone who binged on food
as she gave her tickets to the usher, loaded down as she
was with the super-colossal tub of butter popcorn, a grande
espresso, three chocolate bars, and a Dove bar for good
measure.

Then she found a seat in the middle of the back row and
settled back to wallow in her misery.

The first movie featured an aging French film star she'd
always loved, but the camera was not kind and the role the
actress played unkinder still. Before the movie had reached
its midpoint, Cassie was crying. Not just because the movie
was sad but because the film star's weathered face reminded
her of how quickly life passed one by.

By her third chocolate bar, however, her endorphins had
kicked in sufficiently to raise her spirits to the point where
tears weren't streaming down her face. She was grateful, because she'd forgotten to bring Kleenex and the popcorn napkins were the kind that melted away when they became wet.

The second movie was some kind of horror show and not the funny kind, but the really gruesome kind, so she spent the entire movie looking at the back of her seat. The only good thing about it was she didn't cry once.

By the third movie, she'd run out of food, but all those carbs had more or less put her into a semi-sleep state, so the male coming-of-age film served as backdrop to her nap.

Revived by her brief slumber, she bought some jujubes—the Lagoon's selection of candy was gigantic and dispensed from tall plastic tubes you could manipulate yourself. Her bag of jujubes turned out to be very large because she didn't quite know how to shut the spout. But she consoled herself with the fact that jujubes didn't get old, bought a small cream soda to wash them down, and entered the fourth movie resupplied.

FORTY-TWO

THE AIRPORT WAS DESERTED ON THE AFTER-
noon of the Fourth, which would have been a plus if
the cab stand outside hadn't been deserted as well.

Swearing because he'd spent the last twenty hours in various airports and airplanes trying to make connections on
short notice, Bobby reentered the terminal and leaped down
the escalator to the rental car counters on the underground
level.

Shit. Three were closed. One had a long line. Two shorter
lines. He opted for the shorter line closest to him. And then
he gnashed his teeth as the elderly woman in front of him
insisted on a blue car instead of the white one they had. After way too long, she was finally convinced that insisting on
a blue car wasn't going to make one materialize in the Avis
parking ramp and bitterly agreed to take the white sedan.
Bobby almost said about ten times, "Give her a Mercedes
and I'll pay for it if she'd only move." But he resisted the
impulse because, knowing her, she'd spend another twenty
minutes trying to get the right color upholstery.

When he finally reached the counter, he said, "Give me anything. I don't care."

The clerk's eyes lit up.

Ten minutes later, Bobby was driving out of the parking ramp in a loaded black SUV Navigator that smelled of weed and beer and cheap cologne. Rolling down the windows, he told himself it didn't matter that someone had had a party in the car. He had wheels. He was finally in Minneapolis. And one way or another, he would put an end to the craving that had been screwing up his life.

Although he wasn't unduly optimistic about finding Cassie.

It was the Fourth of July, after all.

And most people other than he had somewhere or something to do.

Or something they *wanted* to do.

He drove to Cassie's first, just in case he was lucky.

He might have known the way his life had been going lately.

No one was home.

He called 411, got Meg's phone number, and struck out. A message machine saying they were up at the lake wouldn't do him much good when they wouldn't be back for three more days.

His tension levels were higher than high. But he'd had plenty of time in the last twenty hours to imagine Cassie in bed with someone else. A whole bunch of someone elses. Why he thought she might be home today anyway made him question his sanity.

But he was obsessed, plain and simple. And sanity wasn't necessarily a player today.

Racking his brain, he discarded the possibility of calling Arthur. As if he'd know anyway where Cassie was. As if he wanted to bring Arthur into his obsession and have him leer at him for the next twenty years. Who the hell else did he know who knew Cassie? It wasn't as though they'd socialized a lot when he'd been in town. Unless talking to people from Cassie's bed counted.

Liv. She'd called. He'd even met her. What the hell was her last name? High-priced lawyer wouldn't work. Tennis player wouldn't fly. Go through the fucking alphabet. A. B. C. D. Dunn, no *Duncan,* as in the dancer who'd died with the scarf around her neck. He saw the film. *Lavinia* Duncan. The name flashed into his brain bordered in gold. *Yessss!*

411 was very helpful, that recorded voice nice and efficient.

His fingers literally raced over his cell phone keys.

One ring, *pick up, pick up,* two rings, *damn,* three rings. What did he expect? It was the Fourth. Four rings and then a small click. It was rolling over. *Thank you, thank you, thank you,* he silently crowed, victory, success, good fortune within his grasp.

Until the rational part of his brain reminded him that Liv might not know where Cassie was, and if she did, Cassie could very well be with *someone.*

His victory parade came to a sudden halt.

"Hello?"

He'd had that chill moment to come down, and when he spoke, his voice was calm. "Liv? This is Bobby Serre. Do you know where Cassie is today?"

"Where are you? Are you here or somewhere else?"

"I'm in town. I apologize for calling. I realize it's the Fourth." He could hear a party going on in the background.

"Not a problem. I think I know where she is," Liv said, deliberately speaking in her expressionless attorney voice, not knowing why Bobby Serre was here and whether he would be good news or bad news for Cassie. On the other hand, there was no way she was going to let him get away without giving Cassie a chance. "I'll give you directions."

"Thanks," Bobby said when she'd finished with the lengthy explanation. "I've been en route for twenty hours. I really appreciate your help."

"Say hi from me," Liv said, feeling better now. Any man who traveled twenty hours on the Fourth weekend must be serious about something. And even if it was just about sex, what the hell, there was no sense knocking pleasure.

FORTY-THREE

HE GOT LOST TWICE, LIV'S DIRECTIONS leaving something to be desired. But he stopped at two gas stations for help and finally found his way to the Lagoon. The parking lot was nearly empty at five o'clock on the Fourth. Most people were where they wanted to be or thinking about supper.

He parked the SUV and seriously thought about leaving the windows open to air it out before visualizing a stripped interior and coming to his senses.

When he reached the theater, he had no idea which movie Cassie was in, although Liv had said Cassie was planning on seeing them all. So he bought five tickets, gave them to the usher, who thought to himself, *two weirdos in one day,* and backed up a step because Bobby Serre was a very large weirdo.

And the usher's assessment held strong as he watched Bobby walk into the first movie, only to emerge ten minutes later and walk down the corridor to the second movie. Another ten minutes and he was back out in the hall. The usher was wondering if he should call 911 and report a killer on the prowl. It reminded him of that film where the ex-wife is hiding from her stalker ex-husband in a movie theater.

As Bobby entered the third movie, the usher began debating the options and or responsibilities required of a minimum-wage job.

Bobby stood in the dark, letting his eyes become accustomed to the gloom, the flickering image on the screen drawing his gaze. A man and woman were standing beside a piano in a bar that had a vaguely Moroccan décor. Their dialogue was familiar, the woman speaking with a taut restlessness, the man only distantly polite, while the piano player kept looking from one to the other. Christ, had someone done a modern version of *Casablanca* in *India?*—a Hindu goddess suddenly coming into his line of vision on the far right of the bar.

Not that unrequited love wasn't a universal theme, he supposed, sort of like—he wasn't about to label what he was feeling as love . . . but something in that general zip code.

Then he caught his breath or maybe he stopped breathing. It was a toss-up. *Exhale, inhale, keep it going,* he told himself, and checked out the back row again.

There she was, crying her eyes out, a Kleenex to her nose. But she looked great. Greater than great—because she was *alone.*

Okay. Relax. Relax. So you've been traveling for twenty hours. If she tells you to go to hell you can always go back to—fuck if he knew where.

And that was the problem with feeling the way he was feeling.

No matter where he went, he couldn't get away from the damnable craving.

The Indian movie wasn't a big winner. With the exception of an elderly couple closer to the front and a couple punkers with spiked hair and chains on the far aisle, Cassie pretty much had the theater to herself.

Okay, gear up. Christ, he hadn't been this nervous since his first date—which had turned out to be a disaster. *Don't go there,* his voice of reason suggested. *Stay on plan.*

That would have been really great, *if he had one.*

Apologize. That always works.

And knowing if he'd had any better ideas they would have come to him during his tedious, much-too-long journey, he decided to go with it.

OHMYGOD, SOME MAN *is coming to sit by me. Don't look. Pretend you're engrossed in the movie. The theater's practically empty. Why does he have to sit here?*

Cassie moved her arm from the arm rest on her left as he approached and leaned to her right, feeling uncomfortable, her pulse racing, thinking this is what came of sitting alone in a movie theater on the Fourth of July when normal people were with their friends or families.

"I want to apologize."

She practically fainted. She didn't, but her arms flew out in some bizarre counterreaction to her fight-or-flight anxiety and her tub of popcorn, or what remained of her popcorn, tumbled from her lap and fell on his feet.

His. Him. *He was here!*

Bobby ignored the slimy popcorn covering his sandaled feet and said, "Do you mind if I sit down?"

"I thought you were some pervert—I mean . . . Thank God you're not. What are you doing here? How did you find me? Where did you come from? You look thinner." The light from the movie screen illuminated his lean form, his high cheekbones starkly defined in chiaroscuro. Maybe he'd been desperately ill and couldn't get in touch with her while he was unconscious in some remote village hospital in France.

He sat down next to her, figuring that long list of questions was a conditional yes at least. "Need a Kleenex?" he said, offering her a pack he'd bought at one of the numerous airports he'd passed through.

Oh, God, she was all tear-streaked and puffy-eyed, and she was still holding the crushed popcorn napkins under her nose, frozen in shock as she was. Sliding her hand beside her leg, she discarded the wet, soggy mess of popcorn napkins as discreetly as possible, dropping them on the floor behind her feet. Then she said, "Thanks," like she was perfectly madeup and self-assured and took his packet of Kleenex from him. "I forgot my Kleenex," she added, mentally bashing herself over the head a second later for sounding so freaking uncool. "I mean—that is—"

"You look great."

Was he saying that out of pity, like you tell a young child their drawing of Mommy is wonderful when she has a stick body and the wrong color hair and only two fingers on each stick hand?

"I missed you."

Hallelujah! It was a *real* great, not a pity great. And he'd *missed* her. How unbelievably fabulous was that?

"I thought of you, too," she said mildly, playing a role right out of some Jane Austen novel where the decorous heroine never actually says what she's feeling to the hero and then the story can go on for another two hundred pages because of all the misunderstandings.

"I'm glad."

Jesus, had he read Jane Austen, too? She wasn't getting a lot of information here.

"I'm glad you're glad," she replied probably because her brain wasn't really functioning after nothing but junk food for the past four hours and had literally ground to a halt. She really wanted to say, *Why the hell are you here?* "Why are you here?" she blurted out, instantly mortified that her sluggish brain apparently had found a spurt of energy.

"Could we go somewhere?"

"For what?" So that was it. He must be in town on some layover between flights and thought he'd have a quick lay. Typical.

"Whatever you want."

She'd heard that phrase before, always in a sexual context, and she really wasn't in the mood to indulge him in his quickie after missing him desperately—and *not* in the quickie context—for weeks. "I'm watching the movie right now."

Her voice had taken on an edge. What the hell had he said wrong? "Do you mind if I watch it with you?" He was walking on eggshells here, he could tell.

"Suit yourself."

Jesus, he hated that tone. And where in the past he would have walked away from female affront in a second flat, he bit the bullet. "It looks like a remake of *Casablanca*. I always liked that movie."

"It's not a remake. It's a new interpretation."

Okeydokey. Maybe he'd be better off keeping his mouth shut. At least she hadn't told him to take a hike. He sat quietly and watched the movie, the dubbing slightly off the mark so the sound came a fraction of a second after the actors' mouths formed the words. That made him zone out real fast, which gave him a better opportunity to surreptitiously watch Cassie out of the corner of his eye.

God, why was she so klutzy? Why hadn't she said something smart and clever and just the tiniest bit cutting instead of the stupid remark she had made that in no way made him understand that she wasn't going to be his Fly-Over Land wham, bam, thank you ma'am fuck? On the other hand, he did look noticeably thinner, so maybe she was maligning him unfairly when he'd really boarded a plane the instant the doctors gave him leave to take out his IVs. Should she offer some sympathetic comment that would allow him to open up and tell her the whole sad story of his near-terminal illness? "Why are you so thin?" she witlessly said, sounding tactless and maladroit instead of poised and concerned in such a way that would indicate not only compassion but a willingness to listen to his sad tale.

He was clearly taken aback, she could see, and in an effort to smooth over her gaucherie, she blundered on, "I mean you look as though you might have been sick or—"

"I was busy and forgot about eating, I suppose," he said carefully, as though he were weighing each word should it be loaded with C-4.

She just hated those male answers that never elaborated in any way and made you more inquisitive than you already were. *Busy with what?* "Busy with what?" she asked bluntly, figuring she had nothing to lose at this point in regard to her image. And if she wasn't going to sleep with him anyway, how could it hurt? *Hey, wait a minute, her inner voice protested. Don't make any hasty decisions.*

"I went up in the mountains in Montana with my cousin last month. You have to pack all your food up there, and I guess I stayed a little longer than I planned."

"What was your cousin's name?" Was she subtle or what? Male or female would be instantly evident.

"Charlie."

Shit. Some women were called Charlie as a nickname. Should she pursue this or pretend indifference. What the hell. "Is Charlie a man or a woman?"

He smiled, feeling for the first time since he saw her that he might have a chance. "A man. You're jealous."

"Am not."

"Well, I'm jealous of you. I've been imagining you out with all kinds of men, and it's been driving me crazy."

"It has?" she cooed precisely like women she'd always found disgusting. "I mean, you have? Thank you."

"You don't have to thank me. To be perfectly honest, I would have preferred not feeling that way."

Was that a rude remark or true and open candor that was the bedrock of any deep and fulfilling relationship? "To be perfectly honest," she replied, "I've spent a moment or two thinking of you with other women as well." Add ten thousand and double it, but it never paid to look anxious in these early phases of a profound and lasting relationship.

"I haven't been dating much. At all, actually."

Was it possible for a choir of angels to appear in a film made in India? Did they have angels per se, or only gods and goddesses? Was it gods and goddesses she heard breaking into song? Was she simply giddy with too much sugar? Or had he really said, *he had not been dating at all!!!* "I see," she said in a cool voice that sounded strange in her ears, like she might have been interrogating a mass murderer and he'd finally given up the location of the first grave, which meant she couldn't react or he'd stop talking.

"Yeah. You've had a real impact on my life."

Ohmygod. *She* had an impact on *his* movie-star life? How could that be? She lived in Minneapolis. But her sugar-saturated brain wouldn't be restrained and she said, kind of dreamily, "I've missed you a lot, really a lot," when any of *The Rules* books would rap you over the knuckles for being so gauche as to tell a man you've only slept with a few times—okay, maybe more than a few times—that you really missed him.

"I thought I might stay in town for a while, if that's okay with you?"

"I'd love it," she said almost shyly.

"Do you want to watch the whole movie?"

Whoa. Maybe there was a small fraction of *The Rules* girl in her after all, because she didn't want to immediately jump into bed with him the very first moment he asked. "I would," she said, ultra politely so he wouldn't take it the wrong way and leave. It was a gamble, and she was already forming some excuse that would allow her to gracefully change her mind when he said, "Okay. Do you want some more popcorn?"

Only if you want me to barf on you, she thought. "No, thank you," she said sweetly, feeling all fluttery inside that he was willing to do whatever she wanted. Feeling like she was in high school again and out on a date.

"I'm going to get some. I'll be right back."

She had a moment of panic thinking he could walk away and never return, but she squelched that pre–*I am woman* sensation. Although she did add for safe measure, "Would you bring me a small Cherry Coke?"

It was terrible, really, that manipulation and subterfuge were so much a part of these dating/sleeping together rituals. But it was all about saving face. And it beat having to run after him and scream, "Don't go!" should he fail to return in an acceptable amount of time.

When he came back, his feet were wiped off, although he didn't mention it and he handed Cassie her Coke and sat down and began eating his butter popcorn. It tasted good, better than anything had tasted for a long time, and he wondered if the butter and popcorn were some special kind or if his taste buds had begun working again now that he maybe had his life back. But even maybe was better than what he'd had the past month or so, and he was grateful.

The movie was terrible, but he tried to look interested.

The movie was terrible, but she refused to say, "Let's go home and get naked." It was a matter of principle.

But when he put his arm around her shoulders, she almost sighed with pleasure.

He could tell. He felt as though he was on safer ground, like he wasn't scaling Everest without a Sherpa guide.

Is this what the Cinderella story was all about? she thought. *About this feeling and not the fancy dress and glass slipper and getting revenge on nasty stepsisters? This warm, sweet, melty feeling of happiness and well-being. Oh, oh, oh and that, too.* With his hand on her shoulder, his fingertips had brushed the upper curve of her breast, kindling an instant, avaricious, lustful need that wasn't sweet and melty at all, that seemed heedless to *Rules* decorum, that was hotter than hot.

She gently arched her back, shut her eyes, and began believing in miracles.

As her breasts rose, his fingers sank into her soft flesh, and her eagerness triggered a flood of feeling—part sexual, part sweet nostalgia, another part end-of-the-rainbow emotion too new to fully understand. But he was very happy to be here. There was no question.

She half turned her head, and he kissed her gently, gently, grateful and content and sexually primed like he was whenever she was near. But he wasn't going there until someone asked. Until it was crystal clear.

He kissed her and she kissed him back, the darkness a benevolent shield against reality, against all the unasked questions and unpalatable answers. And turning in his seat, he pulled her closer, wanting more of her.

The tub of popcorn on his lap tumbled to the floor.

Abruptly curtailing their kiss.

"We're making a helluva mess here," Bobby murmured, kicking the popcorn aside.

"Ick," Cassie said with a grimace. "My feet."

"Want me to wash them?" He held up his hand at her startled look. "Sorry. I wasn't going to make any moves."

She smiled. "I know. Me, too."

"This is very strange."

"How strange?"

Women always wanted to know everything, even when you didn't know yourself. "I'm-walking-on-eggshells strange."

"This movie sucks. What do you think?"

Was this a quiz? "It's interesting, I guess."

She gave him an assessing look. "You're on your best behavior."

"Oh, yeah. Big time."

"Because?"

"I don't want to piss you off."

"Ah."

"Don't say 'ah' like that. I'm not here for sex, okay?"

There were pluses and minuses to his statement, depending on whether she was going to go with her feelings or give lip service to the law of the dating jungle—you know, the one that said you can't look too easy or you'll end up on the wrong side of that Madonna/whore balance sheet. "It looks like you're at least thinking about sex," she said sweetly, reaching over and measuring the length of his erection with a brushing stroke, figuring she'd go with her feelings and worry about male idiosyncrasies about piety at some later date.

"I've been thinking about sex from the moment I met you."

"Sounds good," she whispered, gently squeezing his erection, watching it surge upward, feeling her body open in response—their sexual yin-yang still as fine-tuned as ever.

"Hey," he said on a soft exhalation. "If you don't stop what you're doing I'm going to have a mess on my hands."

She instantly released her grip. "So if I want satisfaction," she murmured with a smile, "I'm thinking maybe it's my turn first."

His grin flashed in the dimness. "Don't be shy."

"Why would I want to be shy?"

His smile broadened, remembering what he liked best about her. "You have to be quiet, then."

"No, I don't."

Okaaay. What the hell, he didn't know any of these four other people. Reaching over, he began to unbutton her blouse.

"Not in here," she hissed, brushing his hands away.

Like there were some rules of decorum. Fine. He was adaptable. No foreplay. Smoothly shifting his focus, he slipped his hand under her short denim skirt and did what he was told. Not that he minded. She could tell him to do this anytime.

Slipping his fingers between her panties and silky curls, he buried two fingers in her hot, wet cunt and instantly wondered if he was going to be able to keep from coming. It had been way too long, and he wasn't a man who had any practice with celibacy. Jesus, she was slippery wet and panting already as though she wasn't planning on waiting. *As usual,* he thought, glancing around to see who was looking, although he was fast approaching the point of no return when he didn't give a shit if anyone was looking or not.

Like. Right. Fucking. Now.

It was going to be both their turns, he decided, or, to be perfectly honest, his cock decided.

Unzipping his shorts with his other hand, he freed himself for action then swung her out of her seat.

She gasped, realizing what he was going to do, but not likely to resist with such a heavenly trade in the offing. Oh, oh, oh—actually in effect, she reflected, sighing with pleasure as he lowered her down his cock with finesse. Not a fumble anywhere; really, he was amazing. Of course, it helped that he was muscled like a stevedore and capable of making her feel light as a feather—a powerful aphrodisiac rarely mentioned in those lists of aphrodisiacs. Or maybe they just were made to fit together superbly—that yin-yang thing. Maybe in all this world, they'd found the perfect match, the perfect sexual wavelength.

He was thinking the same thing, although it was up to him to fine-tune the wavelength so he wouldn't come before she did.

Luckily, he'd had lots of practice.

Ohmygod, ohmygod—was this nirvana or what? She wasn't going to be so crass as to actually consider the word *soul mate,* but primal birds and bees mating as in the animal kingdom was for sure undeniably true. And right this second she had the feeling she was on an out-of-control roller coaster going downhill full speed ahead.

Her climax swamped her a second later, and she screamed just like on a roller coaster; but he was prepared, having been a Boy Scout, or maybe it was the number of times he'd heard her scream that tipped him off. He covered her mouth with his just in time and then allowed his own orgasm to blast off.

He came and came and came, gasping for breath at the end as though his body was drained of everything, including air.

She collapsed on his shoulder, panting, the wild tumult of her orgasm slowly melting away in a blissful glow. "Tell me—no one—saw," she gasped, her breath warm on his throat.

He glanced up to see four moviegoers staring at them. "No one saw," he said, perjuring himself willingly. "Everyone's watching the movie."

"We should go . . . as soon—as I—can walk."

"Want me to carry you?"

"God, no. Everyone—would notice."

They were way past anyone noticing them, but in a situation like this, lying was the only recourse. "Who cares?"

"I do. I live here."

"You come here often?"

"No, but I might."

He laughed softly. "I'm going to lift you back on your seat. If you can find that Kleenex, we'll clean up and get the hell out of here. And if I want to carry you out, I will."

She felt a delicious little shiver at the brusque authority in his tone as he set her back in her seat and all her female power principles packed their bags and went on vacation. Only temporarily and for a very good reason, she told herself, as a sop to her social conscience. "What if I were to say you can't?" It was a teasing, flirtatious query very unlike a female concerned with female power. Those vacationers had hit the road running.

"It wouldn't matter."

Ohmygod, ohmygod, she was going to come again just from the luscious brute command in his voice. There was no excuse for her feminist principles. When those ripples of longing were heating up her cunt, she had trouble remembering the word *principle.* Call her a pushover for a big, strong, take-charge kind of man in bed or, in this case, a very public venue. But at the moment, even the venue was going to lose to her very determined psyche who wanted and *needed,* really *needed* this big strong man to fuck her.

And now was definitely not the time to question unimportant, teeny, tiny little details like why he was here or whether it was strictly proper to be—well . . . so eager or even if it might be illegal to do what they were doing when she was totally *overcome* with lust.

"Let's get out of here."

He was all rearranged and decent, while she hadn't moved. "Do we have to?"

He recognized that plaintive tone. He also took note of the final scene of *Casablanca* Delhi-style being played out on the screen. "The lights are going to be coming on. How about the car?" he offered, looking for some compromise to outright indecent exposure.

"Promise?"

"Absolutely." They were in sync there.

He nodded at the screen. "They're on the tarmac, babe. There's not much time."

Quickly wiping up, she straightened her clothes while Bobby picked up all the Kleenex and popcorn napkin residue and tossed it in a popcorn tub. Then he stood and waited for her to pass by him and move toward the aisle. Following in her wake, he took note of the other viewers' rapt interest in the final good-bye scene, thankful for their benighted taste in movies and thankful most for his own particular movie pleasures—no actors required.

Cassie knew the way to the back door that opened on the parking lot. Once outside, she stopped, blinking against the sun, half-blind after hours in the dark. "Where's your car?"

"Over there." He pointed to his rental. "But if you could *wait* a few minutes, I'd like to take a shower. I've been on the road since last night."

She made a small moue, and he wondered if they were going to have to use his smoky rental. Her car was out of the question. He'd throw out his back.

"I'm sorry. I shouldn't be so demanding. I should be polite."

He didn't know where this was going, but he was thinking rental car.

"Would you mind if we did it in the shower 'cuz I'm really impatient."

"No problem," he said with a smile, having a feeling this was going to be one of his better Fourth of Julys. "I'll follow you."

FORTY-FOUR

HE PULLED IN BEHIND HER IN HER DRIVEWAY, reached in the backseat for his carry-on bag, and turned around to see her leaping out of her car and flying toward the house like she was jet-propelled. Dropping his bag on the front seat, he jumped out of his car and took off after her.

She was already at the door, shoving it open and screaming.

As he raced after her, he saw the red Porsche parked at the curb. Recalling some comments about her ex-husband's Porsche, he almost stopped, wondering if he'd be better off not being involved in what looked to be a God-awful scene.

On the other hand, his jealousy meter was swinging into the red zone, and all he could think of was *Mr. Red Porsche had better not touch her.* That accelerated his pace and brought him into the living room only two steps behind her.

A blond man and woman were standing there, looking fashion-magazine put together in summer casual clothes bearing a distinct Fourth of July red, white, and blue theme.

Bobby's brain registered a moment of shock at such modish ostentation, and he wondered if she dressed him or he dressed her. Their fucking clothes matched. It was Barbie and an older Ken celebrating the holiday in their own glossy way.

The man was holding a painting. A rocky shore, pine trees, a gray-blue lake, and a couple cabins tucked into the trees.

"Damn you, put that painting down!" Cassie's scream echoed in the empty room. "Put it down, or I'll call 911 and report a robbery!"

"It's mine," Jay growled.

"Really, Jay, let the bitch have it," the patently siliconed Barbie said, her perfect breasts holding up a sequined facsimile of the Stars and Stripes on the front of her T-shirt. "It's nothing. I'll buy you another one."

"It's my favorite painting," he snapped.

The Barbie doll looked startled for a second and then pursed her red glossed lips. "I don't like that tone."

"Please, baby, go out in the car," he said, silky smooth and conciliatory. "I'll be out in a few seconds. Be a sweetheart, now."

The blonde shot Cassie a malevolent look, her blue gaze flinty hard. "I don't know why you ever married her," she said petulantly, offering her intended a pouty glance. "She's *old.*"

"Give me five minutes, baby," Jay soothed. "I'll be right with you."

Tami Duvall stood on tiptoe to kiss Jay on his cheek, then turned on her red, white, and blue sandals, puffed up her chest under her sequined American flag, and huffily walked away.

One down, one to go, Cassie thought, that staged kiss that said he's mine and not yours close to bringing up an afternoon of junk food. She swallowed hard, forced her voice to a calm she wasn't feeling, beat down the shriek in the back of her throat, and said, "Give me the painting. And then get out of my house."

"Better do it, mister," Bobby said, irritated by the bitchy remark about Cassie. That blonde wasn't worth a second look.

Jay gave Bobby's pony-tailed, travel-rumpled image the once-over. "Who the hell are you?"

"What's the difference? Do what the lady says."

"Lady?" Jay snorted. "Not unless they grow them in corn fields."

"Listen, prick, give up the painting and get the hell out."

"Or what?" Jay measured Bobby with his hard, gray eyes.

"Or I'll throw you out."

"You and who else?"

"Jesus, Jay, get real," Cassie muttered. Jay had never hit anyone in his life.

"Shut the fuck up."

"Hey," Bobby growled. "Watch your mouth."

Jay glared at him and then began walking toward the door—with the painting.

"Jay, damn you, don't you dare take that—"

Bobby stepped into his path. "Drop it."

Jay stopped, but steam was practically coming out of his ears, his jaw clenching and unclenching. "Stay out of this. It has nothing to do with you."

"It does now. You're bothering Cassie."

"Don't do anything foolish, either one of you!" Cassie exclaimed. "Jesus, I can't believe this is happening!"

"If you'd given me the painting like you were supposed to—"

"You wouldn't have broken into my house and stolen it, you jerk?" Cassie snapped. "And this isn't the first time. I saw your car pull away last week just as I was driving up. You don't give up, do you?"

"It's mine!" Since his company that manufactured putters

had become successful, Jay had increasingly become the little tyrant.

"No, it isn't!"

"Damn right it is!"

Bobby could see this going nowhere and punched Jay hard, once, in the gut, and as Cassie's ex crumpled to the floor, gasping for air, Bobby scooped up the small landscape and handed it to Cassie. "Put it away somewhere safe," he calmly said. "I'll help him out to his car."

Hauling Jay up from the floor, he half-carried, half-pushed him out the door and down the sidewalk to the curb, where his fiancée was waiting impatiently, swinging her shoulder bag in a jerky little arc.

"Jay!" she cried on seeing him. "What happened?"

"He fell," Bobby said. "Nothing serious. He just has to catch his breath. He'll be fine." Propping Cassie's ex-husband against his turbo-charged Porsche, Bobby turned away and walked back to the house.

CASSIE WAS WAITING in the doorway.

Bobby smiled as he reached her. "I'd put away that painting for a month or so, just in case he's stupid enough to try again. He seems to think it's his."

"A small disagreement in the divorce settlement."

"I figured. He's gone for today at least. It takes a while to get over one of those gut punches. It kinda rocks your balls, and not in a good way."

She tried not to smile. "You shouldn't have done that. Knowing him, he might sue."

"Nah. No guy wants to admit he was down. It was time for him to leave; he didn't want to go. I just helped him along."

"Thanks—really . . . thanks," she murmured, not sure it

was politically correct to feel this good after what happened to Jay. But he deserved something for trying to steal her painting, and it was out of her hands. Right?

"My pleasure, babe. He was a real pain." He didn't say "What the hell did you see in him?" because he'd married Claire; he was the last person in the world to talk about making mistakes. Easing her inside, he shut the door. And locked it. "I'm taking a shower, okay?"

"Hey."

"What?"

"That's it? I'm taking a shower?"

"I thought you were in a hurry."

"Tell me why you did that?" She didn't have a knight in shining armor in her house every day. She needed to talk about this, dissect it, maybe revel in it.

"Don't know. Seemed like a good thing to do."

Jeez, that male nonanswer. But she figured she wasn't going to get any more because he was already walking away in the direction of the shower. Running after him, she said, "What if I needed a guard for my painting—say, for a month or so?" You couldn't fault her for trying, when a really perfect man in every sense of the word walked back into your life. There was no point in being a Jane Austen heroine.

"Reporting for duty, ma'am," he said, turning to her with a grin.

"Really?"

"Yeah."

"Why?"

"I started getting hungry up on that mountain." He smiled again. "And not just for food. What do you think about meeting my parents?"

She opened and shut her mouth about ten times before the pathway from her brain to her tongue was cleared of debris from the shock. "You mean it?"

"Of course I mean it. I'm not in the habit of taking women home to meet my parents. Could we continue this discussion in the shower? We both really smell of sex."

Two really fabulous things had just happened to her. One—she was going to meet his parents when he said he didn't usually do that, which caused that Vera Wang gown to wing its way back into her consciousness. Very juvenile for a grown woman who was seriously thinking about taking yoga someday. But nevertheless, freaking wonderful! And two—they'd smelled of sex in front of Jay. She'd never even thought about it . . . but how sweet was that? Because as anyone could see, Bobby Serre was without a doubt God's gift to women. So let her enjoy her spiteful, harboring-a-grudge sort of vengeful quid pro quo. She deserved it after what Jay had done to her.

Really, she was beginning to think there actually was justice in the world.

"Don't go to sleep on me, babe. I've got plans."

Looking up, she realized she'd followed him into the bedroom without noticing, although she *did* notice—wow . . . he was lounging against the bathroom doorway, buck naked with the most beautiful hard-on.

"The shower's running," he said softly.

And she knew he was talking about something else entirely.

"Hurry. I've got a lot of time to make up for. It's cold up in those mountains."

She undressed in record time while he watched her kick off her sandals, practically rip the buttons off her blouse, and wiggle out of her skirt and panties. He was smiling the whole time, one of those sexy, I've-got-what-you-want kind of smiles.

"Are you going to let your hair grow?" she asked, flinging away her clothes.

"Whatever you want, Hot Legs."

His voice was husky and low, and she quickly discarded such superfluous issues as long or short hair. "Maybe we could talk about it later."

He winked and held out his hand. "Good idea."

One never knows if the stars are going to be perfectly aligned like this for long, she thought, placing her hand in his, *but what is happening here right now is a no-brainer and I am going with it for as long as it lasts.*

Because she was happy, really happy.

Who could ask for anything more?

"Where do your parents live?" she asked, not completely capable of jettisoning every last spec of female curiosity even in the throes of Hollywood-style, happy-ending bliss.

"Nantucket at the moment. We'll fly out tomorrow," he said, opening the shower door and holding it for her.

Ohmygod. They were flying out tomorrow!!! Only movie stars could afford those last-minute tickets. They cost a fortune! *Pinch me. Am I in Hollywood?* But almost immediately, the universal female fear surfaced even in the midst of this fairy-tale perfection. "I don't have anything to wear," she said.

He shut the door and pulled her close. "I'll buy you something."

He'll buy her something!!! How cool was that? She was going to just die. Could she send Jay a postcard or something from Nantucket? Then Bobby's lips touched hers and she said, "Mmmmmpffdddwwwp," because her brain was still racing with the sheer, unadulterated glory of him and her, of them . . . and *Nantucket!* She'd have to call Meg and her mother and dad and Liv and anyone else who she knew even remotely to tell them of her good fortune.

And even if it didn't last, think how good her story was *now.*

But then her brain blanked out like cable did when a

storm was passing by because he'd backed her up against the wall and lifted her just enough so he could slide his big cock inside her and she didn't know what was hotter and wetter— outside in the shower or inside, where he was moving really, really slowly so she could feel every luxurious inch of his fine, fine, long, hard cock fill her so full she was standing on tiptoe, gasping.

He made up for lost time.

She made up for lost time.

They both made up for lost time.

Until finally, sinking to the shower floor, they sat with their backs against the wall, their legs sprawled out in front of them, their hearts beating like drums and tried to catch their breaths.

"I think—I'm—in love," he panted.

"How—do—you know?" she gasped.

"I think—I'm in love." He smiled. "That's—all I know."

"Me, too," she said.

"Good."

He didn't ask her how she knew or why. Maybe that was for the best because for once in her life, she didn't have any answer.

"I'm hungry." His appetite was coming back.

"Me, too."

He grinned at her. "I think we've got something going here."

She nodded because she didn't want to say, "Me, too," again but most of her blood had gone to other parts of her body the past hour and her deprived brain was on hold.

"Tired?"

She shook her head.

"Come on, let's dry off and order some food." Coming to his feet, he picked her up and carried her out of the shower. She didn't protest once. She didn't even think about it. As he dried her off while she sat on the side of the tub, she decided she'd have to review the merits of *complete* independence as a woman.

It was rather nice to be dried off by a handsome man who said he loved you after numerous rather sublime orgasms.

But then, feeling a twinge of guilt, she said, "Would you like me to dry you?"

"No thanks, I'm already dry."

Really, was she lucky or what?

And without having to read more than a chapter or so of *How to Make All the Luck You Need*. Okay, maybe just a page or so. Honestly, probably only the chapter headings.

Maybe she was telepathic. Maybe the entire book had just drifted into her brain through her senses. And maybe this feeling she had that she and Bobby Serre were going places was in the nature of a psychic revelation.

She'd better not mention that, just in case he wasn't as spiritually inclined as she. She wouldn't want to scare him away.

"Chinese or Italian or California cuisine? What's your call?" he asked, kissing her for good measure to wake her up. He was damned hungry.

"Are we really going to Nantucket?"

"Yep. What do you want to eat?"

"Tomorrow?"

"Yep. I'm ordering Italian unless you scream." He was standing, clearly on the way to the phone.

"Whatever you want," she said, dreamily. Really, who could eat at a time like this, when she had to plan her travel wardrobe?

Just think, if Arthur wasn't such an ass, his ex-wives would never have stolen the Rubens and she and Bobby would never have met, and they wouldn't be flying to Nantucket tomorrow to meet his folks.

Not that she was going to rush into anything. No, no, no.

But still . . . maybe a long getting-to-know-each-other pre-engagement would give them time to travel. She had plenty of vacation, and maybe she could learn to pack one carry-on for everything if she really squeezed everything into those rolls like they showed you in magazines. On the other hand, it would do her good—exercise wise—to carry a couple suitcases. Think what her biceps would look like. It would be very healthy. Good. That was settled.

She couldn't wait to tell her family and friends.

And most of all—Arthur.

Wouldn't he just die . . .

New York Times bestselling author

Susan Johnson

turns up the heat.

Hot Pink

All Chloe Chisolm wants is a steamy affair with
Mr. Tall, Dark and Handsome. But when an
eventful elevator ride with a seductive stranger
ignites a fiery affair, Chloe finds her desire is
out of control—and her hardened heart
is beginning to melt.

"JOHNSON TAKES SEXUALITY TO THE EDGE."
—OAKLAND PRESS

"SMART...SEXY...SENSUOUS." —ROBIN SCHONE

"EROTIC...SUSAN JOHNSON AT HER HOTTEST."
—SENSUAL ROMANCE REVIEWS

0-425-19682-8

Available wherever books are sold or at
www.penguin.com